STELLA ALLAN

◆

ARROW IN THE DARK

Complete and Unabridged

ULVERSCROFT
Leicester

First published in Great Britain

First Large Print Edition
published 1998

British Library CIP Data

Allan, Stella
Arrow in the dark.—Large print ed.—
Ulverscroft large print series: mystery
1. Detective and mystery stories
2. Large type books
I. Title
823.9′14 [F]

ISBN 0–7089–3900–7

Published by
F. A. Thorpe (Publishing) Ltd.
Anstey, Leicestershire
Set by Words & Graphics Ltd.
Anstey, Leicestershire
Printed and bound in Great Britain by
T. J. International Ltd., Padstow, Cornwall

This book is printed on acid-free paper

I've travelled the world twice over,
Met the famous: saints and sinners,
Poets and artists, kings and queens,
Old stars and hopeful beginners,
I've been where no-one's been before,
Learned secrets from writers and cooks
All with one library ticket
To the wonderful world of books.

© Janice James.

The wisdom of the ages
Is there for you and me,
The wisdom of the ages,
In your local library.

There's large print books
And talking books,
For those who cannot see,
The wisdom of the ages,
It's fantastic, and it's free.

Written by Sam Wood, aged 92

ARROW IN THE DARK

In 1957, when he was serving in the Army in Cyprus, The Reverend Martin Dearsley had suffered the loss of a brother officer and friend. The same incident had bereaved Sylvia Stanton of her lover. Its repercussions brought Martin and Sylvia together and soon after meeting they married, still strangers. They have fashioned a superficially satisfactory marriage until the unexpected arrival in their lives of Stuart Balfour. They become involved in a web of suspicion and intrigue that finally forces Martin to face the past, and the effect that this will have upon their relationship.

Books by Stella Allan
Published by The House of Ulverscroft:

A DEAD GIVEAWAY

For James Leasor who first believed in me as a writer, and whose ever generous encouragement made me persevere — and for Joan — With love and gratitude.

Acknowledgement

My special thanks to John Heritage, with whom I spent an educative and fascinating afternoon at the Limb-fitting Centre at Queen Mary's Hospital, Roehampton, learning about some of the work carried out by him and his fellow prosthetists in the making and fitting of artificial limbs, and the technical and emotional adjustments that have to be faced by amputees.

'Some, when they take Revenge, are desirous the party should know whence it cometh. This is the more generous . . . but base and crafty cowards are like the arrow that flieth in the dark.'

Francis Bacon
from his essay *On Revenge.*

1

AS Sylvia slid a covered casserole into the Aga and slammed the oven door, the bells changed their repetitious bidding for her to 'Come to church' to the monotonous tolling of 'Come! Come! Come!' Over the years she had learned to hide her irritation at their insistence and to comply with their invitation as a matter of course. In the same way she knelt nightly with Martin, the breadth of the double bed between them, while he said prayers aloud for them both. He always left a silence at the end for privately shared supplication — not suspecting that he had been on his own from the beginning.

Taking off her apron, she hurried through into the hall, snatching up her purse as she went. The inner porch door was glazed, and beyond it the front door of the Vicarage stood habitually open by day. The late summer sunshine shone through the glass and, to Sylvia's

1

surprise, silhouetted the figure of a man. At the same moment that she saw him he pressed the house bell, making her start, and those other bells gave up as though in acceptance of her not making Evensong now that she had a valid excuse. Sylvia put her purse down again and went to admit her unexpected visitor.

The man was tall, in his early thirties, bearded in the current fashion, his jeans and T-shirt well worn but clean. The sun behind him tinged his hair, which sprang in short wiry curls, a deep copper, and the exposed skin of his upper features was tanned with the lightly weather-beaten look of a traveller. On his back he carried a hiker's pack which bowed him slightly, so that he was already bending towards her as Sylvia opened the door. For the briefest of moments, before either of them spoke, Sylvia experienced some dim sense of recognition, then it was gone and he was saying experimentally,

"Mrs Dearsley?"

"Yes?" There was a cautious element in her reply, not just because he was a stranger but as though she had some

2

precognition of what was to come. It wasn't so surprising. She had been waiting for the past two years — waiting and hoping every time she answered the door, every time the telephone rang. All the same, she wasn't prepared for the way her heart leaped in her breast when he said with a tentative smile and without preamble,

"I've come about Marian."

He saw her face change, whiten with shock, the large dark eyes grow even bigger with a fleeting hope. Then the light died out of her expression to be replaced by dread and the anticipation of another disappointment.

"What about her?" Sylvia's tongue and mouth were dry, the words coming broken from her parched throat.

"She told me where you lived." His voice was cultured and he spoke easily with no trace of shyness. "At least, she said her father was the vicar of Hanbury, so I came straight here." He was unhitching the webbing straps of his pack first from one shoulder, then from the other as he explained. He swung the bag down to rest it on the polished tiles.

"Marian told you?" Sylvia picked him up sharply. "When?"

He looked slightly nonplussed. It didn't appear to be the question he had expected. "If you mean when did I last see her, it was a few days ago."

He'd never seen anybody go so ashen without fainting. He moved a step forward to catch her in case she fell, but it wasn't necessary. All she did was put the fingers of one hand up to her mouth as if to stem the trembling of her lips as she closed her eyes and whispered, "Oh God! Oh thank God!" Her body was shaking uncontrollably and he felt embarrassed standing there unable to proffer comfort on such unfamiliar terrain. Had she been less attractive he would have found no difficulty in putting an arm around her. But she wasn't what he had expected, with her slim, slight figure and her fashionable dress and the dramatic contrast of her thick black hair against that transparent marble skin. She was young too, not beautiful but eminently desirable, which made it impossible for him to make any physical gesture which might be

4

misinterpreted. Beyond her, he could glimpse doors opening into the hall through any one of which someone might appear. Ridiculously, he already felt guilty.

Sylvia, opening her eyes and sensing his awkwardness, pulled herself together. "I'm so sorry. It's just that it's such a relief. Please come in."

She turned back along the passage and he followed her, taking his bearings as he went. Beyond the first door on his left lay a dining-room. He had time to catch sight of a heavy mahogany table capable of seating at least ten people, a massive polished dresser covered with blue-patterned china, and an ample Victorian sideboard bridging the distance between two windows whose sashes ran the full length from ceiling to skirting. There was a patterned carpet in the centre of the floor and the uncovered boards along its perimeter were stained with a dark varnish. Next, a fleeting view of the drawing-room which looked, if anything, even more spacious than the dining-room. He could smell the fragrance from an arrangement of roses and dahlias set upon a marble-topped table just inside the door, their colours blending with restfully faded chintzes and Chinese rugs. His rubber-soled canvas shoes squeaked on the red and black tiles of the vaulted hall and he was conscious of their noise breaking the silence of the big old house. Some of the paintwork was peeling and the sun showed up smears on the expanses of glass in window-frames that would be bound to rattle at the hint of any wind, yet the air of genteel shabbiness was welcoming. It was a place used to the daily passage of all and sundry and reminded him of the entrance hall at his public school, the one through which parents and special visitors were admitted. It even smelled of the same kind of floor polish.

★ ★ ★

She hadn't invited him to relieve himself of his pack, so he was still carrying it when she took him through into a cluttered study at the very end of the passage. Turning towards him and realizing her omission, Sylvia apologized again. "I'm

6

sorry. Do put that down somewhere. Anywhere."

He looked around, but every available surface was covered with books, cardboard boxes, old clothes and china. The battered leather top of the kneehole desk was submerged in papers, letters, circulars and magazines. A stack of new Bibles perched beside an inkstand and a china mug filled with pencils, ballpoints, paperclips and a couple of staplers. There was an old sofa, its cushions sunk in deep springless depressions, and an armchair that had once matched but that had been recovered in a hideous flowered stretch fabric. Bookshelves covered three walls and the fourth was plastered with photographs above and up each side of a stone fireplace whose aperture was filled by a brass shell case filled with Michaelmas daisies and chrysanthemums. They looked incongruous in this hotch-potch of a room and irrelevantly he thought of flowers being born to blush unseen. She was like one of them. He put the pack down on the carpet and lowered himself into the end of the sofa she had cleared for him.

"This is all stuff I'm sorting for the jumble sale." Sylvia smiled. "People come in and dump it and I'm afraid it hasn't got further than here."

He said involuntarily, "You don't look a bit like a vicar's wife." Seeing her expression change, he added hastily, "I hope that doesn't offend you."

She denied it, though his remark was not original and it and others similar always grated. People said that sort of thing meaning to be complimentary, but Sylvia found them faintly insulting, patronizing. The assumption that everyone could be typified irritated her and perhaps she was more touchy on the subject than she would have been had she ever felt in her heart like a vicar's wife. Leaning against the desk and facing him, she said,

"I don't know your name."

"Stuart. Stuart Balfour."

If he hadn't been facing the window she might have missed the infinitesimal hesitation that preceded the name and the scarcely detectable blink of concentration as he dredged it up from somewhere in his imagination. Her glance fell upon the canvas holdall which she could now see was studded with his initials — S.B. In spite of them she was convinced he had lied. Was it also a lie that he had seen Marian? The hope that had briefly flickered prepared to be extinguished. Better face it.

"You say you have seen my daughter recently," Sylvia said quietly. "Where is she, Mr Balfour?"

"Please call me Stuart. Marian does." The cornflower-blue eyes were transparent as they met hers. Sylvia's confusion increased. She wanted so much to believe him. Perhaps she had made a mistake about the name. Martin had more than once accused her of hasty prejudgements. She called it character assessment while he talked about beams and motes.

She relaxed slightly. "Well then, Stuart."

"Marian is in Indonesia."

"Indonesia!"

"You didn't know?"

Sylvia shook her head slowly. Her knees felt weak. She hitched herself up into a sitting position on the desk. "No," she said dully. "We knew nothing. Not if she was alive or dead. She walked out

9

of here two years ago and hasn't been in touch since. What in God's name is she doing in Indonesia, and why?" She paused. "And if it comes to that — who are you and what, if anything, are you to Marian?"

The dawning note of belligerence wasn't lost upon him. Anger was the natural subsidiary to her relief, like the slap administered by a mother to a child who has recently evaded danger.

"Marian and I were — " he hesitated — "you might say, close for a while."

The pointless euphemism irritated her. If he meant they'd had an affair why couldn't he say so. Afraid of shocking the vicar's wife?

"And what happened to Billy?" she asked. "He was the one Marian went off with."

"Billy?" He creased his brow in an effort to remember. "Was he a little dark guy? Mechanical turn of mind?"

"He *had* been remanded for breaking and entering," Sylvia said tartly.

"Yes, Billy. I've got him now." Seeing he was confusing her he ran his hand through his hair and apologized. "I'm sorry, I'm doing this badly, but there's quite a bit to tell." His hand went to the pocket of his jeans and he pulled out a battered package of cigarettes. "Do you mind if I smoke?"

"No." She gave him an ashtray and watched him light up, refusing the proffered packet herself. She was unprepared for the unfamiliar nauseous pungency of the smoke he exhaled after a first satisfied drag. It was a smell that got right down to her guts and made her want to retch. She must have looked bilious because he apologized again and extinguished the weed, substituting it for one of a recognizable brand.

"I'm afraid the others are an acquired taste. Indonesian spiced with cloves."

She felt like screaming for him to cut the social niceties and get on. "Please tell me about Marian," she said urgently. "Is she all right? She's not in any kind of trouble?"

"You say you've heard nothing from her in two years?" he repeated. "Not a postcard or a phone call? From her or from anyone else?"

He sounded as if he didn't believe her,

almost as though he blamed her for not digging deep enough to uncover Marian's whereabouts. Nobody could accuse Sylvia of not moving heaven and earth in the matter and it was sufficient that everyone else had been convinced that Martin's diligence had equalled hers, though it had been necessary to stifle her own treacherous doubts on that score. Because of those doubts he made her answer defensively, "Who else should I expect to hear from if Marian didn't see fit — " She swallowed the congestion in her throat, unable to finish.

He waited for her to overcome her emotion while he seemed to settle himself more easily.

She went on, "Billy would have been the last person to get in touch. He disapproved of us as much as we — I disapproved of him."

If he noticed the correction he made no comment. He said, "Well, obviously I can't fill in all the gaps but I can tell you that for the past year anyway, Marian has been in a religious community on Durga, Mrs Dearsley. Durga is an island situated between Lombok and Bali, and the Shivine — as it is called — is an enclave embracing beliefs that are a spin-off from Balinese Hinduism. Its leader is a so-called mystic of Malaysian origin who has spent all his life in the islands of Indonesia studying religions and customs among Far Eastern cultures. He is known as the Shivaan — his followers as Shivites." He stopped. "Shall I go on?" He could see that she was flabbergasted.

Sylvia nodded, as yet unable to sort her thoughts into words.

Stuart elaborated. "The Balinese believe in one God divided into a Trinity which they call the Trisakti — that is Brahma, Vishnu and Siwa or Shiva. Brahma is the creator, Vishnu the preserver and Shiva the destroyer. The Shivites have adopted Shiva alone. They say it is because he symbolizes the destruction of all that is evil in a man and the rebuilding of that man's personality after said destruction of all that has hitherto gone to make him what he is. They settled on Durga because Durga was the name of the Goddess who was the consort to Shiva. Like Everest — it was there! Propitious, one might say." He grinned cynically, but Sylvia was far from smiling. She sat there letting it all sink in, then she said at last,

"I'm just trying to understand how the Marian I know could possibly have been taken in by all that — that rubbish. She's such a practical, down-to-earth sort of girl, in fact all too ready to debunk anything that can't be scientifically proved."

Sylvia paused significantly. She was remembering a seventeen-year-old Marian's rebellious answer to one of her own questions.

"Do you *have* to go out of your way to antagonize Daddy deliberately? If you find yourself unable to share his beliefs, why not just keep quiet instead of continually arguing and deriding them?" Sylvia had asked, wearily exasperated in her role as perpetual arbitrator negotiating the terms for every temporary armistice between daughter and father.

"Like you do, you mean?" had been the girl's contemptuous retort. "You don't believe all that stuff any more than I. You go through the motions and just

14

let him think you do. Who is the more honest of the two of us?"

"Honesty can sometimes be ruthless and cruel," Sylvia had countered.

"But you're living a lie — every day. That must be one hell of a strain. OK, so you do it because presumably you love him and you don't want to hurt him, but is it good for either of you? If I were Daddy I'd be insulted if I knew I was being pandered to. If I were you I'd expect to have a right to my own opinion. Besides, if his Faith's worth a row of beans it'll stand being questioned."

Sylvia said simply, "I don't feel I have that right."

"Why not? It's sheer arrogance on your part to think you might have the power to shake it."

"I can't explain. It would seem like disloyalty."

Marian had been bluntly intolerant of that point of view. "For heaven's sake, why? If you'd married a banker or an accountant or a solicitor you wouldn't have been expected to agree with all the rules of his profession. What's different about not being able to swallow the divinity of Jesus Christ, or the virgin birth, or a guilt-inducing concept for life based on a blood sacrifice? Don't you *ever* discuss it?"

"Not in that way — no. And if 'discussing' means flaunting your aggression on the subject, I wish you wouldn't, Marian. It only distresses him, darling."

"But he's so rigid. It's he who antagonizes me."

"He's a man of great principle," Sylvia defended, to which Marian had retorted, "One man's fresh air is another man's draught!"

★ ★ ★

She wrested herself back to the present where uncannily Stuart was voicing a similar opinion.

"You and I know it's a load of old crap, Mrs Dearsley, but that's the trouble with all religions, isn't it? They're emotive. Those outside can never fathom the pull of any particular one. I imagine your husband believes wholeheartedly in what he preaches and that you'd call him a rational man, but there are plenty of others who would say that what he believes is totally irrational. Common sense doesn't come into it."

He could hardly have known it, but what he said was so uncomfortably apt that Sylvia felt herself colour. She dropped her eyes and shifted her position on the desk, clasping her forearms, rubbing some warmth into them with her palms. The Indian summer's day had suddenly turned chill. Stuart regarded her quizzically. Inadvertently he had disturbed her, talking of her husband. Her cheeks were pink now and rose tinged the alabaster white neck and the cleft between her breasts visible in the opening of her shirtwaister dress. A locket she was wearing slid down into the shadow, its flat gold chain catching the light and drawing Stuart's eyes irresistibly to the soft contours on which it lay. For a fraction of a second it was his turn to be disturbed, and intrigued, while momentarily, he dallied with the prospect of unforeseen possible fringe benefits from this operation.

"How on earth did they get hold of

Marian of all people?" she was asking him. "How can we ever get her back?" Her eyes were tragic and filled up with tears that made them like big grey pools. He could see down into the bottom of them and her suffering. "It's been the uncertainty," she excused herself, running a knuckle along each lower eyelid. "Not knowing." Both knuckles came away wet. "Why her?"

Her question collected his thoughts from some other place and he drew on the cigarette, then blew out the smoke in an even flow. He said, "Marian and Billy had been travelling — Europe, India, Thailand, Malaysia. From Singapore they came to Jakarta. While they were there they were approached by a group of youngsters who offered friendship and shelter. The kids said they had established a camp on Durga. It was a great place for a holiday. Marian and Billy went along for the ride and got hooked."

"Brainwashed."

"Brainwashed. Indoctrinated. Converted. Saved. You can use your own interpretation."

His flippant detachment aroused a

sudden suspicion. "You're not one of them, are you?"

He laughed, throwing his head back. "Heavens no! I owe no allegiance to any denomination. If I appear tolerant it's because I don't share the universal paranoia over fringe religion. The established churches are already full of sects. Why should a few more in competition necessarily be evil?"

"But the established churches don't seek to divide families. I presume the Shivites or whatever they're called are encouraged to sever family connections completely or we would have heard from Marian before this."

"Don't they?" He remained lazily amused by her naïvety. "I seem to remember something about 'Everyone that hath left houses, or brethren, or sisters or father or mother or children or lands for my name's sake shall receive a hundredfold, and shall inherit eternal life.' And — 'He that loveth father or mother more than me is not worthy of me.' St Matthew. Revised version. The established churches have closed orders too." His smile faded and he

19

said more seriously, "I'm not trying to be deliberately offensive. I'm only saying there are different horses for different courses. Naturally I can hardly expect you in your position to agree with me."

Something in his tone made Sylvia look at him sharply to see if he spoke tongue in cheek, but once again, how could he know his opinions struck treacherously close to her own convictions — ones that weren't the kind a vicar's wife should entertain or could air if she properly supported her husband? Was it a subject Marian would have mentioned to him? Unlikely. They, no doubt, would have had better ways to spend their time than talking about Marian's mother! Sylvia could appreciate how Marian would have been attracted to Stuart. He was a real man — an improvement at least upon Billy's undernourished, wiry body, his ugly nasal twang and his Borstal background. But then Marian's choice of Billy had been deliberate, a mocking gauntlet thrown down for Martin, and a kind of psychological jemmy with which she had challenged Sylvia to force all kinds of personal issues. It hadn't worked in either case, so Marian had decamped with Billy as a final gesture. Sylvia hadn't been able to bear thinking of Marian in Billy's bed. Just *because* Billy was common and vicious and didn't go much on washing she had bent over backwards reminding herself, as Martin would have done, that he too was one of God's creatures. She'd loathed him but to her damnation she had said nothing. She had been so bloody tolerant in the name of Christianity that it had cost her her daughter. A vivid mental image of Marian's tangle of Rossetti curls and her face pressed to Stuart's naked chest assaulted her. Under the black T-shirt the width of his shoulders and the depth of his chest promised a comfortable strength. His tanned forearms were muscled and the hair on his chest that grew above the shirt's scooped out neck was the same coppery colour as that on his head and beard. It would go right down. Sylvia dropped her eyes before they reached his jeans and slid off the desk, moving over to the window to see if there were any sign of Martin.

Automatically she said, "I don't know

what my husband is going to make of all this. He'll see it as another deliberate slap in the face, I fear. I'm afraid Marian hadn't seen exactly eye to eye with us for a long time. She and my husband got across one another continually. They're both extremely obstinate people when it comes to a showdown on what they call principles. But perhaps you already know that?"

She turned round to challenge him with what Marian might or might not have told him about them to find he wasn't listening to her. She hadn't heard him move, but he was now standing by the fireplace studying the photographs over the mantelpiece.

"Is this your husband?"

He was bending forward attentively over a picture of Martin in profile, surpliced and cassocked, leading prayers at an Armistice parade in front of a poppy-decked urban war memorial. His left hand was raised in blessing. Coming nearer, Sylvia looked over Stuart's shoulder.

"Yes. Taken a few years ago when he had a parish in north London."

His eyes flickered over a male school group, several snaps of Marian at various stages of her development and an unflattering view of Sylvia caught looking surprised at a wedding, to alight on a faintly sepiaed photograph of an infantry officer. The young man was wearing the service dress jacket, Sam Browne, kilt and diced hose of a Highland regiment. The face was the same as the clergyman's but as yet bare of the lines of experience. He was seated with his hands resting loosely upon his knees, holding a silver-knobbed baton.

Sylvia said, "That's Martin when he was in the Army — 1956. Just before we met."

There was a small silence as they both perused the picture and an additional dimension to the atmosphere that Sylvia was unable to pinpoint. Standing close enough to have touched him with her shoulder, she was aware of a rigidity in his stance, almost as if he had suspended breathing, then he suddenly turned round and said, "So you *haven't* always been a vicar's wife. I knew I was right." His smile was teasing and she found him disconcerting at such close quarters. She took a step away from him and said lightly,

"You need many of the same qualities for the Army and the Church."

"Chiefly the ability to adhere unquestioningly to a set of rules?"

Thankfully, she heard the front door open and close and there were steps in the passage. She said, "That will be my husband now. Excuse me." She left him standing there and hurried out of the room.

Tactfully, he remained where he was, allowing time for news of his advent to be imparted and any shock on the part of its recipient to be absorbed. He found his hands were trembling and he clenched them to steady them before moving into the open doorway.

2

AFTER the service Martin had taken the short cut from the church to the house, down across the graveyard and through a wicket-gate in the holly hedge into the vicarage shrubbery. In his predecessor's time an extensive kitchen garden had run right up to the gate, but Sylvia had had it grassed over and planted with laurels, syringa, eucalyptus and laurustinus to save work and the expense of a gardener. The variegated shades of green of the bushes made a more dramatic foil for the rose-garden, when viewed from the house, than straggling rows of cabbages and beans. As he walked in the cool, lush grass the scent of cascading white syringa flowers distilled the essence of an English summer. The roses in full bloom were at their peak and Martin stood still to appreciate the peace and perfection of them and the moment.

The garden was so peaceful. Here at

Hanbury they avoided the flight paths of aircraft, and since the building of the bypass there was none of the traffic noise that had made sitting out of doors in South Hackney an impossibility. Not that there, there had been anywhere to sit. A paved patio and a walled-in square yard of grass had been the extent of the policies. How Sylvia had hated it. Martin knew she had felt confined and like a stranger in a foreign country, establishing no rapport with the parishioners who had embraced him but viewed her with suspicion. She had pretended well enough until his inconvenient principles had affected Marian and her schooling.

"How can I expect the parish to accept me as one of them if my own lifestyle is so far removed from them?" he had argued. "How can I pontificate from the pulpit on the dilemmas of their existence if I live like a stockbroker and send Marian to a private school?" To him it had been a simple moral standpoint.

"But you *aren't* one of them and they know it. They don't expect you to be. They want their vicar on a plane apart — someone to respect for being himself, not a beer-swilling chum," Sylvia had cried.

"I can't entertain double standards," he had persisted stubbornly.

That had made her angry. "I'd like to see any self-respecting stockbroker living here. As for Marian, has she to be sacrificed to save *your* soul? To assist your integration, must she be uprooted from a school where she's happy and successful and brought down to the lowest common denominator so she can be like all the other deprived hordes in this Godforsaken backwater?"

"Marian will survive. All the others have to. She might even learn a more useful lesson."

"Why should she? You must, it's your job. I have to try because I'm part of you, though God knows it's hard enough and I hate it, but Marian has her own life and that's nothing to do with you."

Martin told himself that she hadn't meant the words to come out in quite that way, but it was significant that they had. During the twenty years they had been married, both before and since this particular episode, both had avoided referring to Marian's parentage. Even when he had subsequently been proved wrong and as a result of Marian's new environment she had made the sort of unsuitable liaisons that had led her eventually to Billy, Sylvia unnaturally had not voiced her reproaches. Perhaps if they hadn't been so careful with each other, each bound as they were by guilt and gratitude, they would have had normal healthy rows like other couples, resolving them in the natural earthy spontaneous combustion of the flesh. In the still, dark hours, lying beside his sleeping wife, Martin had remembered the start of the sentence that had finished with the repudiatory "and that's nothing to do with you." Sylvia had said, "I have to try because I'm a part of you, though God knows it's hard enough and I hate it." Was it being part of him that was so hard and hateful, or merely the trying? Did Sylvia really think of herself as part of him?

Bringing himself back to the present, Martin found he was contemplating the heart of a full-blown yellow rose, at the pinnacle of its perfection. Tomorrow it would be spent but at this moment it was sheer beauty. His left hand being encumbered with two volumes and his sermon notes, he reached out his right to steady the bloom and bring it nearer to him, so that he could smell its fragrance. The flower lay against the artificial palm of his new myo-electric hand, and Martin concentrated on flexing the muscle in the stump of his forearm to activate the fingers in the way that he had recently been taught. Miraculously the fist closed and the fingers pinched together, but a shade too quickly and forcibly, breaking the rose's stem and crushing its petals. He swore gently under his breath. Mentally focusing on the opposing arm muscle, he loosened his grasp. His clumsiness had destroyed the magic and the damaged petals fell to the ground. He smiled to himself wryly. It was a fitting allegory but too personal a one to be used conveniently as the basis for another sermon. It still took a conscious effort to motivate the hand but he would soon master it. He didn't quite yet know his own strength. He was more familiar and competent with his alternative, uglier, working arm with its steel attachments, but the new foam hand covered with a plastic skin was aesthetically an enormous improvement. The electronic arm had been a substitute for his secondary cosmetic one which had been due for replacement after five year's usage, and it had been Sylvia who had talked him into 'going bionic', as she had put it. It had been expensive, not as yet being available to adults under the Health Service, but as Sylvia had pointed out, it was useful, whereas the other had been purely ornamental.

"Much less of a shock for strange communicants raising their eyes to see that instead of a hook doling out the Host," she had said irreverently. "Some people are funny about disability." She'd added the rider casually, but Martin knew she wasn't referring solely to his congregation. She had never understood his attitude towards his injury which he wore with an angry shame, like a hair shirt. She had never seen the medal which he had won in the action that had led to it and she assumed that he had put it away out of consideration for any painful memories of her own that it might evoke. It had constituted their first no-go area — others followed — and it included Colin Coleby. Sylvia would have liked to have talked about Colin but when her need to do so was at its most compelling, there had been no one with whom she could share his memory except Martin, and from the first he had made it plain that was taboo.

The evening sun was dying but the air was still humid. Martin's cassock was hot and heavy and the stump of his right arm was sweating and sticking to its new plastic socket. In an hour it would be sore. He would be glad to change it for the comfortable breathing leather of his working arm. Today it would have been a relief to go without either limb but Martin never did that, except in bed. As he went across the lawn and towards the house he was deciding not to ask Sylvia why she had changed her mind about attending Evensong.

★ ★ ★

31

He was barely inside the hall and putting down his books before she came hurrying to greet him and from her agitated expression he could see that something had happened.

"Martin! There's news of Marian. There's someone here who's seen her. She's in Indonesia!" The words fell over themselves and she had lowered her voice conspiratorially. Before she had time to enlarge upon her theme, Martin raised his eyes from her flushed face and saw Stuart standing beyond her, framed in the study doorway. Following his glance, Sylvia turned and took a step back towards their visitor, making a gesture of introduction.

"Martin, this is Stuart Balfour, Marian's friend. Stuart, my husband."

Both men moved forward and Stuart held out his hand. There was a peculiarly set expression on his face, almost in the manner, Sylvia thought, of a man issuing a challenge. She realized that he was not over the stiff nervousness she had sensed in the study. If Marian had portrayed Martin as an orthodox churchman of conservative views, Stuart might well be unsure of his reception. She had evidently neglected to mention her father's disability and Sylvia cursed herself for not priming Stuart. In the photograph he had seen it had not been evident and she could have spared them both the embarrassment of the fumbling handshake they eventually achieved.

They made a striking contrast standing together, Stuart — all tanned and russet and open-air — and Martin, even taller than their guest, darkly patrician. His long, lean face was cleft by two furrows which ran down from either side of an aquiline nose and his green eyes were set widely and severely under thick black brows divided by frown furrows. The mouth saved the whole from uncompromising asceticism and might have belonged to a different man altogether. The top lip curved generously and sharply defined above a lower, fuller, more flexible partner. Its corners could equally well have turned up or down. From habit they were now down, but you got the feeling that if you could turn them right up, then they would also switch on his eyes. His height and the cassock gave him an air of authority. It was a face and figure that would stand out in a crowd and rate a second look — in the case of women, usually a third.

Aware of the green eyes keenly upon him, Stuart countered their penetrating appraisal with an apologetic smile. "I'm sorry to burst in on you like this, sir. I'm afraid I gave your wife a bit of a turn but Marian said . . . I didn't realize . . . " He trailed to a halt.

Unlike Sylvia, Martin had registered neither shock nor surprise, nor had he yet spoken, but then he wouldn't be a man to show his emotions, Stuart gauged. There was about him a controlled, steely withholding, a self-discipline that had communicated itself to the other man in his uncompromising handshake. His voice, when it came, was a surprise, deeply pitched and melodious, richly dark brown and vibrant. Stuart entertained the notion of an Identikit picture assembled from wildly incongruous features.

"Stuart saw Marian a few days ago. Isn't that marvellous?" Sylvia was bubbling now. Her eyes were brightly eager, lit from within. She was really alive for the first time in two years, Martin thought, and he was assailed by a savage stab of jealousy that Marian, and not he, had the power to make her look like that. Marian had always come first. First, last and in between. Putting Satan firmly behind him, he made an effort to show his own relief.

"Yes, it is wonderful," he agreed. "A small miracle and it deserves a celebration. Has my wife offered you a drink yet, Mr Balfour, or was she too overcome?" The smile he gave Stuart flattened out the lines on his brow, creasing his eyes with the swiftly devastating effect of throwing his whole face into perspective. That was how he was meant to look but life had evidently had other ideas.

Sylvia said, "I'm afraid I haven't, but now that you're here you can do the honours. Martin, take him into the drawing-room. There's so much you must hear. I'll check on the supper. You will stay and share it with us, won't you?" She addressed herself to Stuart.

"I'd like to if it's not too much trouble." He accepted without hesitation, adding, "I've no particular plans for the night."

Sylvia wasn't sure if he intended it as a hint or whether he was merely stating he had nothing better to do. Either way she felt faintly provoked at his turn of phrase.

Martin immediately rose to the bait. "Then why don't you stay over? We have plenty of room and there's always a bed made up, isn't there, Sylvia?" He was referring to Marian's bed that had had sheets upon it for twenty-four months. Every so often Sylvia changed them and every other day in winter she turned on the electric blanket to keep the bed aired against Marian's coming. But Marian had never come, nor had she yet. Stuart should have the spare room if he stayed. She heard him saying.

"That's extremely kind of you. Are you sure it's not an imposition?"

"No, of course not. We're used to unexpected visitors here and any friend of Marian's is always welcome." Martin was leading the way into the drawing-room as he spoke. Stuart looked back at Sylvia, seeking her added reassurance.

She gave it. "Of course it's no trouble. Anyway, it's we who are indebted to you."

He smiled, strangely she thought, and said, "That's what I hoped."

He disappeared in Martin's wake, leaving Sylvia standing in the passage consumed by the certain knowledge that he had banked on staying all along. She didn't know why the realization sent a chill whisper along her spine or whether she was falsely attributing the merest implication of a threat to his final remark. She went slowly into the kitchen and started laying the pine table in the eating area with three place settings, without giving the task her full attention. She told herself it was not unreasonable to be disturbed. She had been living on a knife-edge of uncertainty for so long that it took a little time for the fact that Marian was alive to sink in, and that none of the appalling creations of Sylvia's invention had overtaken her. The reaction to Stuart's news was setting in — and there was all the business of this blessed phoney cult and the inherent dangers of Marian's involvement with it to be reckoned with. She'd had too many surprises for one day and they had over-heightened her imagination. Even if Stuart had deliberately angled for an invitation to stay, nothing sinister could be read into that fact. It was typical of the casual manner in which modern youth travelled, and certainly supplying beds for itinerant members of Marian's generation at the drop of a hat was a common enough experience. Not that Stuart was that young. He must be a good ten years older than Marian. Probably only eight or nine years younger than herself. She certainly couldn't think of him in the context of a son. She knew from the way he had looked at her that he didn't feel filial. Sylvia shook herself. She wanted him to stay solely because he was their only lead to Marian. Through him they must find out about the sect and the names of others of her recent contacts through whom she might be traced. He was the only straw they had had for two years and it was right not to let him go before he could help them get her back.

Deliberately Sylvia spun out her tasks

in the kitchen. When she had finished, she poured herself a vodka and tonic with a slice of lemon and a lot of ice which she drank standing against the sink and gazing unseeing into the twilit garden. It was cowardly of her not to want to be present to witness Martin's immediate reaction to Marian's latest escapade, and to save herself the possible embarrassment of a betrayal of her own divided loyalties in front of a stranger. She hoped to God Martin would listen before going off the deep end about the Shivine. If he had listened more before laying down his laws so intransigently to Marian, perhaps the girl would have turned out less bloody-minded. In her heart Sylvia had sympathized with her. It had been a rude and unnecessary awakening for her when Marian had been plucked from her boarding-school and thrust into the State system in Hackney. Martin had never held with private education, being the product of an excellent grammar school himself. It was another point of contention between them that it had been Sylvia's money — or rather her parents' legacy — that had made it possible for her to over-rule his wishes in this respect. She hadn't done it out of perversity or obstinacy as he appeared to think, but from an acute awareness of her personal responsibility for Marian at the time. When the little girl had started school Martin had been a struggling curate and Sylvia ever conscious of the financial burden she and Marian imposed upon him and their debt to him.

Sylvia sighed and poured herself another drink. For the millionth time she pondered on how all their motives might have varied had Martin been Marian's real father.

3

SHE had met Colin Coleby when she was nearly eighteen and he had been twenty-five. She had just left school and was spending the long summer holiday in Staffordshire with her parents, before embarking on the secretarial course which was intended to fill in the time before her eighteenth birthday and taking up her place at Nottingham University.

The second battalion of Colin's Highland regiment had arrived in Staffordshire to regroup and retrain between overseas postings, and for a few months the 'Jocks' were housed in temporarily vacant barrack accommodation on the perimeter of the Ordnance depot that Sylvia's father commanded. Their arrival caused more than a slight flutter in the neighbourhood whose social life they enlivened in a number of ways: There were cocktail-parties to welcome the young officers, a weekly reel club organized in the battalion Mess, and colourful Beatings of Retreat on the barrack square and by invitation in the nearby towns. It was the district's first introduction to the kilt, and for some, to solving the secret of the antique mystery surrounding what Scotsmen wore beneath it!

Sylvia had never been in love before and it was still an age of comparative innocence. The pill was not yet on the market. Contraceptive advice for teenage girls had to be sought discreetly and privately instead of being blazoned on every bookstall, and the day had yet to dawn when the telephone numbers of abortion clinics were advertised alongside the escalators. She wasn't ignorant — she'd done her share of experimental petting — but she was unawakened. Her admirers had all been boys, brothers of friends, unsure and fumbling and, when the pants were down, more eager for their own quick pleasure than hers. Her father's subalterns were chary of getting involved with their Commanding Officer's daughter, and captains and over were married with wives living in quarters on the station.

Colin was neither reticent, nor did her father's rank intimidate him. The first time she met him he came to the house to a welcoming party given by her parents. Their attraction had been instantaneous and mutual though there had been only two brief opportunities for conversation between them that evening. Sylvia had been kept busy acting as hostess handing things round, but she was aware of him every moment watching her, and the way he did it gave her a tight feeling low in her stomach. He wore a grey suit with a blue striped shirt and blue tie that would be termed square by the boys she knew, but then they were still kids and Colin was a man. He was also dramatically good-looking, with fair hair and dark lashes and brows, and his eyes laughed and teased as if he took nothing very seriously. Sylvia appreciated a sense of humour.

For two days and nights she fantasized about him, intrigued and shaken by the effect of their brief introduction upon her emotions. It was her first experience of the onslaught of physical desire and she was shocked and thrilled by the discovery of an eroticism that filled her mind with pictures — pictures of things she hadn't even read about. On the third evening Colin rang and invited her to the cinema. It was the second time round of a film she had seen before but it didn't matter because her mind wasn't on the screen. They sat with their arms linked loosely and hands clasped on the arm rest between them, his right knee a decorous inch from her left, both of them looking studiously ahead. It must show in her face — it must, Sylvia thought, trying to quell the sensations aroused by their casual contact. Her skin was alive and screaming, crawling for his touch, and she hardly knew him. The lights went up for the Intermission and he withdrew his arm and stretched it. When the second film started he made no move to resume their position and she wondered whether he could have sensed her commotion and been embarrassed by it. Feeling awkward and ashamed, she was unprepared for him leaning towards her after a few moments and whispering, "Shall we go?"

It was dark outside and hotter than in

the cinema, with no breath of wind after a sizzling summer's day. In the silent car park there was a couple kissing in the vehicle next to Colin's MG. They were oblivious of spectators just beyond their open window and Sylvia shivered and turned her head away.

"Cold?" Colin put his hand on her bare arm.

"No. I'm fine." She got into the car and they drove away from the cinema and out on to the road towards Lichfield. "Where are we going?" she asked.

"For a drive. Is that OK?"

"Lovely. It's early yet."

He started talking about his family, his mother and father and much younger brother, but she wasn't listening properly, only wishing he would hurry, and watching his hands on the steering-wheel in the light of the dashboard. They were broad and strong and on their backs they had golden hairs which thickened as they ran up his wrists and disappeared into the cuff of his shirt. He made a joke and she laughed and heard herself responding to some light-hearted banter, even managing a witticism that encouraged his admiration.

Somewhere they had turned off the main road and taken a rough track that ran between two narrow hedges and was pitted with pot-holes. The path ended abruptly where the bank of a stream widened in their headlights and the grass looked cool and untrodden, sloping down and away to their right to a thicket of young willows. Sylvia could hear the water rippling over stones, and with the car roof down, the smallest suggestion of a breeze stirred the heavy air that enveloped them. The willow fronds curved invitingly, touching the grass and making a secret canopy. Colin stopped the car and switched off the lights and ignition. It took several seconds to become accustomed to the shadows and to be able to distinguish the outline of his face. There was an interminable moment while they sought each other's features in the darkness and before Colin put out his hand and laid it on the nape of her neck. He exerted a gentle pressure to bring her head closer to his. Her lips were warm and dry and very soft under his, barely parted, and he kissed them experimentally out of deference to her inexperience. Feeling her quiver and respond, he rested his other hand against her bare throat. There was an unsteady pulse at the base of her neck, and he ran his finger up and down its smoothness twice, hearing her breath catch on a small sigh. On its second journey downwards his hand continued to the scooped-out neck of her cotton frock which was ruched into elastic, so that the dress could be worn on or off the shoulder. Insinuating themselves under the gathers, his fingers pushed the material down and found her breasts which were firm and surprisingly full. The nipples felt like stretched silk which, under his touch, immediately puckered and sprang up hard like unripe blackberries. When they did that Colin reached for her more urgently, forgetting the handbrake and gear lever which now rudely impeded his progress. Unromantically, he released Sylvia and swore in pain.

She started laughing, and there was a rueful smile in his voice at his own absurdity as he rubbed his leg and said,

"That bloody well hurt." She sat up straight and adjusted her dress, still giggling, and Colin cursed himself for the ruination of their previous mood. With her laughter had she deliberately broken the spell? He was unwillingly on the verge of calling it a day and re-starting the car when she managed to curb her mirth, and covered with hers the hand with which he was assuaging his pain.

"Let's make it better then," she said, her palm against his thigh. Her voice was still amused. "Where does it hurt?"

The seat of his discomfort shifted with swift importunity and became mingled with an unbearable tantalizing delight. He felt himself stiffen, then go rock hard as, unbelievably, her hand found his erection.

"Is it there?" she whispered. So she had been teasing. She wasn't as innocent as she looked.

"Let's get out," he said unevenly. He reached round to the back of his bucket seat and dragged out an old car rug.

She waited for him on the bank of the stream, shaken with desire and at her own temerity. She had had her chance to withdraw but she hadn't wanted it. She should and could have been on her way back to her waiting, trusting parents had it not been for her deliberate initiative. She felt as if the real Sylvia were watching her from afar. The girl on the river bank was a stranger to herself, a stranger imbued with a sure knowledge of things she never dreamed she knew. It was like suddenly finding oneself fluent in a foreign language without any study, and full of confidence and impatience to try it out. Across the water and over the fields the lights of Lichfield lit the sky pinkly and streakily through the shelter of the willows.

Colin spread the rug, then pulled her down beside him. This time her mouth opened under his, welcoming his questing tongue, drawing it in as deep as it would go. Without releasing her from the kiss, he pushed her dress down to her waist and then down with her pants to her knees. Wriggling free of them, Sylvia felt for the belt that held his trousers. She had difficulty with the buckle, so tugged instead at the zipper on his flies. Colin released her and she heard him fumbling about in the dark before he held her again, this time against his naked body, with electric effect. His hands and mouth were doing things that sent her into such a paroxysm of excitement and abandonment that she found she couldn't wait. "Please — now!" Wrapping herself savagely around his thighs, she pulled him inside her. There was an explosion of stars and every nerve in her body right down to her finger and toe tips seemed to be made of red hot wires. Then slowly, slowly the heat receded and a heavy languor spread and took its place. He was still inside her and in spite of her soreness she was loath to relinquish him. She flexed her muscles to hold on but he slipped out and she groaned in exaggerated disappointment. Colin laughed, still embracing her, and rolled them both on to their sides, his arm under her neck, his other hand in the curve of her hip. Nuzzling his chest, she tongued his nipple with butterfly kisses. He lay quiet in a pool of sensuous contentment. She had astonished and delighted him with the depth of her passion and her uninhibited display of pleasure and pleasuring.

"Was it good?" he asked at last, superfluously.

She snuggled closer. "What do you think?"

He teased her gently. "Judging by the noise, I think it must have been."

"Noise? Me?" She hadn't realized she had made any. She had only been aware of his own urgent, strident breathing, the piston force rammed home with gathering momentum, and at the moment of release, his soft whimpering cries of pleasure that had made him endearingly vulnerable.

He stroked her flank. "Just as well we weren't in your parents' house. Do you always shout and carry on like that?"

"I don't know. I've never done it before."

His hand stayed its course and removing his arm from beneath her, he sat up abruptly.

"What are you doing?" She could hear him rummaging about and tried to pull him down again. "Don't get dressed yet."

He found what he was looking for and

her eyes blinked in the sudden brightness of the flame of his cigarette lighter. He examined her face and she put her hand over it, suddenly shy.

"Is that true?" he asked. The flame played down her body and he saw blood mingled with the traces of their loving smeared on the inside of her leg.

"Oh God! I didn't know you were a virgin. Why didn't you say? You didn't — "

"I didn't behave like one," Sylvia finished for him. She touched him beseechingly. "I didn't feel like one. I'm so glad it was you. I wanted you so much."

He remembered with what abandoned joy she had offered herself and taken him and his heart turned over at the memory and now at the adoration and honesty in her voice.

"I must have hurt you."

"No. No." She couldn't bear his remorse. "It was a lovely hurt."

He took her in his arms and cradled her and said, "Darling," huskily amazed and uncomprehending the evolution of his emotions. For a timeless stretch they lay whisperingly enfolded, the talking and touching and laughing interspersed with contented silence. Before they left that place they made love again discoveringly, then bathed each other in the stream, drying off on the rug.

★ ★ ★

Over the next six weeks they regularly returned to the stream and the willows and fate was kind in providing that August and early September a period of dry, fine weather. Sylvia was deeply, obsessively in love and Colin, who had started the whole thing as a lark, soon found himself seriously enough involved to start thinking in terms of marriage. Brigadier Stanton, who had hitherto adopted a strict, bordering on Victorian attitude to Sylvia's previous boy-friends, welcomed Colin with open arms. Colin was an officer and a gentleman, and as such was of a breed automatically accepted and approved by the Brigadier as a man of discipline and honour. He trusted them both and it would no more occur to him that Colin was laying his daughter thrice weekly than that she would encourage him to do so. Sylvia had more than a few bad moments thinking of her betrayal of that trust and the ease with which she could hoodwink her parents, whom she loved, but her conscience wasn't sufficient to deter her from the grip of her all-consuming fever.

In mid-September she went to London for her secretarial course and was lodged in a hostel in Devonshire Place. At the weekends she fabricated excuses for not returning home and Colin came down to London where he enjoyed the use of a flat in Lexham Gardens that belonged to a brother officer who was serving in Malaya. He would arrive on a Friday evening, which meant that he and Sylvia had two whole nights and days alone together, during which they seldom left the flat. These times compensated for the hurried, stolen moments they were able to snatch when she did go home and which were more infrequent now that winter was upon them and the river bank in the cold was devoid of enchantment.

He began to pressure her to go with him one weekend to meet his mother and also to broach their marriage plans to her parents, but she staved him off, not wanting to share him with anyone else yet and unwilling to waste their precious time together talking about the weather to strangers.

"If we're getting married, you'll have to meet her," he said. "Besides, I want to tell her about you. She'll love you too."

"Soon," she promised. Always there was the feeling that time must not be squandered and that it might be running out.

And then her course was coming to an end and Colin's battalion was posted to Cyprus. EOKA's campaign of violence on the island was in full swing and its attacks were being countered with persistent manhunts by the British Army in the mountains. Anti-Greek riots in the Turkish quarter of Nicosia further inflamed a crucial situation. Colin had been gone seven weeks when Sylvia knew for certain she was pregnant, and ten before she received the news that he had been killed.

* * *

She had been at home when the letter
had come, and she could still recall
that Saturday morning — the breakfast
on the table, three empty grapefruit
shells pushed aside, eggs waiting to be
cracked, the noise of the coffee percolator
breaking the shattering silence in her
brain. The curt, spidery note written
in a wavery, kindergarten hand on a
lined sheet headed 'Queen Alexandra
Military Hospital, Millbank, London,'
and running:

Dear Miss Stanton,

Captain Colin Coleby was killed in
an ambush last week. I believe you
were friends. I have been trusted with
his effects. There are some letters and
things you should have. Can you come
and get them?

M. Dearsley (Captain)

Judging by the writing it looked like an
uneducated hoax. Not even an 'I am sorry
to tell you' or a 'Yours sincerely' and the
letters all higgledy-piggledy. She'd clutch
at that straw and not panic until the

56

existence of M. Dearsley — whoever he might be — could be verified. No panic. It was just someone wanting cruelly to make mischief, to frighten her. A jealous girl-friend of Colin's? A blackmailer? Colin couldn't be dead, especially not now.

"Is anything wrong, dear?" Her mother's anxious voice, sounding as if it came through a long wind tunnel, impinged upon her state of numbness. She looked up vacantly, then down again to the letter. She wasn't ready for their commiserations, and in any case, she couldn't yet discuss the possibility that Colin might be dead. There would be questions and tears and well-meaning prying as to the 'letters and things'.

"Sylvia dear," her mother recalled her gently. She folded the letter back into its envelope. She said, "No, nothing. At least, a friend of Colin's is in hospital in London. He wants me to go and see him."

"That's kind of Colin, isn't it?" said Mrs Stanton, conveniently misunderstanding. "You'll go, as he particularly asks you?"

"Yes, of course." Sylvia pushed her

unfinished breakfast away. "I'll get an earlier train back to town tomorrow and go in the afternoon. Better than evening visiting after college during the week."

Somehow she got herself out of the room and upstairs to the bathroom before the nausea that had begun to dog her these mornings overcame her. When it had subsided she was trembling and deathly cold, and as she hung limply over the basin an initial spiral of fear beaded her body with a chill sweat. "Colin. Colin. Please." She didn't know to whom she was praying — God or Colin himself. She was just willing him to be alive with her and their baby. They were getting married. He had said so. She would cling to that.

Sylvia washed her face and made her bed and pottered about in her room until she heard her father go out and her mother call up the stairs.

"I'm just running down to the nurseries for the plants I ordered, darling. Do you want to come?"

"No, thanks, Mum. I'm busy right now."

She waited for her mother's car to turn out of the drive before reluctantly going down to the phone in the study. Directory Enquiries gave her the Millbank number, then after obtaining it and repeating her enquiry for a Captain Dearsley through four interdepartmental transfers, she was speaking to the Sister in charge of Fleming Surgical Ward. The voice at the other end was businesslike with a faint trace of brogue.

"Yes, we have a Captain Dearsley here. Would you like to speak to him?" she offered.

"No. No, thank you. I just wanted to make sure. When did he come in?"

"Last week."

"Can you tell me, please, what is the matter with him?"

"Are you a relative?" To Sylvia's ear the voice sharpened with suspicion.

She said hastily, "No, a friend of sorts. I had a letter from Captain Dearsley asking me to come to see him."

"A letter?" There was no denying the scepticism this time. Sylvia's heart lifted. For whatever reason this woman didn't believe in the existence or possibility of a letter. It hadn't come from Captain Dearsley. He was probably too ill to write a letter. It was a joke. Hadn't she told herself it had to be a practical joke? She said apologetically, "Well, it says it's from him but I have to admit it doesn't look as if someone like him would have written it."

There was a pause before the Sister replied. "If Captain Dearsley did write you a letter, Miss — I'm sorry, what is your name?"

"Stanton," said Sylvia.

" — Miss Stanton, and it looks a bit odd, that will be because he is learning to use his left hand. He lost his right one in action in Cyprus recently. I am particularly encouraged to hear that he made that special effort. If he did that, Miss Stanton, I think you should certainly come to see him."

Sylvia sat down unsteadily, unable to speak. It *was* all true. There *was* no mistake. Any minute now she was going to have to accept the agonizing fact. She braced herself against the pain of the moment.

"Miss Stanton! Are you there?"

It required a superhuman effort to respond. "Yes, I'm here," she said quietly. To the nurse at the other end Sylvia's devastation was apparent. Attributing her reaction to the news of the patient's condition, she relaxed her professional tone and became confidential.

"I'm sorry if it was a shock, my dear. It was just so splendid to hear that Captain Dearsley had taken this initiative. Quite frankly, he has shown a worrying lack of response since he was brought here, and in the absence of visits from any relatives or friends — it is good to know there is someone — "

Sylvia couldn't summon the stamina to tell her she was barking up the wrong tree. Instead she managed, "I'm in the Midlands at present but I'll be in London tomorrow. I could come in the afternoon."

"Good. I'll tell him you're coming. It will be something for him to look forward to."

Sylvia stared blindly at the dead receiver. Rudely catapulted into reality, she looked into an abyss of loneliness and fear. An hour ago the world had looked sane and reasonably secure. Nothing she and Colin couldn't have coped with. If we could remember being born, this must feel like it, she thought. Beyond the womb responsibility began. It was no good crying out that she wasn't prepared for it when she had courted it. Later there would be plenty of people ready to say she had got what she asked for, whether they meant an unwanted pregnancy, or punishment for her immorality in the loss of Colin. She thought of the child because it was easier than thinking of him and reflected how, ironically, it had been conceived not on that first unguarded night, but later when Colin had been so meticulous about taking precautions. Up to this moment she had thought of it as bad luck but not irredeemable. They would be married and she would have the baby and if anyone raised their eyebrows at its premature appearance, let them. Suddenly it was all quite different. The prospect of being eighteen with an illegitimate child and no job and no training was frankly terrifying. The thought of abortion frightened her as much or more, although it made the only sense. If she got rid of it she could go on to Nottingham as planned, untrammelled and with all her opportunities intact, her parents uninvolved or hurt and no one any the wiser. There must be ways of finding out how to go about it. Perversely, the sensible course was inexplicably unacceptable and the baby unexpectedly precious. It was all she had left of Colin and what they had been to each other. Killing it would be like compounding his own murder. 'Killed in an ambush.' Sylvia's mind shied away from a vision of Colin's bullet-riddled body jerking, then lying still. Had it been dark or daylight? Was he on foot or in a vehicle? Sleeping or waking? Vigilant or unaware? Anything but slow and tortured, please God. She couldn't bear to think, to picture, to remember. She couldn't bear any of it. The tears were now ready to come but she mustn't cry yet. Suppressing them hurt physically. She must keep up a front until tonight at least, until tomorrow when she would be away and by herself. She wished now she had arranged to go today, but it was too late for that without more lies and excuses.

It didn't occur to her to unburden herself to her parents, nor would she unless she absolutely had to. Not that they didn't share a superficially satisfactory rapport, but Sylvia had grown used to shouldering her own problems. Boarding-school at an earlier age than most, occasioned by Brigadier Stanton's peregrinations in the Service, had necessarily distanced her from them at times when she had required a shoulder to cry on. School and home were two separate existences and it hadn't been worth saddling them with school's petty heartaches and tyrannies, however monumental they had seemed at the moment. By the time a letter would have reached her mother and an answer been received, the particular source of pain would have either removed itself or been dealt with. So Sylvia learned to fight her own battles and the Stantons received satisfactory reports of her progress and examination results, together with her own letters crammed with only the happy news of her activities.

It made it worse that they'd always

been so bloody proud of her, Sylvia thought wryly. She had to be alone, had to think. Longing for the anonymity of the hostel and the luxury of breaking down, she had somehow staggered through that hideous day.

4

SHE had reached Euston the next day in a state of refrigerated mental paralysis. After a white night spent alternately pacing and sitting in a chair staring at nothing, sleep had overtaken her soon after dawn. Welcome as the respite it brought her had been, waking anew to the realization that she would never see Colin again only redoubled the aching sense of loss. Before the train drew in, Sylvia went into the lavatory to tidy up and check on her appearance. In the spotted mirror she looked much the same as usual. Paler perhaps, but she had never had a robust colour. It fooled people into believing she was not as physically tough as was the case, and gave her an appealing Dresden fragility. She smoothed some tinted foundation over the purple shadows under her eyes in an attempt to camouflage the signs of fatigue and tucked her silk shirt neatly into the waistband of her pleated skirt.

Smoothing the grey flannel over her hips, her hands rested briefly over her abdomen. She felt like an actress playing a part, whose life depended on going through the motions of such commonplace actions. She was a woman, alone and aloof on a journey, who was now preparing to alight and make her way to her destination. Every movement required concentrated care and attention. It wasn't the time to think of what she had come from, where she was going.

Even in the taxi cruising along the Embankment Sylvia set her sights on the man she was going to see, obscuring the reason he had asked her to come. She had always been squeamish about hospitals — their smell and, once inside, the sense of being ensnared in the mystique of a cult that knew better than you did what was good for you. Not that she'd ever been a patient. Not yet. Everyone said that maternity wards were different. A Happy Event. Not like the medical or surgical repairing of something that had gone wrong. If the corridor hadn't been so long, if the electric light bulbs hadn't reflected so fiercely upon its mosaic of polished lino tiles, and if she hadn't felt faintly claustrophobic in the centrally heated, antiseptic air, Sylvia would have smiled at her unintentionally apt turn of phrase. As it was, she was beginning to remember why she was here and the dormant butterflies in her stomach fluttered their wings and nose-dived.

★ ★ ★

The orderly she had been following thumped his way through a third set of swing doors and did a sharp right turn into a waiting area furnished with tubular chairs and a table supporting a pile of thumbed magazines. With an explanatory "Surgical from here on, Miss. Report to the Captain before you go in," he flashed her a smile and disappeared. Sylvia approached the partitioned office he had indicated and put her head round a partially opened door. The QARANC Sister within rose to meet her enquiry.

"I'm Miss Stanton," Sylvia said. "I'd like to see Captain Dearsley. I spoke to someone about him over the phone yesterday."

"That's right." The Sister smiled. "It was myself." She came round from her position behind the desk. She had the fresh complexion of a country girl and a straight fringe of fine auburn hair poked out beyond her wide, starched cap. She wore three pips on the shoulders of her scarlet cape and her Irish eyes twinkled benignly. "Well!" She looked Sylvia up and down. "You should be a sight for sore eyes. I told him you were coming."

Sylvia cleared her throat and said, "Good."

"He didn't say much, in fact he didn't say anything, but I can't imagine that he won't be pleased." The smile faded and she became serious. "We're hoping very much that you will get him talking. He needs taking out of himself, to come to terms with what has happened to him. He can't do that as long as he is fighting and angry inside. Will you try?" She was taking it for granted that the man was Sylvia's responsibility, one which she was given no chance to repudiate as she was swept out of the office and into a ward of separated wooden cubicles. At the third

69

door they halted. The nurse knocked and entered all in one movement, motioning Sylvia to follow.

"Here's somebody to see you," she said with a false, bright archness that took Sylvia back to the nursery. "I'll be in my office," she told her with a meaning glance that meant she expected a report on their interview later, then rustled out, leaving Sylvia and Captain Dearsley regarding each other in silence.

The man in the bed had obviously been 'tidied up' in anticipation of her visit. There was barely a crease in the top sheet where it was folded over the blankets and pulled tightly across his chest to tuck in neatly under the mattress. His arms lay stiffly to attention outside the bedclothes, the foreshortened right stump bandaged and resting on a honeycombed bedspread. The sleeve of his pyjama jacket had been slit up the seam and rolled back to allow for the dressing. Sylvia's eyes flickered briefly to it, then back to his face which was set no less stiffly than the rest of his body. It was a striking face, not handsomely clear cut and fresh with youth like Colin's. This man didn't look as if he had ever been young like that or carefree. Immobilized in the hospital bed that looked too small and narrow for comfort, there was about him an air of dour unacceptance that screamed of the suppression of some forceful emotion. The sister had hinted at anger, which would tally with the premature, bitterly etched lines around his mouth, but they could equally well have been engraved by shock and pain. His eyes too were vastly more knowing than Colin's. Here was an old soul who gazed out at her remorselessly from the pit. An old soul in hell. Something inside Sylvia stirred, more curiosity than pity. If there was an element of the latter it was better concealed before it was resented. He offered no smile of welcome and as he obviously was in no hurry to speak, Sylvia herself broke the silence.

"I'm Sylvia Stanton."

He nodded.

She waited, then she said, "I got your letter."

He nodded again and she was beginning to consider the possible effects of shell-shock when he cleared his throat and said

71

simply, "I'm sorry."

"So am I." She bit her lip on the ridiculous understatement in connection with both their predicaments.

"How old are you?" The question came surprisingly and surprised.

"Eighteen. Why?"

"Eighteen. Christ!" He shut his eyes, whether on account of her youth or because he was in pain, Sylvia wasn't able to deduce. She took an anxious step nearer the bed. With his eyelids drawn he looked like a death mask. She bent over him and saw that he was breathing, then pulled back feeling foolish. He opened his eyes in time to see her straighten.

She said shakily, "You said you had some things for me."

He seemed to gather himself back from a great distance. "Yes. In the locker." He turned his head on the pillow and indicated where she should look. "The drawer. No, the next one down."

Her hand moved on to the second handle and pulled the drawer open. Inside there was a bundle of airmail envelopes secured with an elastic band, the silver pencil she had given Colin for

Christmas that bore both their initials, and her copy of *The Cruel Sea* which she had lent him and which had her name inside.

"To make sure you're only *reading* in bed," she had joked when he had taken it. It fell open now at random as she took it up and she automatically smoothed out a dogeared corner. She had chided him about that sacrilegious habit. The print blurred and she swayed a little on her feet.

"Here, sit down." She found herself pulled firmly on to the bed.

"I'm all right." She got out her handkerchief and wiped the corner of her nose. "I'll get a chair." There was an upright one at the foot of the bed and Sylvia brought it round and placed it beside the locker. She sat down on it and gathered up those things that were left to her of Colin.

"Thank you for these," she said. "It's not a very nice job for you, especially — " she broke off, not wanting to refer so directly to his own affliction. "Were you close friends?"

"No. I'm first battalion. I was already

out there on the Staff when the second arrived. But we both bought it in the same action. I was being flown home so I offered to bring his things."

"That was kind of you."

There was a small pause, then he said, "It was the least I could do."

"What happened to everything else?" she asked.

"Everything else was sent on to his family."

She stared at him for a moment. "So you — or someone else — sorted these out for me?"

"I did."

It seemed incredible that in the circumstances he had been fit enough or had the will or the interest to do such a thing. By the merest chance her letters hadn't found their way to Colin's family who would have read them — particularly the last one she had written telling him about the baby. Sylvia picked up the letters and checked them. As far as she could remember they were all there. At the bottom of the pile were some folded sheets without an envelope that she hadn't noticed immediately. She straightened them and saw 'Home' written in her own hand, and 'My Beloved Darling — ' she didn't need to go on. She knew what was in it. She felt Martin Dearsley watching her and a hot tide of colour flooded up her neck and cheeks firing her whole body with a burning embarrassment. Had he read this? Had he read any or all of them? Instinctively she looked at him to deduce what, if any, reaction was written on his face. There was no shame, simply the acknowledgement of her silent, accusation.

"I'm afraid I did read that one," he said.

Sylvia turned her head away to hide her mortification. He knew then about the child, was privy to her secret feelings, had read her descriptions of the things she and Colin had done together and the other delights she had promised upon their reunion. Frantically she tried to remember word for word just exactly what it would have sounded like to an outsider.

He was explaining. "His things were in a suitcase. When I reached here it got opened by mistake along with my stuff. The book was on the top and someone put it by my bed. That letter was in the book just like that. There was no address and only an 'S.' for signature. When I read it, it seemed to me better that I should find any others that might be in his luggage. Luckily the rest had your address on the back of the envelopes. I went through everything else with a fine-tooth comb."

She knew she should have been grateful but she found it impossible to thank him again. Irrationally she blamed him for his presumption. She steeled herself to ask what she had come to find out. She said baldly, "How did he die?"

He shifted his closed pallid gaze to contemplation of the ceiling as if she had already taken her leave, and Sylvia wondered whether she could summon the strength to ask again. In profile the hawk-like nose dwarfed his other shock-shrunken features, making her realize how very ill he must have been. She had a moment's misgiving about broaching the subject. He had told her it was the same action that had done for both him and Colin. Perhaps it was wrong to make him talk about it — but the Sister had said . . . Sylvia waited.

"We were moving an EOKA prisoner out from where he was being held to a more secure prison." His voice tailed away huskily and he coughed and continued in a monotone, without feeling. "His name was Jannis Nicolaides and he had been one of Gregoris Afxentiou's lieutenants." He glanced at her and, seeing the name meant nothing to her, elaborated. "Afxentiou was Grivas's second-in-command. A month ago we had a tip-off and we surrounded him while he was hiding in a cave near the monastery at Makhaeras. Five of his henchmen, including Nicolaides, the number one, surrendered, but Afxentiou had to be blasted out. He was burned alive. The incident triggered off a wave of anti-British riots. Increasing numbers of EOKA suspects were being detained and questioned at length and a mandatory death sentence was introduced for a wide range of offences. We were being blamed for brutality and torture of detainees and Greek youths were being incited to clamour for Nicolaides's release as a token reparation. The situation around the Army base where he was being held became increasingly inflammatory. Guards were being baited and stoned and it was only a matter of time before some kind of an 'incident' would be provoked. To defuse the affair, the Powers-that-be decided to move him to a place of concealed security. Colin and I were detailed to escort him secretly under guard. Besides us, there were two soldiers and the driver." He passed his tongue unsteadily over his lips. There was a glass and a carafe of water on top of the locker and Sylvia said, "Would you like a drink?"

"Thank you."

She poured some water into the glass and put it into his good hand. Unable to exert pressure on his stump, he was too tightly bound in the bed to be able to raise himself. Sliding an arm beneath his shoulders, Sylvia assisted him. It was no more than a nurse would have done but she immediately sensed his embarrassed inward withdrawal as if she had committed an unwarranted intimacy. After reading her letters perhaps he thought she was purposely imposing herself physically. He was a big man and her slight embrace brought his head near her shoulder, his cheek in close proximity to her breast. He drank, and she lowered him gently back, feeling shamed and lascivious in his eyes.

"A decoy was set to leave before us and to take a different route to draw off the attention of the demonstrators. Shortly afterwards our reinforced vegetable lorry left by another heavily guarded and camouflaged exit. It was plain sailing until we had been going about half an hour. We were passing through a gully with Bando — bush scrub — rising high on either side, when a mine blew up the road just ahead. The driver managed to pull up in time but both he and his mate up front were knocked out by debris that hurtled through the windscreen. Before we could do anything, the back of the lorry was attacked and prised open. There were ten or twelve of them, all armed. The ones who had forced the doors had axes. They dragged Nicolaides down and me with him, as we were handcuffed together.

Colin would have fired but I stopped him as we were hopelessly outnumbered." His voice drained away and it was a moment before he could go on. "Without any warning they blasted Colin and the other soldier with a machine-gun. He wouldn't — he wouldn't have known anything." He wasn't looking at her — just concentrating on getting it over. "They wanted the key to the handcuffs but I hadn't got it. They were in a hurry. One of the men with the hatchets decided to separate us. He aimed for the links nearest my wrist — and missed." His face quivered with remembered shock and Sylvia closed her eyes on imagined horror. Presently he said, wonderingly, "There was no immediate pain. Nothing straight away. I was high on a terrible anger. We weren't in uniform but we were wearing cartridge belts. I had a grenade pouch. They were running towards the crater in the road. Their transport lay beyond it. I managed to get a grenade out and threw it. They all went up."

He was breathing quickly and unevenly and his face was grey against the starched white pillow-slip. "I tried to wrap something round my hand but when I looked it wasn't there. I could feel it but it wasn't there. I don't know how I made the distance to their cars. God knows how I drove one of them. Managed to get help. The ambulance went back and picked up our driver and the other Jock in time. If they'd gone too — " He gave a shuddering sigh. Perspiration beaded his forehead and upper lip and his dark hair clung dankly to his head. Sylvia felt as numbed as his amputated stump. She could appreciate his awareness of his non-existent ghost hand. Didn't she feel exactly the same about her loss? Colin too had been severed from her but the nerves that said he was a part of her still twitched. They were both cripples in their way.

She got up stiffly and crossed to the washbasin where she ran some water and dampened his flannel. Offering it to him, she waited with a towel at the ready while he made a clumsy one-handed job of washing the sweat from his brow and freshening up. She didn't offer to help this time.

After a while she said, "Thank you for telling me."

"Don't thank me for anything," he said bitterly. "I can't handle gratitude. Giving it or receiving. I know what you're thinking. That I'll need to learn to show it in future to all those kind souls who will offer to help me, like the ones here who cut up my food for me." He wrenched his head round and raked her with a glance filled with malevolence. "I don't suppose you've ever noticed how people do that for the disabled. They mush it all up just like a dog's dinner, not at all the way they'd prepare their own plate."

She knew it was cruel but she said the only thing she could think of to counter what seemed like his crass self-pity. "You are at least alive."

Something shrivelled the expression deep down in his unnaturally enlarged pupils. Drugs probably accounted for their unusual size and intensity, Sylvia thought inconsequentially. Pain-killers that could assist the arm. That was the easy part of the healing.

"I promise to remind you to count

82

your own blessings," he said scathingly, then seeing her wilt, repented. "I'm sorry. We're both a pretty good shambles, aren't we?" His mouth twisted in a sardonic smile and the tight line of her own lips relaxed a little in response. His eyes played over her, really taking her in. Until now he had been more concerned with her impression of himself and how to recount his story least painfully to them both. For all her youth, she was admirably controlled. The grey suit gave her an air of neat efficiency and wryly he acknowledged the professional way in which, with very few words of her own, she had drawn him out. He hadn't spoken more than half a dozen sentences to anyone else since the ambush, and his official interrogators had had to be satisfied with monosyllabic replies to their initial enquiries. She wasn't at all what he had expected. The letters had been unrestrainedly emotional, extravagantly sensuous and unsophisticated in their candour — a mixture of purple prose and touching immaturity. From their author he had been prepared for an open display of grief and desperation, even hysterics. They were not the letters of a person who kept a tight rein on feeling. Whatever impression he had given her, he had read them all. Yet here she was behaving with a discipline and restraint beyond her years while it was he who had been reduced to rubble.

"What will you do now?" he asked.

"I don't know." Her tone implied that it didn't concern him what she did, and she started gathering her things preparatory to leaving.

"About the child, I mean. Will you tell your parents?"

"I don't know."

"If you need money or anything, will you let me know?"

"That's very kind of you but it's really not your business." She said it primly, pulling on her gloves and pressing them down each finger in turn.

"Do you know where to go to get help? You won't go and do anything dangerous or silly?" In spite of himself he had to persist.

"You worry about yourself. I'm not your responsibility." She had replaced the chair and was facing him from the end of the bed. Again her choice of words brought that tantalizing change of expression, as if she had probed an open wound. He looked as if he might have been going to say something else, something important to both of them, but the moment was destroyed by the entry of the Sister. Sensing an atmosphere, and readily construing it as some kind of lovers' conspiracy, she beamed upon them both.

"Time is up, Miss Stanton. It won't do to tire him this time, will it? Don't look like that, Captain Dearsley. She'll be coming every day from now on, I expect." She raised her eyebrows at Sylvia, who stammered,

"Well, I — "

"You're coming tomorrow, aren't you?" It was a command from the bed, although he managed to make it sound as if it was something they had arranged.

She hesitated. She supposed she owed him that much.

"Yes, I'm coming back tomorrow," she agreed.

5

SYLVIA cried all night, worked all day, and went back to the hospital the following evening thoroughly washed out. Martin was up, sitting in an easy chair, wearing a camel dressing-gown and with a rug across his knees. He was still gaunt but there was more colour in his cheeks and he had shed the vulnerability imposed by the confines of the bed. Today it was Sylvia who felt like the patient. This sense of role reversal was pointed by his greeting.

"Are you all right? You don't look so good."

"It's been a long day." She sat down wearily on the edge of the made-up bed and fished a couple of paperbacks out of a carrier. "I brought you something to read." Together the books were too thick for him to take at once so she leaned forward and laid them awkwardly in his lap. He didn't look at them but said again,

86

"You look all in."

She hoped he wasn't going to be solicitous. She could take anything but kindness.

"You haven't *done* anything?" His face was suddenly alight with suspicion.

Anger welled in her at the suggestion of condemnation. Who the hell was he to censure any step she might take? Anyone would think it was his baby.

"I'd hardly be here tonight if I had," she said tartly. "I don't know why I did come."

"Why did you then?"

The reason she had was because he was the only person who knew the truth and therefore with whom she needn't pretend, which was ridiculous because he was still a stranger and an awe-inspiring one at that. He probably thought of her as a loose, silly little chit. His aura of aggressive cynicism made him an unlikely candidate for the role of father confessor. She countered his question with one of her own.

"Why did you ask me — no, *tell* me — to come?"

He said, "Someone's got to keep an

eye on you now Colin's not here."

"I'm quite capable of looking after myself." She said it haughtily to cover the effect his mention of Colin's name had upon her.

"You could have fooled me."

His sarcasm had the effect of damming the threatening tears and stinging her to retort, "I don't see what you think you could do about anything." She hadn't really meant it as a jibe at his disability — not really. But he had indirectly taunted her with hers.

And then he had absolutely floored her by saying, "I could marry you."

Every other emotion evaporated and she was swamped by astonishment as she saw that he was serious. "Marry? *You*?" Her incredulity was little short of insulting but he made allowances for shock. All the same, he flushed.

"I'm aware that like this I'm not much of a catch. But it appears you urgently need a husband and I'm available."

She just stared at him, so he went on. "What are your other options? You can go home and confess to your parents. No doubt they'd stand nobly by you, but afterwards either you or they will be saddled with the child. If it is you, your career prospects will go up the spout — at least be seriously handicapped — unless you intend the burden of nappies and broken nights and cots and prams and schooling to start all over again for them in middle age. You'd still have to tell them if you had the child adopted. You're still a minor. At your age you wouldn't get through the pregnancy and confinement without them getting to know. Of course there's abortion, but that's illegal and dangerous."

Still she said nothing.

"I can see that none of those courses appeals to you." He waited. "Do you want to keep the baby?"

"I didn't think I did." She shrugged hopelessly. "It isn't feasible."

"It is if you marry me."

There was a silence which lengthened as he watched the wheels start going round in her brain. After the initial shock, his bizarre proposition was receiving tentative examination. She looked up sharply, exploring his sincerity. "Is it a joke?"

His good fist clenched and he said grimly, "Believe me, it's no joke."

"But why?" She looked childishly perplexed, trying to fathom the puzzle. "You can't want to marry me. You don't know me. You can't possibly care what becomes of the baby."

"I'd rather you didn't kill it." He looked away from her and a tendon in his neck tightened and stood out like a thick cord. It conveyed to Sylvia his tension and she couldn't understand why it should matter to him so much. Unless the baby was the excuse and it was he who needed the help.

She said, "You haven't any family, have you? Where will you go when you get out of here?"

He looked back at her coldly. "I'm not asking you because I need a nurse, if that's what you're thinking. I shall understand if you find this — " he indicated his empty right sleeve — "too distasteful. Although there's no reason for you ever to . . . I shall learn to manage."

There was no reason for her ever to what? See it? Touch it? Come near him physically at all? Sylvia thought of Colin's arms, the touch of his hands. She'd never allow herself to feel that way about anyone again. Once had got her into enough of a mess and it hurt too damn much ever to risk again. There wasn't just herself to consider. She had the responsibility of Colin's child, what was best for him or her. Colin wouldn't have wanted it to go to strangers any more than she did. Colin would have urged practicality. He'd always teased her about her romanticism. "We can't live for always in our own little rose-coloured vacuum," he had told her when she had wanted to prolong their secret idyll. "We've got to mingle and survive in the real world out there." Well, Colin hadn't survived, but he would have wanted them to, even if survival meant grasping so unlikely a lifeline. And was it so unlikely when it came down to it? She would be marrying into the same kind of Army life that she had anticipated with him. She'd make a good Captain's wife. It was her milieu, the only one she had known. The exigencies of the Service — of packing and moving, being separated and coping independently, were disciplines learned at Mrs Stanton's knee, along with the wives' clubs, welfare work and not being able to run twelve thousand miles home to Mother when the overseas postings got rough. Sylvia knew she could make a go of that side of things. Surely that was half the battle. That was the devil she knew. As for the devil she didn't — her train of thought led her back to the reality of the haggard relic of a man confronting her and waiting for her answer. It was mad. They knew nothing at all about each other. Arranged marriages worked in other parts of the world, she reminded herself. Her bemused mind darted backwards and forwards between the pros and cons. She was too tired to reason against the lure of beckoning security.

"I'm sorry. I can see I should have led up to this suggestion but there wasn't time." Martin's voice broke into her distracted reverie. "I didn't just say it off the top of my head. I did think about it most of last night and all of today."

"I don't want to be married out of pity." It was a stupid thing to say, voiced out of a need to resurrect her self-respect. She had actually half-persuaded herself to enter this soulless union. She heard his small intake of breath before he said quietly, "Nor I," and realized she had been clumsy.

"I mean," she stammered on, "the advantages to me are obvious but what on earth are you going to get out of it?"

He looked amused and suddenly half-way human. "You do yourself an injustice. For my part I can offer you my protection, consideration, duty and loyalty. I should hope to receive the same from you. That doesn't seem too one-sided a bargain to me." He paused. "Added to which you are a whole lot prettier than I am." His smile broadened persuasively. The list of virtues pledged had tripped off his tongue lightly, almost flippantly, yet Sylvia had the distinct impression that her agreement to his terms was in some way vital to him. It strengthened her conviction that whatever he might have said about not needing a nurse, he was afraid of the future alone.

"How on earth could I explain it to my parents? I'd need their consent, wouldn't I? They'd want to meet you." She looked at him doubtfully, wondering what ever they'd make of the situation.

He said, "All being well I shall be out of here next week. They tell me I shall then have a couple of weeks to wait before reporting to Roehampton for limb-fitting. We could see your parents during that time and get a special licence. I imagine time is of the essence. How far — ?"

"Nearly three months."

"Forgive me asking, but you are quite sure?"

"Quite." She hesitated. "What if they say 'no'? It's a bit much for them to swallow after so short a time. I suppose I could say I had met you a few times before — since I've been down in London. I hate lying." Distress and shame clouded her eyes. "We shall have to go on lying, shan't we? To the child? Why should I involve you in deceit?"

He dropped his gaze and she saw him swallow. He said, "It won't be a lie. We'll make the child ours. Eventually we'll both forget."

His magnanimity overwhelmed her, and for it she forgave him the impertinence of suggesting that she could ever forget Colin. He was already taking charge — assuming shared responsibility for breaking the news to her parents. For the first time since hearing of Colin's death some of the frightening loneliness receded.

★ ★ ★

In the event there had been no confrontation. After the first surprise, Sylvia's mother and father had accepted without unnecessary objection her implausible transference of affection from Colin to Martin, and her desire to be married to the latter in such unseemly haste. Sylvia's story of having been introduced in London to Martin by Colin and their attraction for each other before Martin preceded Colin to Cyprus was swallowed hook, line and sinker. They appreciated how the ambush had made Sylvia realize how nearly she had lost Martin and how badly she wanted to be with him now and help him to recover. Brigadier Stanton allowed that she was very young but that she had always had her head screwed well on to her shoulders. Sylvia was full of good sense and had never given them a moment's worry. Martin had proved what sort of a chap he was. A character possessing the brand of loyalty and courage he had demonstrated in action could only be admirable. Mrs Stanton hadn't said much. Privately she was capable of the addition of two and two. Making the calculation and not liking the result, she preferred to ignore it and go along with her husband's general sentiments. Only a fool sought unpleasant reality when a convenient shield was at hand. Sylvia, as always, knew what she was doing.

Sylvia, who had not expected but was grateful for so easy a passage, irrationally resented the ostrich stance of her mother. Mrs Stanton's speculative perusal of her and Martin, and back to Sylvia's waistline, had not escaped her daughter. Brigadier Stanton would be protected and spared his wife's suspicions. Shotgun marriages occurred in other families. Privately Sylvia congratulated Martin on playing his part so well, and then remembered that she didn't know enough about him to gauge whether he *was* actually acting. From his easy conversation to her parents she was learning all kinds of things about him that he and she hadn't yet got around to discussing. His parents had been dead some years and he was an only child. His father had been a Scottish minister from Nairn who had moved south to Gloucestershire shortly after the boy's eighth birthday. Martin had been raised on a mixture of evangelical fervour and Calvinistic presbyterianism, which influences held sway until his parents' deaths in an accident during his first year at Cambridge. He supposed, he said, he was a late developer. The wider world of University encouraged him to question his father's tenets and he went a little wild in the sense of his new-found freedom. It was at Cambridge that Martin had met Ian Forsythe. Ian was destined for his father's regiment. General Roderick Forsythe and his wife lived in ramshackle feudality in a huge converted manse on the Black Isle, and the vacation that Martin spent there immediately following his double bereavement was the forerunner of many. The Forsythes lived larger than life in the manner of money comfortably taken for granted. From the look of their threadbare furniture and antediluvian kitchen and plumbing arrangements a stranger might assume there were not two bawbees to be rubbed together. However, there was a ready income for the necessities of life — stacked larders, a well stocked cellar, hunters in the stable, guns in three shooting syndicates, lavish entertainment of guests and gambling on cards and horses for the sort of stakes guaranteed to spin the Reverend Dearsley like a top in his grave. Under the Forsythe's influence Martin began to think seriously of abandoning the academic career his father had visualized for him and going into the Army. With his Scottish parentage and the backing of General Forsythe, his candidature was approved and he and Ian both entered Sandhurst and were subsequently commissioned on the same date in 1952.

* * *

They had travelled up to Sylvia's home together the day after he had been discharged from Millbank. She had grown used to him in the intimacy of the hospital cubicle where they had inhabited a private world, so it gave her a jolt seeing him dressed in a suit and sitting among their fellow passengers in the carriage. He was the man she was going to marry but she knew him no better than she knew them. She had wondered how he would manage his first foray into normal living and had been prepared to assist discreetly if the need arose, but she needn't have worried. He was already amazingly competent with his left hand. Little did she know what grim satisfaction it afforded Martin to be able to take charge of the taxi fare and train tickets without fumbling. Sylvia was unaware of the slavish hours occupied in practising dressing, tying laces, buttoning flies, using a comb, toothpaste and lavatory paper, re-learning every action hitherto automatic and taken for granted. Eventually no doubt they would come easily, but now he felt clumsy and conquering each new gesture brought him out in a sweat. With his remark about dogs' dinners fresh in her mind, Sylvia had primed Mrs Stanton, who thoughtfully produced dishes which required no cutting and were easily manipulated by use of a fork.

"They've taken it pretty well," he said on their way back to London.

Sylvia agreed that they had. It was what she had prayed for but she didn't know whether to be pleased. If her parents really cared about her would they have been so easily indulgent? In her heightened state of emotion she saw their reluctance to stir themselves to any real investigation of her feelings, her motives, as unwillingness to disturb the superficial calm of their own lives. She knew she was being contrary.

"Your father was unexpectedly understanding about my temporary financial embarrassment," Martin was continuing.

"Oh?" This came as a surprise. They hadn't talked about money yet, but in her naïvety Sylvia had assumed he could afford to marry.

"Well, of course he wanted to know what we were going to live on. I was quite straight with him and I want to be with you, Sylvia." The carriage was empty this time and they occupied corner seats opposite each other. Martin leaned forward earnestly. "I haven't any investments or income apart from my army pay. We'll get marriage allowance now so that will help. We'll be able to manage, but I have got some debts that I want to clear off as soon as I can. Out of what my father left me I did buy a small house in Inverness which I've rented out through the army hiring system. I shall sell that now to settle up. Its value together with the family bits and pieces in it should cover what I owe, but it means whereas I could have offered you a small foot in the property market, I now can't."

It was her turn to feel awkward. "That's none of my business, Martin. But I am sorry to think of you getting rid of family things because of me."

"It's not because of you. Not specially. And anyway — " his eyes travelled beyond her and out over the passing countryside — "it'll do us both good to have a break with the past and start anew, don't you think?"

She wanted to agree but to do so seemed a treacherous negation of Colin. Following his gaze, she numbly beheld some sheep in waterlogged discomfort in a field and cars on a distant road running parallel to the track. It was settled now. Her parents' blessing and talking about finances seemed to seal the whole crazy project with a certainty and inevitability. Impulsively she opened her mouth to say that she didn't think she could go through with it. A sudden rush of air sucked at the train as it was plunged into the dark, reverberating clatter of a tunnel. The carriage lights dipped and extinguished themselves as the roar of their progress came magnified through the half-open window, precluding any attempt at conversation. The tunnel passed — and so did the moment. She saw that Martin had settled back and his eyes were closed.

★ ★ ★

They were married a fortnight later in a register office in Barnes and the Stantons came down for the brief ceremony. Martin, using the excuse of the second battalion being in Cyprus and the first in Scotland, was unattended.

"I would have liked Ian to have been here, but as for anyone else — well, it's probably better this way," he had said, making Sylvia feel more than ever responsible for pressing him into something furtive and 'hole and corner.' He had sought the customary formal permission to marry from his Commanding Officer, who had signalled back his blessing with expressions of pleasure at Martin's satisfactory progress. Ian's own telegram, couched in sexually ribald vein, he kept to himself. Had he shown it to Sylvia she might have thought he was using it to force some kind of an issue, and anyway, it was one upon which he hadn't yet sorted his own feelings. At the present moment Martin couldn't imagine himself ever desiring a woman sexually again. Desire was dead.

103

Cyprus had killed all that. Stone dead. It relieved him to fancy that Sylvia probably felt the same. He was hardly appealing to any woman in his present condition, and her own would most likely have put her off all that kind of thing. But somewhere, somehow, it was a subject that would have to be broached between them and preferably before confronting each other in the honeymoon hotel in the New Forest which had been arranged for them as a surprise by Brigadier Stanton. Martin would have preferred to have gone straight back after the wedding to the flat in Putney he had rented for a three-month period to tide them over his sick leave. Putney had the advantage of being within spitting distance of Roehampton and the limb-fitting centre where he would shortly be spending two weeks at the training school when he was fitted with his arm. When he had suggested such a course, Brigadier Stanton's determinedly well-intentioned generosity would brook no refusal, and after several attempts at polite resistance to his plans for them, the bridal couple had been forced either to capitulate or to appear impossibly churlish.

"Poor Daddy. He meant to be kind. He obviously took what you said about financial embarrassment to heart. They were disappointed enough about the church, but they were determined we'd have a honeymoon. I'm sorry about all the confetti." Sylvia was driving her mother's car, lent to them for the occasion, and she glanced anxiously across at Martin to see if he had been put out by it all. To her relief, he was laughing, and she allowed herself to relax for the first time that day. She had dreaded the actual wedding, but it had all been so much less than majestic, the few short sentences binding them as banal as applying for a driving licence. She had felt no great sense of occasion nor had it seemed like taking a step of any great magnitude.

When they got further into the country, they stopped and shook out their clothes and Sylvia swept the car free of the multitudinous little bits of coloured paper. By the time they reached the hotel, the chilly April day had turned decidedly bleak with a freshening wind and flurries of sleet. Some thicker white flakes settled on the windscreen, then melted.

"Lambing snow. That's what they call it at this time of year in Scotland," Martin said.

There was a huge log fire alight in a cosily panelled hall to welcome them, and polished oak stairs and chintzes and bowls of flowers. Upstairs there were books in the bedroom and wallpaper to match the curtains, latticed windows and a window-seat, tapestried chairs and a fourposter bed. Martin looked at it. Still he hadn't said anything and if he was going to it had better be now. He cleared his throat, but Sylvia forestalled him.

"Which side of the bed would you be more comfortable?" she was asking. She had unpacked her nightdress and was waiting to stake her claim with it. He looked at the plump, frilled pillows lying side by side. If he slept on the right then his stump would be away from her, but if he turned in the night he would be facing her.

He said, "I don't mind. What about you?"

"I'll take the left side then. It's nearer

106

the bathroom and I sometimes have to get up in the night now." She gave studied consideration to the arrangement of her nightdress on the pillow. "Before we go any further Martin, I'd like to know — "

"It's all right. You needn't worry. I don't want you that way." He blurted it out in his anxiety to reassure her. Strain and fatigue etched his face in a cold severity which she read as distaste. He saw her whiten and blink as though he had struck her. He kept forgetting that she was only eighteen. "I'm sorry," he apologized. "That was clumsy." His arm jumped uncontrollably in his empty sleeve as it did when he was particularly tense or overtired. He turned away to hide its involuntary movement from her and jammed his shoulder against the lintel of the adjoining bathroom door to quell the life it appeared to have of its own. "I thought you were afraid of me demanding my marital rights." He took a Dunhill packet out of his pocket, snapped it open with his thumbnail and flipped up a cigarette towards his mouth, The lighter responded first time. He took a couple of deep drags before facing her. "You needn't be."

Sylvia swallowed. "Actually, what I was going to say was, the thing I'm afraid of is us not talking about all this. We haven't so far. Don't you think we should?"

"All what?"

"Well — this." She indicated the baby. "This," making a gesture towards the bed, "and — " she hesitated before ploughing bravely on — "that," referring directly to his arm.

"What is there to discuss?"

"Everything. It would help us both. I'm a person who needs to have things out in the open. I want to make a success of this, Martin, for both of us. We need to get to know each other." She sat down on the bed and waited hopefully for his response.

"I don't see that it does any good talking things into the ground. What's past is past. As far as I'm concerned, the child is ours. Confessions and soul-searching aren't healthy, Sylvia. As for the arm, that's something I have to live with."

"We," she corrected him.

He raised his eyebrows.

"We have to live with," she repeated.

"Yes, I'm sorry that it will affect you." He was immediately uptight.

"You're not being fair. You know I didn't mean that. It's nothing to be ashamed of. I'm going to have to see it some time, Martin. And you're going to have to see me as well, when I'm thick and ugly, when I'm being sick in the morning. I'm shy too. It'll only get worse if we hide from each other, undressing in the bathroom, sleeping apart — too damn polite to fart."

He was listening to her, frowning. He couldn't handle her frankness and was obviously embarrassed by it. There was no way of knowing if she had got through. It hadn't been easy and the least he could do was acknowledge her attempt. Most likely she'd frightened him right off. It would have been nice if he could have shown her some demonstration of friendship, an arm round her shoulders, a compassionate hug, a humorous slap on the bottom. Apart from the time when she had lifted him up that first day in his bed they had not so much as touched each other. He had side-stepped the obligatory kiss at the end of the register office proceedings. If there was to be any real communication between them she was going to have to make the running. But if she made a move he might think she expected a demonstration of his sexual prowess which he was not ready to give. She kept thinking of that damned letter that he'd read. There was a lot she would have liked to explain but she had evidently said too much already.

She stood up and smoothed the bedcover and finished her unpacking. He watched her and when she looked up at him the frown had vanished and there was a kinder expression in his eyes.

"You are an extraordinary girl."

She smiled slowly, relieved. "I know I'm extraordinarily hungry. May we have dinner early — with champagne?"

"I shall have to teach you to appreciate whisky as well now that you're a co-opted Scot."

She hadn't realized quite how empty she was. After the wedding the four of them had lunched at a hotel in

Richmond, but Sylvia hadn't then had the stomach for avocado pears, fresh salmon and strawberries. It was noon most days before her morning nausea receded and usually well into the afternoon before her appetite sharpened. Today nerves had made eating mid-day even more of an impossibility. A delicious dinner of Parma ham and chicken Kiev washed down by Moët and preceded by a couple of malt whiskies at Martin's instigation, did much to revive her confidence and flagging spirits. The alcohol helped, though she knew she would pay for it in the morning, but it was worth it if it could get them through the night. When Martin ordered a second bottle of wine she held her tongue and pretended to keep pace with him glass for glass. Later, when they collected their key at the desk, Sylvia purposely allowed herself to be waylaid by the proprietor's wife and engaged in a discussion on the history of the hotel which had once been a coaching inn. Martin went on up and when she reached the room he was sitting on the bed unbuttoning his shirt.

"I think I'm a bit sloshed." He

111

struggled to get his arm out of the sleeve.

"Let me help."

She thought he was going to refuse, but after only a second's hesitation, he sat passively and allowed her to slide the shirt off his left shoulder and then the right. His skin was very white in contrast to the dark hair that covered his chest and which came as more of a shock to her than the sight of his stump. Colin's body had been smooth and tanned. There was something aggressively male and primitive in the thick black thatch that tapered down to his trouser band. The arm itself wasn't at all repugnant — no discoloration or open wound, just a neatly puckered drawing together of skin over the bone like the finishing off of the toe of a knitted sock. She knew he was waiting for her recoil. She held out his pyjama jacket and he put it on and went off into the bathroom. When he came back she was undressed and in her robe.

"I shan't be long. I'm going to have a bath. Are you all right?"

"Fine. Just tired and a bit the worse

for wear. I may be asleep when you come in. If so, goodnight, Sylvia. And thank you." His words were just the slightest bit slurred.

She didn't know whether he really was asleep twenty minutes later, or pretending.

6

MARIAN had been born in Germany and when she was three months old they had brought her home to be shown off to the Stantons and to be christened. Their posting to Munster on Martin's resumption of service after his sick leave had come as an unforeseen blessing. Under her parents' noses it would have been harder for Sylvia to pass off her new eight-pound daughter as premature, whereas at twelve weeks the baby could reasonably have been expected to have made up a normal weight and size for that age. Upon their arrival in Germany Martin and Sylvia were known to be fairly recently married, but no one had taxed them with an exact date. As Martin's was another Staff appointment, he was among a strange crowd of officers from a mixed bunch of regiments who were meeting him and Sylvia for the first time, so there were no awkward questions to be answered from that direction. Martin had been right. With the passage of time it became harder to believe that Marian didn't belong to them both equally. At least Martin seemed to have no difficulty in deluding himself. He adored the baby and never privately nor publicly gave any sign that he was anything but her proud and doting parent. It was an attitude of which at first Sylvia found herself perplexingly resentful. He had no right to be possessive of Marian. By assuming possession he was crowding Colin out. Sylvia knew she was being ridiculous and grossly unfair, that she was incredibly fortunate that not only had he taken her and the child on but that he actually loved the baby — all the same it was hard to rid herself of this feeling of vexation every time she saw him with it. Marian seemed to release in him the taut spring of tension within which he was coiled all the rest of the time. About him there was always that same sense of a force withheld that had struck Sylvia so potently when she had first seen him in the hospital bed. It made for a total lack of the kind of communication she had optimistically expected could eventually grow from their shared extremities. Martin was not ungenerous with his money, his goods, but when it came to himself he simply didn't know how to share. Sylvia had learned not to press too far. Any probing on her part would shut him up like a clam and precipitate one of his dark periods of silence, during which she was excluded even more completely from his thoughts. Patiently, she attributed these to the trauma of his arm and the barbarity of the action that had deprived him of it. The nightmares too were deeply rooted.

He had suffered them from the beginning — recurring dreams of fending off a murderous assailant from which he awoke alternately shamefaced and sheepish for appearing foolish, or sweating and gasping until Sylvia had soothed him into full wakefulness. It was the nightmares that had kept her in the double bed. There had been singles in the flat in Putney which they had both viewed with relief, but on the second night back from their honeymoon Sylvia had awakened suddenly in the middle of the night alerted by a sixth sense of some unnamed danger. She had sat up and reached for the lamp switch when she had been halted by Martin's whisper, hoarse and wary from somewhere in the room.

"Don't put on the light."

She had obeyed, dry-mouthed, her eyes searching the dark for a possible intruder. There was a commotion in the shadowed corner near where a french window opened on to their third-floor balcony and where a table had evidently been overturned.

"Martin!" Terrified, Sylvia had struggled out of bed.

"Stay there! Don't come near! I've got him!" The curtain was wrenched away from the window and against the background of the upward filtering light from the street lamps Sylvia saw Martin clearly lunge against the catchment and stagger out on to the tiny railed verandah. By now she was fully awake, and fear and sudden reason gave her the impetus to make the dash towards him to grasp his pyjama coat with both hands and pull him backwards into the room. He was struggling wildly as he threw a punch at her with his left hand which missed and swung him off balance. They both crashed to the floor with Sylvia still hanging on like grim death.

"It's all right. It's all right, Martin. There's nobody there." Her voice was calm and clear and she went on repeating her reassurances until she felt him quieten and cease fighting. "You were dreaming. Are you all right?"

"Of course I am," he snapped. "There's no need to make such a fuss."

Sylvia smiled to herself in the darkness. She could sympathize with him feeling all kinds of a bloody fool. If anyone could have seen them they would no doubt have made a comic sight. Extricating herself from their entanglement she got up and put on the bedside lamp. A leg had broken off the pedestal table lying on the floor, otherwise no damage had been done. She propped it up, wedging the splintered member under it and closed the french window, redrawing the curtain. Her heart was racing but she pretended a calm she was far from feeling. The balcony was a mere four feet wide, the wrought-iron safety rail waist-high. Martin was still unbalanced on his damaged wing and any sudden turn to the right could have toppled him, flailing as he had been. Her knees suddenly shook and sweat prickled on her forehead and in her armpits.

He had hauled himself to his feet and pulled himself together enough to remember her condition. "I'm sorry. It was a bad dream. I've had them since — I didn't hurt you, did I?"

She shook her head. "No, I'm fine, but you could have killed yourself. Just as well that I was here. I think I'd better sleep between you and the window from now on. Until you grow out of them. We'll push the beds together in the morning." Seeing his face close, she added, "You can pinch me to shut me up when I snore and I'll prevent you from committing suicide." She grinned at him and got back into bed.

He never had grown out of them. They had gradually become less frequent and Sylvia learned how to wake him and calm him before they were in full spate. On a visit to the Stantons he had 'fought' and shattered a cherished alabaster bedside lamp to his shamed embarrassment, and on another occasion he had sent the Teasmade flying before Sylvia could grab him. They never discussed the incidents next morning. Unlike Sylvia, he couldn't see the funny side of any of these episodes and she soon learned that he regarded the nightmares as some unmentionable practice like bedwetting or masturbation. She found it hard to understand his attitude, but then he was full of complexities she couldn't fathom.

★ ★ ★

He had lived up to his side of their bargain. He had promised her his protection, consideration, duty and loyalty, and those she received in abundance. It had really all worked far better than either of them could have prophesied. There was a lot of shared humour, although in that as in so much else, Sylvia felt Martin let himself go so far and no further. She knew she expressed herself more broadly and frankly than he did but she wasn't convinced he found her earthiness as distasteful as his expression sometimes made out. They both enjoyed similar tastes in books and art, the theatre and music, and with his superior academic knowledge he could be fascinatingly informative without being in the least didactically pompous. In discussions on these subjects his natural enthusiasms shone through and he encouraged her opinions and arguments and enjoyed her shared appreciation. Those were the times when she felt they had what mattered most in common. He was a more knowledgeable, much more interesting man than Colin, but she was conscious of always feeling her way with him whereas with Colin she had been completely herself. And there remained those other times when Martin retreated into himself and she tiptoed on a quicksand in fear of rebuff or cold rejection.

During the first tentative weeks enough of the shyness had worn off between them to make their relationship companionable and they were not left much to their own devices. The superficiality of Army social life abroad helped patch any cracks that might have been more obvious if Sylvia had been sitting at home in a two-up, two-down house waiting for a nine-to-five civilian husband, and she threw herself avidly into the military swim. It helped too that Service life ensured a niche already carved for newcomers, a welcome into a community of people with a common bond and no time for loneliness. Martin had arrived in Munster with the reputation of something of a hero and for the first two months out there he and Sylvia were wined and dined around the Brigade in warm and touching hospitality. Reciprocating all those invitations, coffee-housing, looking after the families' welfare and supporting Martin in attendance at Brigade sporting and other events filled two-thirds of her time. The other third was occupied in preparing for the baby and keeping house. There were eight quarters on the 'patch'. Six were allocated to Captains in semi-detached pairs, identically designed and fitted. Sylvia spent hours turning the W.D. furniture round in an effort to keep a sense of separate identity from numbers one to five. Numbers seven and eight were Majors' quarters, detached and boasting a fourth bedroom and double garage, and their drawing-room suites were loose-covered in Sanderson's chintz instead of being upholstered in serviceable dun-coloured moquette. Seniority even extended to the cup hooks in the kitchen.

"Marjorie's got four more on each shelf than we have, and Isobel's got eight more than Marjorie. I wonder where it's all worked out and who lays down how it shall be. Do you suppose it's all handed down like holy writ from Quarter Master Generals immemorial?" Sylvia pondered. She had never thought to count the cup hooks in her mother's kitchen.

Martin said, "I hope you don't call her Isobel to her face."

"Why not?"

"Well, she is the Colonel's wife."

"She's still a human being," Sylvia said reasonably. "Marjorie's a Major's wife and I call her by her christian name."

"You aren't the Brigadier's daughter now." Martin's rebuke was unexpected and uncalled-for. It was also unjust. Nobody understood better than she the structured class divisions of army rank.

Being a Brigadier's daughter had put her on a pedestal not of her choosing and other people's deference had often left her in splendid isolation. Seeing her chastened, he tried to make amends. "I'm sorry. I didn't mean that as it sounded. The truth is I'm probably jealous of the way you get on with all and sundry. I must seem very conventional to you."

"Sometimes."

"I'm sorry if that makes you unhappy." His voice was stiff and polite.

"Only sometimes," Sylvia said again.

It was the nearest they had so far got to a discussion of their feelings.

She was healing at a pace that made her feel guilty, and on a day a bare eighteen months after Colin's death she was able to acknowledge to herself that she was happy most of the time. Marian was largely responsible for that. She was a gorgeous bouncing, bubbling baby with a cluster of coal black curls and the bluest saucer eyes, thick fringed and wickedly endearing. A true love-child, Sylvia had thought when she had first held her, but only because she was so beautiful and not because there was anything of

Colin in her looks. Sylvia had dreaded the baby would present a daily reminder of past grief, but in the way the devil has of looking after his own, she had been spared that. *Past* grief! She hadn't realized that sorrow had been relegated until she had used that term. She chided herself with being so shallow in having come through without even realizing that she had. For how long had she been goading herself to Colin's memory out of a sense of loyalty? She asked herself that question again next time she felt a pang seeing Martin lift Marian from her cot. If it wasn't Colin she was jealous for, was it herself? Deeply shocked by the implications of such a suggestion, she hadn't been ready to examine them. All the same, something had stirred within her or she wouldn't have been prompted to behave as she had several nights later.

★ ★ ★

Martin had never given any indication that the non-consummation of the marriage was anything but an accepted condition of the terms they had agreed upon between them. Lately the subject had come to occupy Sylvia's thoughts more cogently. After her attempt on their wedding night to make her case clear to him and his rebuff, she had coasted along on the excuses of her pregnancy and his recuperation for doing nothing further about their sexual relationship. However, now her confinement was well past, and as far as she could judge his wounds, mental and physical, had had time to heal. It would be unreasonable to expect either to go on living their present brother- and-sister existence forever, but the longer they left it to try to get things together, the more impossible it would become to do so. Sylvia knew enough about Martin by now to know it was a subject he would never bring himself to talk about. She couldn't categorically state that he hadn't had a woman in the past eighteen months, but she would have bet her bottom dollar he hadn't. He had promised her his duty and loyalty and implicit in those was fidelity. He was the sort of man who subscribed to rules of conduct. Sometimes she found him hard to live up to in this way and he made her all the more aware of her own baser instincts and shortcomings. It was a situation from which, if neglected, all kinds of dangers might arise. Sylvia knew her own nature. She didn't trust herself to remain celibately faithful forever, nor, after what he had done for her, did she want to betray Martin's faith in her. Lately desires which she had considered dead had begun to flicker and tease her, and she wondered whether it could be the same for him. She had never seen him fully naked nor had she ever openly undressed before him. Between them they had observed a tacit acceptance of each other's privacy and the thought of being the one to initiate the breaking of the habit frightened Sylvia more than a little. They had achieved a delicate balance of tolerant comradeship which she might smash if she were clumsy or, in his eyes, too forward. If he rejected her she knew she would never try again, and if she never tried again there would inevitably come a day when there would be another man. After eighteen months she was still a stranger to his emotions and awed by what at times appeared as his strict, paternalistic attitude to her. That particular night, with these thoughts occupying her mind for the hundredth time, Sylvia had prepared for bed and slid down between the sheets, wished Martin a chaste goodnight and turned out the bedside lamp.

The nightmare had crept stealthily upon him in its usual way. He was somewhere in the sunlight and the birds were singing. The world was wearing a mask and only he knew that the radiance and brightness cloaked the growing menace of something threatening and evil. He wanted to shout a warning but no sound came from his open mouth, yet still he must keep trying. People about him were in danger and they must be made to disperse before the light reached its pinnacle at which point it blinded him and he had to put up his arm to shield his eyes. It was his right arm, whole and unimpaired, but it couldn't keep the light out which burned down into his eye sockets, then swam and diffused, forming itself into a man's shape which grew and dwarfed him. The man was there, and Martin shouted unavailingly again for people to look and see him because when the darkness came, the man would be hidden and in the dark he would accomplish his terrible purpose. And then it *was* dark, pitch black, which hurt after the light, and the terror of the unseen enemy lent strength to Martin's limbs as he leaped up to grapple with it, preferring to chance his arm than lie waiting for its bestial attack. His head was pounding and the smell of his own fear filled his nostrils and began to suffocate him like vomit as he gasped for breath. The thing closed with him. It was pushing him backwards. He put up both hands to enclose its throat and in the middle of his panic he exulted in the strength of his right hand. He always knew it was still there. Couldn't he always feel it? The thing was calling out for mercy now but he wouldn't let go. It screamed his name — and then it hit him. He was falling out of a window and he waited for the crash on to the concrete and oblivion. He hurtled down and gave himself a tremendous jerk at the last moment to save his head from connecting with the pavement.

The shock of waking was like the impact of a car smash. It took a moment for the blood to creep back up into his drained skull and the pain of his tensed neck muscles to subside. He was lying face down, half on the bed with his legs trailing on the floor. As he raised his head the light snapped on and he groaned, turning over and trying to sit up to regain some dignity. Sylvia was standing over him looking anxious, one hand to her throat, the other pushing back her hair which she then wore loose and long. She irritated him standing there but at least she had learned to say nothing.

He said finally, "You'll get cold." He hoisted himself tiredly up on to the bed. She bent to tidy the rumpled bedclothes and he saw in the lamplight five ugly red blotches on her neck. His irrational annoyance fell away to be replaced by remorse. "Oh God, did I do that?"

"It doesn't matter. It doesn't hurt." She said it brightly, not looking at him, reaching out to switch off the lamp quickly, but not before he had caught the glint of tears in her eyes. She was ashamed of herself for being so unnerved, but this had been a bad one, and in spite of what she had said her throat was sore and he had frightened her. And then, amazingly, before she had time to straighten she felt his hand in the darkness touch the bruises apologetically.

"God, I'm sorry. I wouldn't hurt you deliberately. You know that, don't you?"

"Of course." She stood up jerkily, expecting him to have retracted his hand, but he hadn't, and her movement caused it to brush down over the rounded top of her breast, where it hesitated, making her catch her breath. Involuntarily, taking her courage and his hand in both hers, she kept his fingers there, swaying slightly curved above him so that the weight of her breast fell cupped into his palm. She hadn't bargained for the electric effect of her action. His arm slid swiftly round her back in a steel grip and pulled her peremptorily with startling speed down on top of him. She fell against his body which was bony hard, unyielding like an iron cage imprisoning some dangerously excited animal. It was as different from Colin's body as could be, as was his approach which savoured no slow sensual build-up and which lacked Colin's tenderness. Yet she was immediately, unbearably aroused. Clamped to his chest, her head lying beneath his chin, she felt the black hair coarse under her cheek where his pyjama jacket had fallen open during his nightmare, and lower down where her short nightdress had rucked up above her waist, his penis was urgent and ramrod stiff against her stomach. Moving her free hand down she grasped it, then sliding her knees forward she put him inside her. He took her fiercely, quickly and angrily, but after the long abstinence she was as ready as he and when she came it was with a hurt and a glory and a degree of sadism that appalled and thrilled her. This time she didn't cry out, nor did he, and the feverishly charged silence lent their activity a curiously furtive exhilaration. Although she was in the dominant position it was he who possessed her, authoritatively and with the passion of one driving out a demon, as if wanting to prove that it was his arm that they had cut off, not his manhood. Later she would have liked to have spoken about that, in the same way that afterwards she had felt moved to put her lips against his stump — but she had done neither. When it was over he didn't speak, nor did he relinquish his hold on her while she lay against him listening to his breathing regain its normal pattern. Presently she felt him slip out of her on a quivering sigh. The silence lengthened until he drew a breath to speak and she was suddenly afraid that he was going to apologize. Before he could do so, if indeed that had been his intention, she got up and laid her fingers gently against his lips. He made no move to kiss them, so, daring, she bent and laid her own mouth lightly for a second on his cheek. With a stab of dismay she tasted the salt wetness of tears and cursed herself for her gesture which, in his pride, he might take as an intrusion. She felt lost and bewildered and out of her league, unable to behave spontaneously as she had with Colin. Long after Martin slept she could still taste his tears.

7

THE shrubbery was dark now and the light in the kitchen showed Sylvia her own reflection in the window above the sink. Remembering, she smiled ruefully at her own naïvety so long ago in believing that physical intimacy automatically unlocked any relationship. The act in itself had solved nothing then or since. If, as a result of it, she had expected the kind of post-coital mental union she and Colin had shared, she had been disappointed and baffled. Opening her body to Colin had been synonymous with opening her mind to him, and his to her. Not so with Martin. The following morning there had been no acknowledgement from him that anything had changed between them, and Sylvia eventually resigned herself to the fact that his reserve was unbreachable. Subsequently, when they made love at longer and longer intervals it was always in silence, and in the dark and, as Sylvia was careful to ensure, only at Martin's instigation. It was something that had been a bitter disappointment at the time but to which she had adapted and grown used. She had, she told herself, much else to thank him for, and any time she was tempted to feel resentful that she had so much more to offer than he wanted to take, she reminded herself that half a loaf was better than no bread.

Shaking herself from her reverie, she left the kitchen and went upstairs to prepare the guest-room. When she came down she could hear the men still in conversation in the drawing-room. As she entered they rose, and she looked swiftly towards Martin.

"Has he told you?" she asked anxiously.

"Some of it. We'll discuss it later, shall we? I expect Stuart would like to wash and brush up before supper. Would you like to show him his room while I get out of this cassock into something more comfortable?"

Relieving Stuart of his empty glass, Martin stood aside to allow him to follow Sylvia. She waited while he fetched his rucksack, then preceded him up the wide oak stairs which were carpeted with a worn Axminster. He followed her, watching the sun-burned calves of her legs going up ahead, and her skirt swinging against them. They were smooth and shiny, each tapering into a neat ankle that he would easily be able to span with the fingers of one hand. Lingering a little, he indulged himself with a view of the tantalizing sway of her buttocks as she mounted. At the top the landing divided into two corridors running left and right, and the staircase continued upwards, narrower and uncovered, to what presumably must once have been the servants' quarters. There were a good many doors to choose from and Sylvia, selecting one facing the stairhead, opened it saying,

"Here you are. I hope you'll be comfortable. If there's anything you need that I've forgotten, just ask. There's a shaver point over the basin. The bathroom's next door, the loo two doors down. Come down when you're ready." She smiled at him and crossed to the door.

He halted her. "Mrs Dearsley — Sylvia

— I'm sorry if I was ham-fisted down-stairs when I met your husband. I didn't realize when I went to shake hands. I hope I didn't embarrass him."

"Not a bit." Sylvia shrugged it off lightly. "Martin's used to that. I should have warned you but I suppose I thought Marian might have said."

"How did it happen? An accident?"

"No. It was before we met. When he was in the Army."

"What was it, a bomb or a grenade?" He seemed not to care that he sounded inquisitive.

Sylvia said curtly, "It was chopped off during what the media would describe as an 'incident'."

He looked shocked. "Not deliberately?"

"More or less."

"Where?"

"Cyprus. It's a long story. I might tell you sometime but not now because my supper is spoiling."

He said gravely, "I should certainly be interested to hear it."

She left him, and a few moments later he could hear her running downstairs as he unpacked thoughtfully.

* * *

Martin was in his dressing-room as she passed. Sylvia went in and found him, cassock discarded, in the act of unharnessing his arm. He gave a small sigh of relief as he disengaged himself from the plastic socket.

"That's better. It's been clammy today. I'll have a quick shower." He disappeared into the adjoining bathroom and Sylvia sat down on the window-seat that overlooked the side garden. When the noise of the water ceased she called through to him.

"How did the service go? I'm sorry I couldn't make it. I was just leaving when he turned up."

Martin returned with a towel wrapped round his waist. He busied himself selecting the clothes he was going to wear.

"It was all right. About twenty in church."

Sylvia got up, realizing this was not the moment. She couldn't help asking, "You're not angry, are you?"

He looked up, genuinely surprised.

"With you? No. With Marian — furious."

"At least we know she's alive."

"No thanks to her," he said grimly. "I'm livid at what she's put you through. And I've a feeling it's not over."

She noticed he didn't say 'us'.

"All the same, it's such a terrific relief."

His attitude relaxed as he admitted, "For me as well."

He didn't know whether she believed him. Sylvia had always thought him harsh with Marian, but if he had been strict it had only been meant for the girl's own good. She might not be his own flesh but Martin saw much of himself in her. Without self-discipline she had too much spirit to keep her on the straight and narrow. He had only wanted to save her from his own mistakes. It was apparent that he had failed, and that hurt him. Not just the fact of failure, but that he couldn't communicate his sense of regret. Once you started shutting doors on feelings they couldn't get out, however hard you tried to set them free. It was a lack in him that he felt acutely but about which he was helpless to do anything. He doubted whether Sylvia dreamed he was even aware of it. He had wanted to comfort her many times during the past two years but had not known how to make the simple gesture. Her unspoken accusation that he had driven Marian away lay between them. Bringing the subject into the open would have involved cracking the behavioural pattern of their marriage and that was something they were both too reticent to dare. They were used to each other as they were.

He had made it doubly difficult for her, coming out of the Army when he had. Sylvia had survived a couple of big enough adjustments at that time — marriage to him in difficult circumstances and having a baby — and she had just been settling down in a milieu in which she felt confident again. His decision had come as a thunderbolt, no less the fact that he had taken it without consulting her.

"You mean you've actually sent in your resignation and it has been accepted?" She had been stunned. "Without telling me?"

"I had to thrash it out in my own mind. I didn't want to be influenced against what I know is the right thing to do," he defended himself.

"But for God's sake, why? You love the Army. All your friends are in the regiment."

"It's not the same now — with this." He indicated his hand and despised himself for using it as the main excuse. It was true that it hampered him on exercises and training and that he could no longer shoot or tackle an assault course as of old. Neither could he stand the noise of thunderflashes or bullets exploding without experiencing the cold sweat of remembrance. Because he couldn't tell her the complete truth, he magnified these frailties.

She had tried to brace him. "You're giving up too soon. Look at Roger Packer in the Black Watch. He's got a gammy foot but he's still serving. You haven't given yourself time to get adjusted. Tell the Colonel you want to reconsider. Give yourself a chance."

"It's not only that. I've lost my nerve. I'm not fit to command soldiers and they

141

would be the first to discover that fact. It wouldn't be right for their lives to be in my charge."

"If that's true," she had persisted, "put in for sick leave. We'll go away together and you can get things into perspective. Don't throw your whole career away."

"I've *had* sick leave. It's no good, Sylvia. The truth is that I'm afraid. I'm a coward. I want to get out."

They had stared at each other through a long silence. Martin remembered how she had looked, standing there with a dawning compassion in her eyes which he didn't deserve. He could see she thought she understood. Finally she had said, "Have you thought at all of what you will do?"

He had drawn a deep breath and cleared his throat. "I want to go into the Church. After all, I'll be following family tradition and that's what I intended originally when I got side-tracked by Ian into the Army."

"The Church!" It was the last thing Sylvia had imagined and it represented everything foreign to her way of thinking. Instead of breaking down the barriers

142

between them he intended erecting more. She had been raised in the Church of England, to whose practices Brigadier and Mrs Stanton had paid token service at Sunday church parades, and she had endured Chapel twice daily and three times on Sundays at school, but she was no longer, if she had ever been, an orthodox believer. Through experience she had evolved a faith acknowledging a power or life force beyond her comprehension. For want of a better word Sylvia called it God. Experience too suggested that there were 'more things in heaven and earth' than she might have dreamed of, so that an after life could not be discounted, but there it stopped. Experience and intellect combined refuted one solitary path to salvation and the hidebound rules of a man-made hierarchy for its achievement. When she had recovered from the initial shock of Martin's revelation, Sylvia had accepted that his choice was in character. Since birth he had been part of one institution or another. Primarily it had been the Church under his father's narrow influence, then school, university, the Army — and now once more, the Church. The security of a laid-down code of conduct evidently furnished his sense of stability and was necessary to him. Sylvia rationalized. She was good at making the best of things.

* * *

It wasn't until the end of the meal that the subject of Marian was broached. Sylvia thought: Here we are, the three of us, with Marian uppermost in all our minds and dying of curiosity, and we have to play this absurdly British game of well-bred, side-stepping small talk.

Martin eventually led into it in a roundabout way. Stuart had commented upon a series of regimental prints lining the wall beside the staircase and expressed a fascination for military memorabilia.

"If you're really interested you must see our collection in the dining-room," Martin said. "Sylvia calls it the regimental shrine. We've got a few nice statuettes, medals, that kind of thing."

"Did you miss the life very much when you came out, sir?" Stuart asked. He had worked his way through Sylvia's casserole with relish, completely at home.

"It was harder for Sylvia than for me. I'm afraid it still is at times. Of necessity I get very engrossed with my flock and it's a round-the-clock job." Martin put his knife and fork together. "What sort of work do you do, Stuart? By the way, I'd feel far less ancient if you dropped the 'sir' and called me Martin."

Stuart said, "Thank you, sir — " hesitated, and then they all laughed. Pushing his plate away from him, he rested his elbows easily on the table and answered Martin's question. "I sell agricultural machinery. Mostly in the Far East." He mentioned the name of an internationally recognized firm. "We manufacture and have our head office in Birmingham. I work for Malcolm Quennell, the managing director of the London department at High Holborn."

Martin said, "I see." He surveyed Stuart over the top of his wine glass. He had insisted on opening a bottle of Mouton Cadet in celebration. "And is agricultural machinery what brought you in contact with Marian?"

"Hardly. Actually it was quite by coincidence. I was in Java and Sumatra on business which I had arranged to round off with a week's holiday in Bali. I've got a girlfriend there who works for the Garuda airline. A grumbling appendix that had troubled me from time to time blew up and I was taken into hospital in Denpasar, where they whipped it out. While I was recovering, Marian was brought in for surgery. The hospital there is small and it was full, so she was put into a curtained-off cubicle at the end of my ward."

"Surgery? What was wrong with her?" Sylvia's eyes and voice were full of alarm.

Stuart looked grave. "She, as it happens, also had an appendicitis, but in her case the appendix had burst. Peritonitis and complications had set in and she had to have a piece of the bowel removed." He hurried on, forestalling their horrified questions. "Apparently she hadn't been well, but the cause of the trouble hadn't immediately been diagnosed because there was a gastric bug going around the commune in Durga at the time and Marian's symptoms of stomach ache and vomiting were put down at first to that. She told me there is no qualified doctor in the Shivine, only one or two nurses and a couple of drop-outs from medical school. However, once her condition was realized they did pull out all the stops. The Shivine has paid for all her treatment so far and seen her through."

"Praise heaven for that at least," said Martin.

"Yes, but the problem now is that they want reimbursement, and Marian is broke."

Sylvia said whitely, "She drew every penny she possessed out of her account and her savings banks before she left. We discovered that much after she had gone. She had a little money of her own from my parents. What has happened to that?"

"I'm afraid that's all gone to the Shivaan already." Stuart made a face. "He milks his adherents of whatever they've got. What was intact of it when she and Billy got to Jakarta went in registration fees for them both and into the communal kitty."

"Damn little fool!" Martin's exasperation and anxiety boiled over to the extent of uncharacteristic expletive. "I suppose she sent you to ask us for the money. How much does she need to be free of these people?"

"Two thousand pounds. They had to fly a specialist in from Singapore to do the job. Marian was too sick to be moved."

"Two thousand pounds! And what if they don't get it? They'd have no legal hold on her, I dare say, if their activities were investigated. I imagine investigation would be the last thing they would seek. Their case would never stand up in a court of law. What's to stop her just walking out when she's fit enough? She'd need her fare home. That we could find somehow." Martin looked at Sylvia for her agreement but she wasn't listening. She was turned towards Stuart fearfully.

"A piece of the bowel removed, you say? But that's a major operation. Why didn't you say so at the beginning? Do you mean she's still in hospital? How did she take it and is she going to be all right?" In her rising agitation she made a gesture towards him which knocked over her glass. The wine spilled, trickling off the edge of the table and on to Stuart's clothes, and the next few seconds were occupied with Sylvia's apologies and joint mopping-up operations. She jumped up to get a cloth and behind her back Martin said, "Well, is she?"

Stuart said, "Don't worry. It's all over now." He took the cloth from Sylvia and wiped his trousers.

"But where is she? Can we get her home? Can she travel?" She couldn't understand how he could have sat there allowing them to exchange pleasantries when all the time he had news of this importance to impart.

Stuart said, "I'm afraid it's not quite as simple as that. As you say, there's be nothing to stop her walking out. Except herself." He paused significantly. "It's not a case of her wanting to be free of these people, as you put it." Sylvia and Martin both stared at him. Stuart nodded. "She is dead set on going back to the Shivine when she leaves hospital. They won't readmit her until she pays her debt to them, but she's determined to do so and to stay with them."

"But she can't," Sylvia said incredulously. "She can't be that crazy. They've cheated her already and now they're extorting more."

"She doesn't see it that way. She says what she gave them was a gift. Repayment for the operation is a moral obligation."

"That's all very well, but if she can't repay they'll kick her out, and as far as I can see that would be the best thing that could happen for Marian's sake. She may not appreciate it immediately but she'll come to her senses eventually. Even if I could, I wouldn't give her any financial encouragement to remain mixed up in all that rubbish." Martin closed his mind to occasions in the past when his confidence in Marian's 'coming to her senses' had too often proved falsely optimistic.

"I don't think you quite understand, sir. She's rabidly fervent, in the way of converts. She's threatened to get the money by hook or by crook. To give her her due, it was she who refuted my suggestion that you might cough

150

up. It was when she told me how she intended to lay her hands on it that I found myself in a cleft stick." Stuart looked at Sylvia. "As far as the Shivine goes, as I said, if that's Marian's choice, then that's her business. We all have the right to choose, and if she's prepared to be fleeced in what she regards as a vital cause, then that's her prerogative. Like Martin's parishioners who are encouraged to join the planned giving or save the church tower." He paused, and Sylvia could see that Martin did not appreciate the analogy. "You may rightly ask why I chose to make her my business or why what happens to her should be my concern," Stuart continued. "Well, when she was brought in she was in very poor shape. She and I were the only English people there. I spoke to her before she went down to the theatre and I sat with her when she came back. She was very homesick during the days immediately after, though people came to see her from the Shivine. That's when I met Billy. That's when she told me she had quarrelled with her parents. She was too

151

proud to send for you and too afraid you would haul her back home if she did. When you get to know someone in those circumstances you short-circuit the preliminaries. Hospital is like being on board ship. No other world exists." He stopped. Sylvia avoided looking at Martin and wondered if he too was remembering. She thought about Stuart saying that he and Marian had been close for a while. He hadn't meant then what she had assumed. She ridiculed the fact that her own heart lightened at the realization, suffocating a dangerous fantasy.

"She was wary of me at first," Stuart went on. "Like a timid animal. They're warned to be on their guard all the time and that's why the Shivites came in daily. Always in twos and threes. There have been attempts by relatives to kidnap some of them back into their old world. There are organizations who send de-programmers, and to a Shivite, to be snatched by one of them is the same as the surrender of your immortal soul would be to you, Martin. She gradually learned to trust me. I put no pressure on her by questioning her about the past or the present or her motives in giving her life to the Shivine. I would have given her the money she needed to get back in with them myself, but I hadn't got it. Then one of them came in and told her there was a way. Someone he knew who organized couriers carrying cannabis, heroin and cocaine between Singapore and Bangkok. He said one run would see her clear. Two at the most. She was quite calm and detached about it. She told me with a quiet, innocent fanaticism. I told her that the penalty in Bangkok was death if she was caught. She said that outside the Shivine it would be a living death and she preferred to take the risk. She'd see herself as some kind of a martyr — they're all that crazy."

Sylvia shivered. "She's got to be stopped. They're using her. They probably use others. It's a cover for running drugs. Martin, surely the police . . . She's done silly things before but this is criminal."

Stuart said, "For whatever cock-eyed reason, I tell you she's desperate to get that money. And if you aren't thinking straight and you're desperate, you'll do anything, won't you?" His question was rhetorical and Martin didn't answer. He was fiddling with the stem of his glass, absent-mindedly aligning its rounded base with the whorled pattern of the folk-weave tablecloth. When he raised his eyes to find them both staring at him there was a strange, vacant expression in them. He blinked.

"How do we know it's all true?" he asked.

"Martin!"

"No, it's a good question, Sylvia." Stuart seemed not at all put out by his host's scepticism. "I suggest you ring the hospital for yourself — Denpasar 5602 — and — " he reached into the back pocket of his jeans and produced a plastic wallet that he flipped open and dropped down on to the table — "here's my identification."

Martin pulled it towards him and glanced at an array of credit cards, a kidney donor authorization and a company identity plaque.

"I've got a passport upstairs — and there's always my operation scar!"

Sylvia wasn't sure whether Stuart was

mocking himself or them, and she felt embarrassed as though she had been forced into a breach of good taste.

"Why don't you put the call through now?" Stuart consulted his watch and made a rapid calculation. "It will be early morning there, but not too early."

"Martin, please do."

Martin looked from Sylvia's tense, white face to Stuart's faintly challenging expression.

"All right." There was a telephone extension on the wall by the door and he went over to it and lifted the receiver. While he was waiting for the international operator Stuart sat relaxed, his arms folded, and Sylvia stared fixedly at the table. When the answer came and Martin had dealt with the preliminaries, he mouthed at Stuart who supplied the number once more.

"Denpasar 5602," Martin repeated into the instrument.

They all went on waiting, then Martin suddenly said, "Hallo. Hallo. Is that the general hospital in Denpasar?" He turned and nodded at Stuart and Sylvia. "I believe you have my daughter as a

155

patient. A Miss Marian Dearsley. Yes, Dearsley. You have? May I speak to her, please?"

There was a silence while Martin listened.

"I see," he said. "Yes, I understand." He looked towards Sylvia and then turned back to face the wall. "Well then, can you tell me how she is? Is she recovering well? Mm. Yes. Good. Good. Thank you. When would be a good time to speak to her if I rang again? I see. But she's definitely all right? Mm. One more thing. What is the situation as regards payment for my daughter's medical treatment, the operation, anaesthetic, etc?" A lengthy silence ensued. "It has? Yes. I understand. Thank you. No, no message. Goodbye." Martin hung up, leaving his hand resting against the wall, assimilating what he had heard. After a second he turned slowly.

"Well?" Sylvia couldn't contain her impatience.

"They're very pleased with her. She's going to be all right. She was having a supervised bath, that's why I couldn't speak to her and perhaps it's just as well I couldn't. We don't want to frighten her off. The woman I spoke to says it's not all that convenient as they only have one portable phone. Marian might have been afraid we were going to pressure her and go and do something hasty. I thought it better to say no message." He looked at Stuart. "You're right. Her expenses have been taken care of by her friends. Approximately £1,985 sterling."

An embarrassed silence was broken by Stuart's movement to replace his wallet.

"I would have to find a way of raising that kind of money, if we decided that was what needed to be done," Martin mused aloud. "On a clerical stipend I hardly have £2,000 lying spare in the bank," he said drily. "I have no shares, and this house doesn't belong to me so I can't raise a mortgage."

"What do you mean, *if* we decided?" Sylvia demanded.

He made a gesture. "Well, how long does one go on? I'm not unaware or uncaring of the dangers into which Marian may foolishly be running herself. Set against that, there comes a time when people have to take individual

157

responsibility for their actions. As you yourself pointed out, Stuart, Marian is free to choose and she is very nearly twenty."

"It's not old enough to expect a high degree of maturity," Sylvia defended.

"You took some big decisions very much younger," Martin reminded her. "We both did," he added.

"You expect a lot. You can't judge her by your own strength of character. Most of us are weaker vessels." Stuart weighed in on Sylvia's side.

"You were the one who said she was responsible enough to decide to stay with the Shivine, now you are saying that she is not mature enough to take responsibility for this other decision. You can't have it both ways," Martin said quietly.

Stuart flushed. "Obviously it's up to you to decide what's to be done — if anything. I merely came here because I felt I had to. I don't mean to interfere, but I grew fond of Marian."

Sylvia jumped into the breach. "We don't think you're interfering. We're eternally grateful to have news of any sort, and for what you did to help Marian through her illness. Aren't we, Martin?"

"Very grateful," Martin said formally. "You've given us a lot to sleep on, Stuart." He pushed his chair into the table to indicate the end of the meal and the subject. "I imagine if you have been travelling you'll be ready to turn in early yourself. We mustn't forget that you are also convalescing."

There were a thousand more questions Sylvia wanted to ask but she could see from Martin's face that he didn't want to pursue the subject further in front of Stuart.

Stuart said, "That's all right. Whatever you decide, I shall be going back to see Marian before her discharge. I promised her that. She gave me her word she would do nothing foolish until we had talked again."

"You're going back then, soon?"

"I have a business meeting in Jakarta on Friday morning. I shall go to Bali immediately afterwards."

"So you'll leave UK when — Thursday?"

"Yes."

"And you could take the money back with you?" Sylvia persisted.

"I could — but I don't think — "

There was a ring at the doorbell and Martin went to answer it.

She said, "Will you please stay until then? Just give me time. He's not as unsympathetic as he sounds but two thousand pounds is a heck of a lot of cash to us. This isn't the first time he's bailed Marian out and there's nothing to say that it will be the last. There are reasons why I can't put too much pressure on, but if you are here . . . What Martin said was true. He has no private income and what I was left by my parents was exhausted long ago. We've got one or two decent bits of furniture, family heirlooms, which would raise a bit, and there's my jewellery, but that doesn't amount to much. We are the proverbial church mice."

He said casually, "There was a Russell Flint in the drawing-room and the two bronzes in the hall must be worth a bob or two." Before the presumption had time to jar he added, "You look expensive. That's a nice dress."

Rather primly she said, "I make my own clothes."

"Congratulations. You're more than just a fascinating face."

It was such a blatant and well-worn line as he ran an openly approving glance over the rest of her, but somehow it was robbed of oily impertinence by his frank and smiling appreciation. There was a warm, easy-going friendliness in his manner, the confidence of liking and expecting to be liked. That was the way of the young nowadays, Sylvia thought. She envied them. They were sometimes tactless in their honesty but you knew where you were with them when they went straight to the point. She recalled a time when she had been like that. Conditioned to caution as she now was, would she have befriended a mixed-up stranger far from home and put herself out to save her from herself as Stuart had Marian? Far more likely Sylvia would have avoided involvement with an embryo delinquent like the plague. She had grown too accustomed to weighing her words and actions.

Impulsively she said, "I'm so grateful

and glad you came."

He began to help her stack the dirty plates and carry them to the draining-board. He was beginning to be especially glad himself.

8

STUART lay on the bed smoking and letting the night breeze waft in gentle puffs over his naked body. He was cooling down after a hot bath which had been a luxurious experience after a restless night in flight and twenty-seven hours' solid travel. A blissful lassitude crept into his muscles, making his limbs heavy and torpid, but it did not extend to his brain which remained keen and resolutely wide-awake behind his unclosed eyes. He had extinguished the bedside light against its invitation to the moths and other flying creepie-crawlies of the late summer's night, but there was enough light in the room from an unclouded moon to reveal the shapes of heavy mahogany furniture, and the glinting glass covering a panoramic watercolour reproduction of the British Fleet in Malta Harbour. The Stantons had served in Malta before the war, some years before

Sylvia's birth. Through the lower half of the open sash drifted the scent of the dew-dampened garden — a peculiarly English smell which beat all your bougainvillœa and hibiscus and frangipani wilting after a day in the heat and humidity and dust. It seemed strange to think that all that was only twenty-seven hours away. Unreal as all the other links in the chain of events that had led him to this evening — this moment.

He had been twelve years old and in his first term at Stowe, standing in his housemaster's study while 'Badger' Brock clumsily broke the news to him that his brother was dead. The nickname was particularly apt, not merely on account of the master's name, but also because of his dark brows arching low and slanted highly back, his pointed nose and chin, and the way his dark hair sleeked down and over the flattened dome of his skull, disappearing into the collar of his black gown. His shoulders hunched, and he snuffled and grunted, usually with impatience at a dull-witted boy too slow to supply an immediate answer. Badger snuffled now, but in embarrassment and in search of appropriate condoling clichés. Being a plain mathematician, he wasn't much of a word-merchant, he was fond of saying. He said it now. Stuart had felt no blazing personal grief. Colin had been double his age and their worlds had not yet merged. His prime emotion was anger at the futile waste of a life lost for no particular cause — Cyprus wasn't even a patriotic war — and later, a bitter antagonism for the unknown person or persons who destroyed his beloved mother as surely as if she as well as Colin had been their target.

Stuart had been a 'mistake', born on his mother's change, but after her initial shock, he was none the less loved by her for that fact. In fact he had been spoiled as an only child and allowed to get away with behaviour for which Colin would have had his knuckles rapped a decade previously. His father had died of a coronary four years before Stuart stood fidgeting on Badger Brock's carpet, so the news that morning filled him with a double importance — as an object of curiosity and sympathy from the rest of the school, and as his mother's prime support and the man in her life. Once she got over it, she would enjoy things again, they would do all kinds of things together and have fun, and it would be all the better for being just the two of them. Stuart had respected but not loved his father, who had been a more remote figure, not always agreeing with the way his wife indulged Stuart. Now there was no one to come between them. But she hadn't got over it and because she hadn't, nothing was fun — ever again. Oh, she had relied upon him as he had wanted her to, but reliance became total dependence and not wanting to let him out of her sight. He was growing, and so was resentment. But it was not a resentment with his mother whom he loved best in the world, and understood. No, his loathing was reserved for that unknown person whose action had changed her and turned her sweet nature in upon itself. He found it necessary to blame someone, and guilt wouldn't allow him to lay it upon his mother for not attempting to snap out of it herself. His muddled adolescent emotions were unable to admit the disloyalty of criticism of her. He gorged on her venomous hatred for the man who had pulled the trigger on Colin, and with her he went through over and over again the War Office's letter describing Colin's part in the action. She still had the case of Colin's effects that had been returned to them posthumously and which she took out and handled and stroked, then laid reverently back. When he was older and he could recognize her obsession as the unhealthy product of an unhinged mind, he found her no less pitiable or lovable, nor did he ever quite outgrow it himself.

Why else had he eventually gone to Cyprus in adulthood with the express purpose of looking for the site of Colin's death? He had made the pilgrimage to lay his mother's ghost, not Colin's, and if he preferred to tell himself it was merely a holiday, that was because he wasn't a sentimental man. He smiled privately at the chance of being described as such by any of the people with whom he presently had dealings. There was scant room for sentiment in business, least of all his kind. It was a long time since he had felt any real emotion towards another human being, not since his mother's death. Even before that, there had been only her. Appetites — yes, in plenty, but no love except for himself. That was the safest way to be. He had seen love destroy her. At too early an age he had been filled up with a poison that had stunted his capacity for feeling. A cloud obscured the moon, blackening the room. He drew the sheet up over the lower half of his body, staring beyond the pitch, seeing again the heat haze and the dusty road and a handful of wilting flowers adorning a garishly painted Cypriot wayside icon.

He had hired a car and travelled east from Limassol, armed with a map, a compass and the memorized bearings detailed in the Ministry of Defence account of where and how Colin had met his death. It was the penultimate day of his holiday and he had resisted until then the call strong within him to exorcize his obsession with Colin and to find the place. He couldn't have said what it was he had expected to discover, if anything. He was merely following an instinct that had dominated him since setting foot on Cypriot soil — if he were honest, since entering the travel agent's office in Berkeley Street. Yet still he procrastinated as the clapped-out rented Citroën churned its laborious way towards its goal, stopping to admire here a mediaeval castle keep, there a village pottery, or the baskets of split reeds and willow twigs made by the peasants at Livadhia. After lunch he turned off the main tourist route, heading north. Eventually the road narrowed to a single track and then the thin strip of tarmac curved eastward, running parallel to the busier coast road which he had left. It rose to peaks from which the sea was visible and plunged to depths where it snaked along gullies between the hills. On the upward gradients the Citroën hesitated between gear changes, pinking and spluttering with the effort of responding to Stuart's foot on the accelerator pressed to the floor. Going down, he had difficulty in controlling a determined pull to the left when braking, and he mistrusted a compensatory swing at the back as he slithered gingerly along the melted tar in the centre of the road, doing his best to avoid the dangerously

169

crumbling camber at each edge. Coming to a halt in the second valley, he got out and surveyed his surroundings. If the chart was right, it had to have happened somewhere near here. It was a Godforsaken enough spot, hemmed in and desolate, perfect for an ambush. The rocks and brush around him afforded cover for a hundred unseen eyes and Stuart's flesh suddenly crawled. The sun was dipping westward, shadowing one half of the mountain to his left. The noise made by the cicadas accentuated the utter stillness in which he was entrapped. A sixth sense told him that if this wasn't the place, then it was at least very near, and as in a dream he had begun to walk away from the car with his eyes on the road. Foolish as it was, he was looking for signs of a crater repaired, a fresh-looking piece of tarmac, any evidence that at some point one piece of the road had been mended. Reason insisted upon the insanity of any such expectation after this length of time. It was eight years since the explosion and he couldn't be a hundred per cent sure that he was even in the right valley, yet he didn't feel ridiculous.

He had come so far and there *had* to be something. He could sense his mother's presence, her gratitude. "At least I came, and for your sake I got as near as I could to the truth," he told her silently. And then, like a miracle, he had rounded a bend and seen the little bridge, and the girl with the flowers in her hands.

She was only a child, about nine or ten years old, in a faded pink cotton skirt and skimpy blouse. Their surprise at seeing each other was mutual. He had come silently up behind her in his canvas shoes, and now he smiled to allay the look of sudden alarm in her pointed little pixie face caused by his strange presence. She was attending to a wooden icon set back into a niche in the stone parapet of the bridge. A plaster madonna gazed blandly up from the foot of a chipped cross at the tortured body of her crucified son. The figures were cracked, but a recent attempt had been made to touch up the blue of Mary's gown, the golden haloes and a vivid scarlet background. The newness of the paint was already overlaid with gritty dust, and a daisy-chain wreath of multi-coloured wild flowers adorning the Madonna's neck was faded and brittle. It was these flowers that the girl was in the act of replacing when Stuart had come upon her, and once she had accepted his greeting she turned back to the task he had interrupted. Beneath the icon there was some Greek lettering cut into the stone. She was the first human being he had seen since he had turned off the main coast road and her presence denoted the existence of a village or some kind of habitation nearby, as she had no visible means of transport and had evidently made her pilgrimage on foot. Stuart's eerie sense of isolation fell away and he began to feel faintly idiotic. What the hell was he doing here anyway? He watched her twitch a flower into place. Looking back and seeing him still standing there, the child made a gesture for his approval.

"English? Nice — eh?" she said.

"Very pretty." He nodded agreeably.

She had used up all the flowers. She put her head on one side contemplating her work. "Is necessary more."

Below the bridge the river bed was

dry, but there were small bright patches of colour growing out of the stony bank where the water had been and would rise again. The girl jumped down to gather more flowers and Stuart turned back towards the car, all melodramatic fancies fled, dispersed by common sense.

★ ★ ★

He started the engine and went forward. A staccato knocking became audible under the bonnet, increasing in volume and rapidity as the car's pace accelerated. By the time Stuart reached the corner and had decided upon the wisdom of stopping before worse damage was done, there was a loud crack and a bang and the car slewed far to the left, coming to rest broadside across the road.

"Hell and damnation!" He got out and gave vent to his anger with the contraption by futilely kicking the front wheel with all his night, practically fracturing his toe.

"Hell and damnation!" He nursed his foot, muttering further imprecations. Hearing the child laughing at him did nothing to improve his temper. She danced across the road and surveyed the situation. He simmered down. She would surely know where he could get help.

"Finish. Broken. Kaput." He smiled at her ruefully. "You," he pointed to her, "take me," indicating himself, "to get help?" He waved his hand to encompass their surroundings hopefully and raised his eyebrows in exaggerated enquiry.

"Kaput!" That seemed to amuse her greatly. When she had finished giggling she volunteered, "I understand small piece English. Come." She skipped down once more into the river bed on his side of the road and beckoned him to follow. Stuart hobbled after her, wincing each time the cushion of his big toe encountered a stone under his thin sole. The wadi twisted through a break in the hillside and a quarter of an hour later came out the other side upon a huddle of white flat-roofed buildings. The buildings lay on two sides of a breaker's yard in which a couple of haulage vehicles were parked. An unmade track meandered into the distance to join a main road some three hundred yards distant. This side of the hill the sun was still hot on the plain. A pie-dog ambled lazily from the shade of the doorway of the biggest building and made an unconvincing display of aggression. The child ignored it and ran through the doorway calling out to someone inside. Stuart heard an animated exchange of Greek, then a woman emerged, shielding her eyes from the sun. She was about forty, with a firm, ripe body and thick hennaed hair, bronzed like her skin. As she approached Stuart saw that her face was older than the rest of her, lined about the forehead and eyes, and there were already cracks running up from her top lip into which her lipstick had smudged. Her mouth had pulled itself together tightly too often to let go into its natural shape. She looked suspiciously at Stuart as he started to explain his predicament.

To his immense relief she spoke good enough English to understand his difficulty and she said her husband would help him by taking his truck and towing the car round as soon as he returned. Stuart thanked her and mopped the inside of his collar and his forehead with his handkerchief. The woman said he had better wait inside and, taking him into the house which was considerably more comfortable than its exterior suggested, she gave him an iced beer and sat down at the table with one herself. She child sidled up to Stuart, watching him with darting, birdlike gaze. He discovered her name was Melina.

"Lina for short," the woman volunteered.

"It was lucky for me that I met Lina. I would have had a long walk, not knowing the short cut."

"In summer — every day I go. In winter — water comes, I go once a week in papa's truck," the child piped.

"To the valley, she means. To put the flowers."

"For Uncle Jan."

Stuart looked at the woman enquiringly.

"My brother Jannis," she explained. "He was killed in the troubles." Her voice was hoarse and heavy — without expression.

"Is it some kind of a war memorial?" Stuart remembered the inscription which he hadn't been able to decipher.

"He and many of our people killed

there." She looked at him dispassionately as though she had long since become inured to tribulation. Stuart felt his heart stop — and start again jaggedly.

"Jannis." He said it almost under his breath. "Jannis — Nicolaides?" He tentatively tried the taste of the name out loud.

Her eyes sharpened, narrowed. "You know Jannis?"

He shook his head. His throat was dry and he had finished his beer.

"I think I have read about him," he tried experimentally. "In the history books. The history of EOKA."

"History!" She spat the word and wiped her mouth with the back of her hand where the beer froth glistened. "My husband, Costas, he talk of history. Is proud of history. All men make wars for history. Better history forgotten. No wars then. History dead. Jannis alive. Crazy men never want to forget. Same for British, eh? You not want to come and throw away lives here for history. Hatred no good."

"No." He hardly knew what he was saying. All he could think of was that he had been right to feel as he had about the valley. His intuition had not failed him. Fate had led him not only to the site, but incredibly to this woman who belonged to the enemy. Something must have showed in his face because she leaned forward and studied him closely.

"You hate. Why?"

"I have good reason to." He had forgotten caution. "Is that where your people ambushed a British truck to free Nicolaides?"

She didn't have to answer. He could see from her eyes that it was, and that she was wondering just what was his connection with it all. Was his story of the broken-down car a fabrication? Where was Costas? He should be back and she was alone here with the child and with this stranger. She half rose from the table but he prevented her, grasping her by the wrist.

"My brother was the officer in the truck," he said bitterly.

She caught her breath and he saw that he had completely knocked the wind out of her sails. He let her go and she subsided back on to her chair.

"Your brother?" Her hand fluttered to her ribcage as though he had dealt her a blow in the solar plexus. Under her tan her colour drained, giving her face a muddy tinge, bereaving it of vitality. She whispered a name. "Martin!"

Stuart had to bend forward to catch it and it didn't make sense. Nonplussed he said, "My name is Stuart Coleby. My brother, Colin, was the officer your people killed."

She blinked at him, but didn't speak. Absent-mindedly she smoothed her hand up over her breast and down again in a stroking movement as though a pain there could be soothed or erased. At last she said, "So — you still hate." She nodded and shrugged her shoulders as if she accepted the inanity of the male. She was regaining her composure. "What you want we should do? We killed your brother. You killed mine. You want now you and I should make war because of History? Men! Always like little boys." She slapped the palm of her hand down on the table in a gesture of contempt.

"Don't tell me there wasn't a time when you didn't want revenge for your

179

brother. *You* may have forgotten now, but I cannot," Stuart said hotly.

"Revenge?" She spoke the word quietly, and her mouth twisted. Getting up, she went over to the refrigerator and got out another couple of cans of beer. With her back to him she said, "Who's to revenge? Where is the man?" She snapped the rings back on the cans and brought him one. She looked at him mockingly.

"I don't know." She made him feel silly and immature with her tolerant philosophy and those eyes that had seen everything.

"I do not want to know where is the man. Once perhaps — " she ran her finger up the side of the beer can, dispersing the chilled beads of condensation contemplatively.

"What man?"

She raised her eyes and looked at him seriously. "Is the same man. You do not know?"

Her use of the language muddled him. "I don't understand," he said. "How should I know?"

"Is the same man," she insisted. "Same for you. Same for me."

He felt even more at sea, like a man trying to grasp a lifebelt floating just out of reach. Impatiently she thrust her face close up to his to hammer home her meaning, both arms braced and grasping the table between them. He remembered afterwards the damp spreading stain on her cotton shirt where she had held the been cans against her, a whiff of garlic on her breath, strong white peasant teeth marred by a tiny chip out of a central lower incisor.

"Same man killed your brother — my brother."

It was a let-down. He had been expecting some kind of revelation, but she had, as he had suspected, got her wires crossed.

He said, "My brother was shot by your people."

For the fourth time, "Same man," she said. "He did not pull trigger. Oh no." A wagging finger dramatically denied the actual deed, then knowingly touched the side of her nose. "But because of him both died. British traitor."

He stared at her. "British?" He remembered the name that had been wrung involuntarily from her. "Dearsley?" He accented the name incredulously. "Martin — Dearsley?"

It took a few moments to try the idea for size, then he said,

"Tell me."

Ariana told him.

9

HE had somebody real to hate and blame now, but there wasn't any way in which Stuart could use the information to harm Martin Dearsley. If he had taken such a cock-and-bull tale to the Ministry of Defence it would have been his word against the records, and Ariana, if approached, would deny everything. She had too much to lose. She had spoken in an unguarded moment, visibly regretting the indiscretion afterwards, and she had more than one good reason for letting sleeping dogs lie. For all her talk about forgiveness, she was motivated like all the rest of mankind by self-interest. She adored the child, and Costas was a muscular traditional Levantine male chauvinist, jealous of his masculinity and his womenfolk. She would be out on her ear in two seconds flat if he started delving. There was the Press, but they would have been unlikely to back Stuart's story uncorroborated. He had been alone and only twenty years old. Besides, by then, there were beginning to be reasons why it might be unwise in the long run to invite investigation into some of his own activities. He was already in tow with Malcolm Quennell.

His mother had died just after Stuart's A-levels. He had been destined for the Agricultural College at Cirencester, and was working for a local farmer, doing his preliminary statutory practical period required by the College for entrants. With his mother's death and the rupture of their emotional interdependence he was feeling rudderless and uncertain now about the future. Besides, he very soon found that there was more to farming than stalking the hedgerows with a twelve-bore or ferreting and harvesting in clement weather. There was backbreaking hedging and ditching and mucking out pigs, and getting up at cock-crow on ice-bound mornings, and renouncing social engagements for sows that farrowed at inconvenient times. It was all a sight too disciplined for Stuart who had been spared any suggestion of the rod. He suspected that there must be easier and more profitable ways of earning a living. And then he had met Malcolm Quennell who, though only a few years his senior, wore handmade shirts and custom built suits and who drove an E-type Jaguar. For his part Malcolm appreciated a bright, ambitious lad when he met one.

They had run into one another at a county show where Malcolm was demonstrating the merits of Handyside and Bennett's revolutionary new crop rotovator. Handyside's had been threatening to provide Malcolm with an assistant for some time, and he had brought them round to agreeing to give him a free hand in making his own appointment. Their business took him abroad several times a year, whence he had developed private side-lines unrelated to Handyside's. Whoever he appointed would have to be relied upon to close a blind eye — better still become involved himself, so that each had an equal amount to lose should one of them be tempted at any time to pull the carpet out from under the other. A couple of meetings had been enough to convince both men that Stuart was right for the job.

Under Malcolm's tuition he had grown up fast. Under Handyside's impeccably respectable umbrella, his and Malcolm's side-lines had expanded profitably in the three years since Stuart had thrown in his lot with the latter.

"Just remember to keep your nose clean. A low profile, and no courting of any undue publicity in your private life that might rock the boat," had been Malcolm's stipulation when he had taken him on. "In our line we need to be faceless. You're not the sort of bloke likely to get into the gossip columns, are you?"

Stuart had assured him that he was a nobody.

It was therefore plain that any follow-up to the information Ariana had given him would, of necessity, have to be secret, discreet and personal.

On the pretext of chronicling Colin's brief Army career for the purposes of a family history he was meant to be writing, Stuart travelled to Inverness to the regimental depot. There in the library he

186

was given access to back numbers of the regimental magazine which he scanned diligently for any mention of Martin Dearsley, or clue as to where he might presently be discovered. It turned out to be a disappointing exercise in that apart from a reference to the action in Cyprus and Dearsley's decoration consequent upon it, the records revealed nothing more than that his quarry had retired from the Army the following year and seemingly sunk into obscurity. Nor had the Secretary to the regimental association any constructive suggestion to offer when Stuart had asked if anyone knew what had become of Martin Dearsley either.

"He was the last one to see my brother alive, and as I was only a kid when it happened, I'd rather like to trace him and get his version."

Duncan McAlpine had frowned and pursed his lips. "I can't say there's anyone here now who would have known him. He's been retired ten years, and unless he had kept in touch with the depot or attended regimental dinners, it's unlikely we'd know who his friends were or have a record of any address.

Some keep us posted — others drop right away. I've been doing this job five years and during that time I haven't heard of him."

Discreet enquiries made at the Ministry of Defence produced equally abortive results and Stuart soon got tired of perusing random telephone directories on the outside chance of running his man to earth. The obsession, fanned by the encounter in Cyprus, flared hotly for a few months and then had cooled and lain dormant for ten more years, buried under the more urgent business of living. But you never quite buried those ways you had been brought up with. They were so much a part of you, those early attitudes instilled.

★ ★ ★

There were eight cigarette butts in the ashtray by his bed when Stuart leaned over to stub out his ninth. It was overloaded and smelled stale. He got off the bed and emptied it into a waste-paper basket under the washbasin. The clouds had ridden away and a shaft of moonlight spread across the carpet where he stood. The garden was brilliantly lit, the roses uniformly ghostly pale, their colours diluted, shrubs and trees etched blackly, mysterious. Silvered, his naked body looked like dead flesh, like the white underbelly of a fish, and he shivered involuntarily, reminded of his own mortality — and of Marian. Her face, when they had brought her into the hospital, had been that colour.

She had been admitted in the middle of the night in a flurry of activity. After some of the excitement had subsided Stuart, unable to recapture sleep and returning from a visit to the urinals, had stopped out of curiosity by the open door of Marian's cubicle. She had been lying facing the door, attached to a drip, and a Balinese nurse was monitoring her heartbeat on a screen. The machine was emitting a series of irregular bleeps, and they must have given her something to kill the pain because earlier she had been audibly distressed. Marian's hair, brushed out on the pillow in a huge Afro-Asian cloud of natural corkscrew curls, made her face look elfin, and there were great bruised shadows beneath her closed lids. She looked about thirteen years old and in a bad way. Stuart had been about to tiptoe on when she had suddenly opened her eyes and looked straight at him. He had smiled. He didn't know whether she saw him but she told him later that she had and that his smile had immediately calmed her and given her courage. He had sat with her for many hours and talked. Marian had done most of the talking. It had seemed natural that they had exchanged only Christian names. At the Shivine, she had said, they were known simply by their first names to remind them they were individuals without appendages. Equally, it suited Stuart to preserve his anonymity. His passports provided him with a selection of surnames to choose from, depending upon his location. At Handyside and Bennett his secretary, Daphne Gates, manned his private line that bypassed the company switchboard and took messages for his various aliases. Daphne was a cool blonde with ambitions of her own. She had long shared Malcolm's confidence as well as his bed and knew which side her bread was buttered. With his own early promotion, Malcolm had engineered his and Daphne's and Stuart's migration to the London office where they more or less ran their own show. Seemingly there were no limits to Malcolm's ingenuity. He also knew where he could lay hands upon a number of useful friends to suit any contingency. He was acquainted with a genius in the electronics business, sundry photographers, engravers, suppliers, pushers, even Customs officials. The commodity didn't exist that he couldn't buy. Malcolm put up the cash for lawyers, the police and the information. Stuart's responsibility was recruitment of couriers.

"You're tailor-made with your sunny, easy-going, open temperament, dear boy," Malcolm had congratulated him. "People take to you. I can just hear them pouring out their troubles to you and you showing them an easy way out of them. You'd do any one of them a good turn." Malcolm had pioneered the British end of the operations while Stuart was responsible for the trafficking of the merchandise between Singapore and Bangkok. He hadn't actually got around to suggesting to Marian that she might be enlisted as one of his couriers, but that had been his intention. She'd have been a pushover, with her fanaticism for that pot-bellied, greasy old charlatan who had made a million out of kids like her. Stuart was sick of hearing about his theology and his purity and his noble design for the salvation of mankind. Talking about it was the only thing that put colour back into her cheeks — and she was very pretty when that happened. Her friends who came to visit her were all the same. He could see they viewed him with suspicion, as well they might. He had plans for her. She was an attractive little piece, or would be when she'd got a bit more meat on her bones. She could be an amusing challenge. If she did one run and Stuart saw to it that the Shivaan was tipped off how the money had been come by, that one would either be greedy for more, or he wouldn't want to be contaminated with suspicion of drug-running. If she found herself being used she might easily become disenchanted. If they dropped her like a hot cake she'd be out of the Shivine for good. Whichever way it happened, Stuart would take good care to be around. She had broken with her family, so there was no one to ask questions about her back home. He'd set her up in a flat in Singapore, dress her decently, give her a cover, as he had other girls before her, including beautiful Balinese Daisy. He'd had all these marvellous ideas for Marian's future, then what did she do? On the eighth day after her operation when she had seemingly turned the corner to renewed health, she had confounded all his plans by upping and dying. It had been a terrible shock.

He had been discharged from hospital at the beginning of that week and he had been coming in daily thereafter to see Marian. Arriving that day at his appointed time he had found her cubicle empty, the bed stripped and freshly made. A Eurasian woman in a white coat was clearing Marian's locker and her few paltry possessions. The contents of her locker were scattered on the honeycombed counterpane. There was a handbag, scarf, a battered purse, a nightdress, a sponge-bag, a brush and comb, a pair of thonged sandals and a pathetic half-packet of peppermints. Stuart, in shock, took in what the woman was saying.

"But she was all right when I left last night. She even ate her supper."

"I know. It was very unforeseen." The woman dispensed her brand of official sympathy. "She rang the bell in the night complaining of nausea and faintness. She began vomiting continuously. The repaired bowel ruptured. Peritonitis. They operated immediately but it was all too sudden, and after the first big operation — " she was making a list of Marian's effects as she spoke. "Were you a close friend of Miss Dearsley's?" She looked up, pen poised.

He dragged his gaze away from what she was doing. He said slowly, "Did you say Dearsley? Was that her name?" He realized that he must sound strange. "I called her Marian."

"Dearsley." She spelled it out for him. "So you didn't know her well?"

"Not all that well. We met in here."

She clipped her pen efficiently into

her top pocket and suddenly noticed his pallor. "You look frightful," she said. "Hadn't you better sit down?"

"I'm sorry," he muttered, taking her advice and thinking he was going mad. "I've only just been discharged myself. Appendix."

"Of course, I remember you now. You were in the end bed, weren't you? I didn't recognize you without your pyjamas."

There was an answer to that one but he hardly felt up to making it, nor did she look likely to appreciate vulgarity.

She said, "I'll just get something to put these things into. You rest there a moment." She bustled out, her starched coat crackling, leaving him sitting on the bed.

He took up the diary, riffling through its pages, throwing it down as it yielded nothing, then picked up the handbag. It was of tattered hide with three divisions and a zipped compartment in the lining. The zip caught, then acquiesced. He dug his hand in and drew out a passport. The almoner's footsteps were returning. Hesitating only fractionally, he closed the zip, replaced the bag and slipped the passport into his pocket. When she came into the cubicle he was standing breathing deep draughts of air at the window.

"Better now?"

"Much, thank you." He asked casually, "What are they doing — with her?"

"We've notified her friends. She put them down as her next of kin. They're arranging for her to go back with them."

"I see." He wondered whether the Shivites believed in cremation Balinese-style with all the trappings of paper tower, bull sarcophagus and the myriad offerings? Would Marian's ashes be gathered in coconut shells and sprinkled in the river to be carried down to the sea? Stuart had been present at one such ceremony, his Western concept of death unprepared for the incongruity of a funeral conducted in carnival mood. Maybe these people had something after all. If his mother had been Balinese . . . He pulled himself together. If his aunt had had balls she would have been his uncle! He was deliberately filling his mind with jumbled, unrelated thoughts. He could feel the passport lying tight against his hip and he hoped it didn't make a noticeable outline. Stealing it had been an involuntary act, and much later, back in his hotel room, he marvelled that the name, leaping out at him in such totally unexpected surroundings after all these years, had produced so determined a reaction. He hadn't consciously considered Dearsley and Colin and Ariana for longer than he could remember. Aeons ago he had accepted that any deployment of his energies in that direction were futile and, more to the point, non-productive. Stuart had learned in the interim that time was money and any time or passion wasted contributed nothing in hard cash. He corrected himself. He *thought* he had learned. Looking at that standard- type passport photograph that made even Marian look like a grim-faced custodian of a concentration camp, he realized he had actually learned — accepted — forgotten nothing. One word — one chance mention of the hated name, and the flame flickered and rekindled. He could rationalize all night, all week, all year, but for all that, he knew he was going to have to follow it up. Concentrating his mind back, he tried desperately hard to recall what Marian had said about her home life. Not much, as far as he could remember, except that she and her parents had parted company and that her father was the vicar of Hanbury. 'Hanbury in Sussex — not Staffordshire,' that bit came back and he blessed his memory for storing the then irrelevant detail. It was a start. Although, would the sort of man who became a vicar be the kind to have behaved as *his* Dearsley had done? Might the priesthood have been embraced as a penance? More likely because it was a better cover than a great many professions. Vicars were honourable men. Like Brutus!

Stuart pulled himself up. He had been disappointed before. No point in having his man mentally hung, drawn and quartered before knowing that he *was* his man. He had no clear idea what he intended, or what plan his revenge might take. If the vicar turned out to be Captain Hook, only then was he in business. On the plane and train, and walking up from the station, he had to discipline his thoughts to prevent them jumping the gun. He had dressed purposely casually for the occasion, deliberately coming without his own transport. If it turned out to be a dead-end he could make up some message from Marian and fade away into obscurity. If it didn't, being without wheels would provide a more plausible excuse for accepting a bed for the night. He didn't doubt his ability in manœuvring the offer of one.

He would never forget the moment he had seen Martin in the hall. He still couldn't believe that the long search was over. A chill frisson, a mixture of excitement and anticipation, chased the shadow of a ghost across his grave, bringing his body out in gooseflesh. Stuart pulled on a pair of pyjamas and got into bed. This time he drew the blankets up over him as well as the sheet. That was better. Somewhere in the old house a cistern flushed and in the stillness there came the sound of a tap turned on and water running, then it ceased. For a short while afterwards the system knocked as particles of scale shifted and settled in the pipes. So he wasn't the only one awake.

They would have been discussing him and what best to do. They really didn't have very much choice. They'd find the money somehow, in spite of anything Martin might have said. Whether they gave him cash for Marian or sent him with a banker's draft, either way it was Stuart's. The passport would come in useful if it was a draft. He had only to show that on presentation and copy Marian's signature to cash it. Of course they'd have to be sure of him before they handed him the money. He had purposely given them clues that they could check up on. Martin was shrewd enough. He'd proved that in the past with a vengeance. He hadn't been all that smart over the phone call to the hospital, though. Stuart smiled. He had to admit that he hadn't been smiling at the time. He had been sweating when he had given Martin the number, but he needn't have been. People were sometimes more gullible than one gave them credit. Thank Martin's God for that! Daisy had come up trumps. Stuart hadn't been able to hear her, but she had obviously played her part well enough. He must remember to give her an Oscar! He didn't really know how he had thought of it all without even a rehearsal. It was true he had dreamed long of blackmail, but making Dearsley sweat and suffer and break would yield an infinitely sweeter satisfaction than all the money in the world. Stuart intended to string him along with a series of raised hopes and disappointments leading up to the moment when he would tell Martin about Marian's death. Even after that, when Stuart had revealed himself and his motives, Dearsley would still have to dance to his tune or be exposed. He'd have to check to see whether Martin could still be accountable under military law after all this time, but even if not, it was reasonable to assume that the threat of the scandal, the fall from grace and respectability, would put him into the strait-jacket of Stuart's design. People didn't change. A man who was capable of sacrificing a friend's life for money to save his own skin would surely betray a mere principle in the same cause. And just for good measure — there was Sylvia. That would indeed be delightful. There had been a sensual recognition between them. He was aware of that and he was seldom wrong about those things. It hardly seemed likely that she would . . . and time was short . . . and it would be mixing business with pleasure — but what a way to round off the complete destruction of his victim. As he toyed with the fantasy his groin and his resolution hardened. By the time he finished with him, Dearsley would be bankrupt — financially, morally, emotionally, spiritually. It would be worse than being dead.

"It's so much worse for those who are left!" How often had he heard his mother say that? Stuart gritted his teeth.

He'd see that it was for Dearsley. A bloody sight worse than death!

10

STUART was right. He was not the only person in the house keeping a moonlit vigil. Sylvia, tiptoeing back into the bedroom from a trip to the lavatory, had paused to look out upon the beauty of the illuminated garden. Martin had been late coming upstairs. His visitor had kept him and when he did come to bed he had looked pale and strained.

"That was Dan Rowson," he said. "Annette has left him. She went off after breakfast today to deliver the children to her mother. She and Dan were due to leave on Wednesday for a trip to the States. Apparently she dropped the kids, and when she didn't return, Dan assumed she'd stayed for lunch. Later on he got a phone call from some man telling him she wouldn't be back — ever. Dan made a few enquiries. It seems it's been going on for some months and all their friends knew but nobody liked to tell Dan." He passed a weary hand across his eyes. "It would have to be this evening."

Wouldn't it just! Sylvia thought. Not for the first time, and God knew it would be the last, their own personal drama had had to be subordinated to one of the parishioner's.

"Let's talk about Marian in the morning, shall we? I don't feel as though I can think straight tonight."

Resenting the Rowsons, and even more the way in which Martin had rolled over and been snoring within five minutes, Sylvia had lain with her thoughts in turmoil, incapable of sleep herself. After ignoring a call of nature for what seemed like hours for fear of waking him, she had eventually got up, and now didn't feel like going back to bed again. She drew her cotton dressing-gown tightly around her. Behind her she heard Martin stir.

"What's the matter?"

"I can't sleep."

The sheets rustled as he raised himself in the bed.

"Nor can I."

She laughed shortly. "You give a very

credible performance."

"You think I'm not concerned?" he asked quietly.

"Well, she isn't really your worry, is she?" She hated herself for saying it, knowing it was unjust, but she owed so much already where Marian was concerned. It made her want to blame him. "I'm sorry, but that's what you seemed to be saying when you told Stuart she ought to be left to stew in her own juice."

"I didn't mean it." He sighed. "But our resources aren't limitless, and there comes a point where enough is enough, Sylvia. Marian will have to learn that."

"She never has learned your way, has she?"

He sounded weary. "No. I seem to have done it all wrong, but I wanted to give her a discipline I never had."

"You?" That *had* surprised her. "You're the most disciplined person I ever knew."

"That sounds like an indictment. You think I don't understand? You think I don't wish I could put you on a plane tomorrow and send you out to talk some sense into her? I can't afford the fare, even if I thought she'd listen. I don't know how much it would cost — I can find out tomorrow — but I guess the return would be well over a thousand pounds."

"I know. I know." She wished he wouldn't make her feel so rotten. "Even if I could go, there'd be no point in rushing out there unless I were welcome. She's done without me for two years."

"That on top of the £2,000 plus it looks as though we're going to have to find would be an even tougher struggle."

"£2,000 plus?"

"Well there's the money for the operation and some for a one-way ticket home, if she's sane enough to use it."

Sylvia turned from the window. Her figure was silhouetted, her face a dark shadow. "You'll send it?"

"What else can we do? If we don't and she gets herself into something criminal, the consequences will be much more horrific. If we do and she stays with that bunch, then that's tragic but that's her choice. We at least will have done all we can. What I'm banking on is her paying off the debt and Stuart's powers of persuasion. I have to. What I must make quite clear is that it's the end of the line financially if she persists in getting herself into further trouble."

"You'll send it with him?"

"I think I'll have to. Time is so short and he will be quicker than a letter. I'll have to find out the best way."

"That means you'll have to trust him. Do you?"

"He seems genuine, but I'm not such a fool that I'd hand over £2,000 without checking. We know where he works and the name of his Managing Director." Martin paused for thought. "There was also an office phone number on his ID card. I made a mental note of it and jotted it down. There's an organization that's been set up to deal with families affected by these quasi-religious sects. I think it's called 'Animus'. Ken Hartwell told me about it when they had all that trouble with Keith, do you remember? They may know something about these Shivites. I could check out those three items and that would be about the best we could do. Would you put your faith in him?"

"I want to. He has helped Marian. He didn't have to come here."

"It could be a confidence trick to get the money. But if he really does work at Handyside's and they vouch for him, would it be worth his jeopardizing his job that way? It sounds like a good job too."

She felt humbled and ashamed that she could have accused him of not caring. He was continually contradicting her expectations of how he would react. She was so used to the stony, pebbly look on his face, the flinty tones that presaged the sudden changes of mood to which she had grown so accustomed. An incident, a remark, even a change of weather could effect an almost immediate transformation from sunshine to days of impenetrable fog. She would have bet on this present trauma sending him into complete withdrawal.

She said, "Where's the money coming from?"

"We'll have to sell something — probably things in the plural. In the meantime we'll need a loan."

"Alan Spencer?"

Martin drew in his breath. "No. I don't want to ask him to extend the overdraft again. It was embarrassing last time. He was very nice about it but he made it clear he was stretching the bank's facility to accommodate me because I was a personal friend. If I hadn't had the new arm — "

"Who then?"

"There's only one person I could ask. Ian Forsythe. I don't know anyone else who might have that kind of ready cash."

"Ian? But you haven't seen him for years." She knew that Martin and Ian Forsythe had exchanged Christmas cards over the past two decades, but their ways had long since diverged. Ian's good-natured attempts at effecting a reunion had been balked by Martin enough times with excuses for his friend finally to give up. Ian was a part of that other life that was dead and gone. A reminder of times that Martin preferred to forget. He too had left the Army three years after Martin, and had accepted a 'golden bowler' on the amalgamation of the regiment with another in the Highland Brigade, going into the drink business with Distillers.

Martin said, "No, but I know where to find him. I may have to go to London tomorrow. It's as well that it's Monday. There's the confirmation class in the evening but I'll be back for that. If I'm not, Peter can take it. I'll warn him in the morning."

Peter Cummings was an accountant and a lay reader at the church. His wife, Alison, was a friend of Sylvia's and her closest contemporary in the parish.

Martin continued along his train of thought. "Jack Bradley is coming up in the morning to see me about the awnings and trestles for Saturday's Michaelmas Fayre, but you can tell him what we want, can't you? The Parish Council meeting isn't till later in the week. I'll prepare my notes for that on the train."

His attitude, and the fact that he was six jumps ahead of her in practical planning flooded Sylvia with immense gratitude and another emotion for which she had no name. She said huskily, "You are a strange man — and kind. You've got it all worked out, and I thought . . . I can't live up to you, Martin."

"Don't ever say that." He spoke sharply and she heard him shift uncomfortably, as he always did when she threatened to get under his cover.

"Why not? It is true that you make me feel very unworthy sometimes."

"I don't know what you're talking about."

"Don't you? Or do you just pretend not to?"

"I don't pretend anything." His voice was patient, bearing with her.

"You're always pretending." His tone and some devil made her press him although it was an insane moment to seek any kind of a showdown. She didn't know what had got into her, except she suddenly had the strangest feeling that this business of Marian tonight had brought them to some sort of watershed and that she was all mixed up with feelings that had been dammed over-long. Life never managed to time its really important moments right, Sylvia thought. One mentally rehearsed for hours or years, waiting for the psychological moment to raise a topic, and then it would pop up unexpectedly and have to be dealt with in inauspicious circumstances, and nearly always in a hurry. The absurd memory of Marian, aged eight, standing beside her at the check-out in Sainsbury's and asking at the top of her voice, "What's masturbation, Mummy?" was a case in point. The child's direct question had made mincemeat of evasions and Sylvia's carefully plotted lecture on the facts of life which she had intended to introduce in some quietly chosen moment. Shock tactics. They worked.

"Put on the light."

"What?"

"Put on the light," she insisted.

He did so, humouring her. The light was bright and he turned away from it to lie down.

"You're pretending now," she said ruthlessly. "Look at me."

He obeyed, feigning sleepiness.

"Open your eyes, Martin, and look at me." He looked, bewildered as well he might be, she thought, almost pitying him. "What you see is me. ME! I'm here. A very surface person. Nothing tremendously complicated. I don't like having to hide myself from you but I have to, because you're always pretending with me." On a flood of emotion she came and knelt by the bed.

"I feel as if I'm always in the dark, Martin. We even make love in the dark and you pretend it hasn't happened in the morning. I want to be loved and talked to in the light. Now." She knew she was being dramatic and unreasonable and that he was tired and that it had been a long and trying day for them both, but she was inexplicably shot through with a nameless fear and the need for the closeness of his body to assuage it, the comforting touch of his hand and the untasted generosity of the sort of kisses they had never shared. "We never talk about us," she said coaxingly "You never say what you feel about me."

"You're my wife." He said it baldly, as though that should be enough.

"That doesn't tell me anything."

"I don't know what's brought all this on," he said wearily. "What are you trying to do, Sylvia? I know you're upset, but it's no good letting all this make you overwrought. Come to bed. Come on. We're both exhausted. You need your rest."

She had asked for bread and been given a stone! What a damned fool she was! What had she expected? That she could force him into saying that he loved her? He had never said it, any more than she had. She had been on the verge of breaking the habit of a marriage but he certainly had a choice knack of turning one off. He had once told her that he didn't understand the meaning of the word 'love'. In usage 'love' had been debased to cover sex, lust, possessiveness, infatuation. To him love was respect, a negation of self, and if his actions towards her didn't speak louder than words, then he was sorry. She didn't know what was the matter with her tonight. She was too old by far to expect palm trees waving, the moon and stars and a pair of romantic lovers locked in silhouette against a tropical sunset! She rose from her knees and went round to her side of the bed. Obediently she lay down beside him and closed her eyes.

After she slept Martin remained awake. His hand only had to reach out to feel her skin. One move from him was all she had asked. Would she have asked it if she had known what kind of a man he really was? He couldn't take that risk. He couldn't afford to lose her. Encouraging her inevitably would have led to letting her inside his mind.

★ ★ ★

There was no sign of Stuart until midday next morning. By the time he did eventually surface Martin had gone and Sylvia was immersed with her working Committee in the study. They were inspecting, sorting and boxing up some of the mass of jumble to be distributed upon the stalls for Saturday's Fayre. Earlier Martin had made three phone calls, shortly after which he went to find Sylvia to report upon his activities. She was in an outbuilding attached to the garage, getting down boxes for her working party.

"I've been on to Alan Spencer," he

215

said. "I didn't go into details, but I asked him what the form would be if we wanted to send some money out to Bali. As it's unlikely Marian has an account out there and she closed her one this end, it would have to be cash sterling or a bank draft in Indonesian currency. The snag with applying for a draft is that it takes at least two working days to get it through from the bank's international branch. It probably wouldn't arrive by Wednesday and Stuart leaves Thursday."

Sylvia brushed her hair back out of her eyes with a dusty hand, leaving a mark across her forehead. "But it would be legal for him to take out so much cash?"

"There's no restriction now." Martin frowned. "I won't get the money from Ian until tomorrow earliest. We're meeting tonight at half past six, so I shall be going to London. And I've got an appointment with 'Animus' this afternoon. I caught Ken before he went off to work and he told me where to find them."

"You managed to find Ian then?"

"Quite easily. He's at the same office. I got straight through."

"Did you say what it was about?"

"No."

She knew how difficult it was going to be for him to sink his monumental pride and go cap in hand to a friend who justifiably could resent being used after a lengthy period of having been dropped.

He added, "I've told Peter I might have to stay up the night. He says he'll take the class tonight anyway. If I do have to stay, will you go over to the church and see that it's locked when he's finished? I told him you'd have the key."

She nodded.

"I'll call you one way or the other."

"Thank you." Sylvia jumped down from her perch among the crates and dusted her hands off. They went out into the sunlight.

"I also rang the travel agent. I'm afraid I was right about the fare. £1,359 at least return. I'm sorry. If I hadn't spent all that money on this wretched arm — "

"What about the other enquiries?" she asked.

"Better to make them from London. I wasn't sure if our guest was about." He

217

looked at his watch. "I think I'd better get off now."

"Good luck."

He stooped. By the merest movement she offered him her cheek. The gesture managed to emphasize an aloofness though she tried not to let it, but he recognized it. He hesitated and saw her watching him dispassionately.

"Sylvia, last night you — "

"Last night I was overwrought. You said so. You were right. I'm better now."

He looked relieved.

What humbugs men were, she thought, watching him go. For a quiet life they could make themselves believe anything. She felt rebellious and lonely and angry and hurt. The sunshine glancing off the glass of the conservatory dazzled her eyes and made them water.

11

THE hands of the grandfather clock in the hall stood at ten past twelve as Stuart came down, his sneakers soundless on the carpet. From the study came the sound of women's voices and a fair amount of activity. Sylvia's helpers were on the point of leaving, and while they were about it Stuart slipped into the kitchen and made himself a cup of instant coffee. When they had gone, he wandered out to find Sylvia tidying up after the morning's work. She was bent over a tea-chest packing into it remnants of china left over for the White Elephant stall, and she didn't hear him until he had enjoyed the benefit of a full sixty seconds' contemplation of the rounded cheeks of her bottom encased in tight blue denim.

"Good morning."

Sylvia started violently. The heel of her left shoe caught in the neck of a particularly hideous blue vase lying at her feet and for a moment she strove to maintain her balance.

"Steady!" It was a great excuse to plant his hands lightly on her hips to save her from falling, nor did he immediately remove them when she turned. For a second they were standing very close to one another. She could feel the pressure of his palms through the cotton fabric and he smelled of peppermint and some kind of spicy after-shave, though there wasn't much scope on his bearded face for the use of a razor.

"You scared the living daylights out of me. Good afternoon." She corrected his greeting emphatically.

"Yes, I'm sorry about that. I seem to have overslept. It was a very comfortable bed." He released her.

"It doesn't matter a bit." She smiled up at him. "I've been pretty tied up."

"So I see." He surveyed the boxes lined up in the hall and this last one obviously destined to join them. "Shall I shift this one out for you?"

"Please, if you will. Mind your operation! We are lining them up out there, then Jack Bradley and his merry men will take them out later this week. It's the Michaelmas Fayre on Saturday."

"Ah! The Michaelmas Fayre. Spelled with a 'y' no less. I saw it advertised on the parish notice board when I wended my way here." The gleam in his eye invited her to share his amusement at the Fayre Committee's literary pretension, and she laughed out loud. He liked making her do that. She would have a nice sense of the ridiculous and he was ready to bet she'd be someone who could laugh a lot in bed. In her jeans and blue shirt she looked even younger than she had last night. He hoisted the box up on to his knee, grasped it and carried it out into the hall.

"Thank you. That's it then. Do you want anything to eat? It's a bit late for breakfast."

"I had coffee."

"I could do with one myself."

He followed her into the kitchen. "Where's Martin?"

"He's gone to London. To see about arrangements."

He nodded. "When is he coming back?"

She was busy with the kettle. "He may come back tonight or he may have to stay over."

Stuart assimilated this. "Will he mind me being here if he's not?"

"Of course not. We've asked you to stay."

"He must be a fool, or incredibly complacent. If you were mine I wouldn't trust a complete stranger alone with you for the night."

She poured boiling water into two cups and stirred in coffee granules. Smiling, she handed him one. "How old-fashioned of you. What's so special that happens at night that can't take place in the daytime?"

It was his turn to laugh. They sipped their coffee companionably.

"When did he decide to go?"

"In the night."

"I see."

"He's got a friend who might help. He's gone to see him."

"A friend?" Stuart kept his voice carefully neutral.

"Someone who may lend him the money — until we can get a few things valued."

"I see." That was a relief. Nobody connected with the authorities. "Last night I thought — "

"Oh, you don't want to take any notice of Martin," Sylvia said hastily, then added, "He's not always easy to understand."

"No?"

"No." She probably said it with more feeling than she intended because she was still deflated after the previous night. She frowned at her thoughts, then looked up to catch him watching her. "It's his arm, I think," she explained. "Losing it gave him a bit of a chip. At least I always think that's what it was. I didn't know him before so I couldn't say what he was like then."

Stuart doodled a cat with pricked up ears on a piece of paper on the kitchen table. "That was a long time ago. I should have thought he'd have grown out of it by now."

"You might have thought so, but he still has nightmares about it."

"Nightmares?"

"Yes." She laughed. "Sometimes they're quite comical." She recounted a couple of

223

episodes when Martin and she had ended up in particularly ludicrous situations after some of his dreams.

Stuart, enjoying the joke said, "Aren't you ever afraid of him? He sounds as if he could be quite violent."

Her face clouded. "Yes, he can, but it's not directed against me. It's inside him and it's got to get out. I suppose if he could talk about it he wouldn't have the nightmares. They're a form of release."

The cat had whiskers now and a long tail which Stuart carefully thickened to make it bushy. "Haven't you tried talking?"

"Of course."

"But it doesn't work?" He looked up from the drawing, penetratingly. "No, I can see it doesn't. That must be difficult for you, being a demonstrative, outgoing sort of person."

"You seem to have summed me up in a short time," she said lightly. "Actually, it's probably just as well Martin is more phlegmatic and withdrawn than I. I tend to go at everything like a bull at a gate. I'm far too romantic and impulsive and he keeps my feet on the ground."

"Is that what he says?"

"No. But I know myself pretty well."

"So you feel safer being chained down — to the ground I mean?" he ventured.

"Most of the time."

"Don't you ever want to fly?"

"A vicar's wife doesn't get many opportunities for aerobatics." Spooning the sugar out of the bottom of her cup, Sylvia glanced across at him. "You don't waste time in getting to know people, do you?"

"Not if I'm interested in them. Life's too short. And you interest me, Sylvia."

The banter had died out of his tone and it was a straightforward statement of fact. She had the feeling she might not be able to handle the conversation if it got heavy. In an attempt to restore its levity she said lightly, "You're too young to be flirting with me, Stuart."

"Is that what we're doing? I'm certainly too old to be patronized. Incidentally, how old are you?"

"I'm forty."

"There you go! There's only five years between us — give or take a month.

What's the age gap between you and Martin?"

"Seven."

"Well then. Same difference almost."

"Yes, but the wrong way round."

"For what?"

She coloured. He had led her into a trap and caught her out.

"It's refreshing to find a woman who can still blush," he said. "You're much prettier than Marian. More sexy." His eyes appraised her openly, completely frank in his admiration, never doubting that his candour could be taken as anything but complimentary. It was impossible to resent his familiarity and equally ridiculous to feel disturbed, but she was disconcerted. She was out of practice at this sort of thing, being herself and directly communicating aloud. At the mention of Marian, anxiety shadowed her expression.

"Poor darling," she said. "I don't suppose she *is* feeling particularly attractive after what she has been through." She sighed. "We seem to have made such a mess of things between us. What really hurts is her total rejection of us. Even at death's door she didn't want us. That's very hard to take. One inevitably blames oneself." Sylvia took her cup to the sink and rinsed it so that he should not see the tears that suddenly welled to choke her.

"I'm sure you've nothing to reproach yourself about. This thing Marian has for the Shivine — it's like an infatuation, a love-affair when someone is temporarily prepared to throw everything overboard. You know the feeling. It doesn't mean she hates you or even that she won't remember that she loves you again. This is all-absorbing at present. The trouble is, people can take some ill-judged and dangerous steps when they're infatuated."

Sylvia watched the water curl and swirl down the drain. Yes, she knew the feeling all right. In the aluminium sink bowl she fancied she saw Colin's reflection, and beside him, Marian. What kind of a father would Colin have turned out to be? Would Marian have disowned him and taken herself off out of both their lives if things had been different? Was this Sylvia's punishment for denying the child the knowledge of her true parentage? It had been Marian's right to know. But Martin had been her father in every way that truly counted, barring the act that had created her. Ten minutes — against a lifetime's rearing as Martin's own child. An insignificant ten minutes. But who were they to have decided Marian shouldn't know? She had obviously been searching for something. Whatever it was, all Martin's religion and Sylvia's philosophy had been unable to provide it and she had renounced them and turned to the Shivaan. She and Martin had failed her. Would she listen to them now? There was no guarantee they could buy back her affection, but if there was a chance Sylvia wasn't above trying.

A tear dropped into the sink in spite of herself, and then another. To her dismay more followed and her shoulders heaved on a convulsive sob.

"Hey!" Stuart was on his feet and beside her. He put his arm across her shoulders and turned her to him. The simple comforting gesture was her undoing. It was what she had so badly needed from Martin last night, the luxury of breaking down helplessly and being consoled. She let go and cried silently and messily all over her clean blue cotton shirt, sniffing and gulping unromantically, unable to release her pinioned arms to wipe her face.

"Hey," he said again, drawing her head to his chest where she spattered his own T-shirt with salty tears. It was a red one today and it felt soft against her cheek. His beard was scratchy on her forehead and his arms cradled her gently against him. After a minute the worst was over, but she stayed quite still in the shelter of his arms. He handed her a tea-towel on which she wiped her eyes, then went on holding her.

"Thank you." She smiled tremulously, and met his eyes.

Slowly, and very deliberately, he bent his head and kissed her. Her first instinct was to pull away, but for fear of appearing gauche and giving his gesture an undue significance, she accepted the caress. His lips were warm and full and firm, and it was strange kissing a man with hair on his face, tickly and tingly. She hadn't been kissed with that degree of tenderness since Colin. With him so lately in her thoughts Sylvia allowed herself to linger two seconds longer in the embrace than a kiss of mere friendship dictated. An echo of those other kisses sounded faintly in her memory and, cataclysmically, the tingling electrified, stabbing through her breasts and down into her loins. She stepped back and he let her go immediately, watching her while she made a production of finding her handkerchief, blowing her nose and straightening her hair.

"OK?"

"Yes, thank you," she affirmed nervously, not quite looking at him. "I'm sorry for going all tragic on you."

There was a tapping on the kitchen window and the moment was broken by the ludicrous spectacle of a man's head bobbing up and down outside. It appeared, then vanished as its owner jumped up and down to attract attention.

"It's Jack Bradley," Sylvia said. She reached over the sink and opened the window, calling out a warning. "Mind the new panes of glass for the greenhouse, Jack."

"It's all right, Mrs Dearsley. I seen 'em here stacked up right by the wall. On account of 'em I couldn't get up to the window. Vicar said you'd be wanting to see me about trestles."

"I'll be right there." Sylvia closed the window. "Do you want to come and help?" she asked Stuart.

"Sure." He sounded perfectly natural.

She went to the door and looked back over her shoulder. "Are you coming then?"

"Yes." She hardly needed to ask him. Any more of that and if she gave him half a chance he reckoned he'd be coming all right!

★ ★ ★

By five-thirty in the afternoon Martin was ready for a cup of tea and a place where he could quietly put his feet up. There was still an hour to go before his appointment with Ian at the Inverdonian Club in Chesham Place, and he wasn't much looking forward to the encounter. Not that Ian had given any hint that his call, out of the blue, was anything but welcome once Martin had run him to earth.

"Martin! I don't believe it! How splendid to hear you. Where are you?"

"I'll be in London for the day. I don't get up often. I wondered if you could spare a moment for a meeting."

"Splendid. Splendid." Ian positively purred. He sounded benign and prosperous. "Let me see. Lunch is out, so is dinner, I fear. Dorothy has asked people in for bridge. I could manage a snifter at the club when I finish here. By the way, do you still belong?"

"No," said Martin, "I gave up my membership years ago."

"Not to worry. Be my guest. Shall we say half six? Grand to see you then."

He would have preferred to have met Ian in some anonymous bar and he hoped that at the club he wasn't likely to run into anyone else he had known from the old days. He passed a cafeteria and went in, selecting a doughnut with his tea and carrying both to an unoccupied table for two. The doughnut would act as blotting-paper for the dutch courage he'd need before he came clean with Ian.

Looking around at the other customers, an unremarkable, nondescript crowd of varying ages, their shopping-bags testifying to their day's activity, he felt divorced from them, unreal. It was a feeling he was used to — being on the outside. He sipped his tea and thought about his day.

As soon as he had reached Victoria he had rung the number memorized from Stuart's card.

"Good morning. Handyside and Bennett. Can I help you?" A woman's voice, well modulated, efficient.

"Good morning," Martin had said. "I wonder if I could speak to Mr Balfour."

There was no hesitation in the reply. "I'm afraid Mr Balfour is on holiday at present. This is his secretary speaking. May I take a message and get Mr Balfour to ring you. Who's calling?"

"It doesn't matter, thank you. It's a personal matter. When do you expect him back again?"

"Next week. If you care to call Wednesday or Thursday you should catch him."

"Thank you." Martin rang off and

233

juggled with the telephone directory to find Handyside's High Holborn number. No harm in having a double check. Anyone could fake an ID card and flash it around. He dialled and got answered by a switchboard operator repetitiously rattling off, "Handyside and Bennett". In the background there were other voices and the faint sound of a radio.

"May I speak to Mr Malcolm Quennell, please?"

She barely allowed him to finish his sentence. "Just a moment."

There followed two clicks, a dead silence, then a short ring.

"Handyside and Bennett. Mr Quennell's office."

Martin repeated his request.

"Who's calling?"

Martin was ready for her. "Mr Stanton. Mr Quennell doesn't know me but it is a personal matter." He banked on the girl being cautious of overstepping her authority and Malcolm Quennell's curiosity getting him through. He judged right.

"Quennell speaking." It was a no-nonsense voice.

"Oh, Mr Quennell. My name is Michael Stanton and I am an acquaintance of Stuart Balfour's. We met recently in Singapore. I believe he works for you, or at least with Handyside's? He mentioned your name as a colleague."

There was a tiny pause, then carefully, "Yes, that is so. What is the nature of your business, Mr Stanton?"

"Not business at all," Martin said in a manner intended to be disarming. "Stuart and I spent a pleasant interlude at the bar in the Marco Polo and after he had gone I picked up a Dupont lighter he had left behind on the counter. I would like to see that it gets back to him, but I had no reference as to where I could find him except for the firm's name. I thought I had better check that I had got the right branch. When we met he said he wasn't coming straight back to England." He hoped it didn't sound as thin as he suspected it might, but it didn't really matter because he had already found out what he wanted to know.

"That's very civil of you, Mr Stanton. I'm sure Stuart will be very grateful. If you like to post the lighter to this office — " Quennell's voice was overlaid by a series of staccato 'pips' as Martin's ten pence in the coin slot ran out. He replaced the receiver and left the phone-box. He was sneakingly ashamed that, having just proved what a consummate liar he was himself, he had suspected Stuart of not being on the level. His entire life was a lie. No amount of confession could alter that. There was no merit in confessing when he went on repeating the sin. Feeling depressed, he opened his diary and found the page where he had noted down the location of his next port of call. It was seven stops without changing on the Circle line. He would take the underground and walk.

The headquarters of Animus was lodged in a private three-storey house tucked in a once salubrious, but now slightly seedy square between Paddington Station and Sussex Gardens. There was no plate outside No. 23 to advertise the organization's presence, and when the front door was opened in response to Martin's ring, he could see the hall was furnished in the style of a private house rather than offices. A comfortable woman with a fresh complexion and wispy hair caught up in an untidy bun accepted his self-introduction, and admitted him immediately on the strength of his dog-collar. Martin was glad he had worn it in preference to 'mufti'. The drawing-room of the house was given over to Animus's investigations. These were multiplying weekly as more people got to know about them, the woman informed Martin as she took him in and presented him to two other members of the staff.

"I am Eileen Jenks, this is Ann Weston, and that is Frank Stebbing." She lowered her voice as she indicated a spare-looking man who was conducting a telephone conversation. He went on talking but acknowledged Martin with a nod and a smile. "Frank is our legal eagle. Ann deals with finances and travel arrangements. I do most of the preliminary interviews and am general dogsbody. There are more of us but we're all on a part-time basis and voluntary." She sat him down. "Would you like a cup of coffee?"

Martin said that he would, and the Weston woman went away to make it. She was tall and rather gaunt, of academic mien with straight, dark hair severely fringed, and circular owl-like spectacles that marked her prominent cheekbones.

"How did you hear of us, Mr Dearsley?" Mrs Jenks was asking.

"Through a parishioner whose son became a disciple of the Moonies. His son had disappeared and this is what he had suspected had happened. Animus was able to locate the young man and verify that he was at least alive and well."

"Did we manage to restore him to his father?"

"Sadly, no. But at least they are now in limited contact. A postcard now and again. It is better than the uncertainty although it is a poor substitute." He paused. "Mrs Jenks, I now find myself in a similar position and remembering what my friend told me about your organization, that's why I am here. I believe it is not just the Moonies you have dealt with?"

"Indeed no." The coffee arrived. She took a cup after he had accepted his. "No. We are being asked all the time to investigate a growing number of sects.

Forgive me for saying so, but as the churches empty this seems to be a growth industry." She smiled apologetically. "We are compiling our own dossiers on as many as we hear about. I don't think there is anyone else engaged in quite the same degree. We feel it is essential to air these matters and make people aware. Some of these institutions are harmless enough, some may even be a force for good, but there's no doubt about it that some need exploring. I am not entirely disinterested, Mr Dearsley. I lost my own son to one such a few years ago."

"I'm sorry," Martin said inadequately.

She regarded him quizzically. "And now you are in the same boat?"

"I'm not sure. I have heard about a cult in Indonesia. Its leader calls himself the Shivaan. Its followers are Shivites. I wonder, would you have anything on them?"

"Just a moment."

She got up and went to a filing cabinet. Pulling out a drawer, she lifted out a file and returned with it. She ran her forefinger down a list on the inside cover. "Durga. Is that the one?"

He was surprised and showed it. He had expected a lengthier search, a few blanks drawn. "You've heard of it? Such a community actually exists?"

"We've not got very much, but yes, we have had enquiries about a couple of people there." She was reading now. "Followers of Shiva. Offshoot of Balinese Hinduism. Mm . . . Mm . . . Mm . . . so on and so forth." She looked up and saw his face. "Weren't you expecting us to know about them?"

Martin said slowly, "I suppose I was hoping it was all a fantasy. It sounded like the sort of place somebody might have made up."

"It always does — to the parents," Eileen Jenks said sadly. She gave him a moment. "Would you like us to make enquiries about someone?"

He thought quickly. Better not. Not yet anyway. It might upset the applecart. A sniff of anything official might drive Marian into God knew what ill-conceived action.

"Not just at present, I think," he said. "There are one or two other avenues I have to explore and then I'll come back to you later, if I may. Thank you for your help so far." He gave her a grateful smile and Eileen Jenks found herself wishing that it was Martin's church brasses that she assiduously polished instead of her own dried-up old stick of a vicar's!

★ ★ ★

"Excuse me, is this seat taken?" A young girl, laden with a tray was asking permission to share his table.

"No. Please sit down." He moved his things to make more space on the table for her. He saw her look at his hand and look away.

"Look at me!" Sylvia had demanded. "ME!"

He had understood.

"Look at *me*," he wanted to say to the girl at the table.

There was no one to whom he could relieve himself by extending the invitation, but a perfect stranger, and she would have thought he was mad. A perfect stranger — or God. The unsatisfactory part about that was that you could only imagine God's response.

241

12

THE Club hadn't changed much in twenty years. Coming in off the street and going through to the bar, Martin had the most vivid sensation of having been petrified in time. The etching of Prince's Street circa 1898 still hung in the foyer along with kilted presidents of the Inverdonian past and present, and tartan-mounted views of Lochs Ness and Linnhe featuring the occasional stag. The top half of the reading-room door was glass-paned and, peering through, he caught a glimpse of half a dozen tweed-clad septuagenarians behind their papers, suspended in time and a deathly hush. It was easy to believe that they had been sitting there without moving since the place had existed. On his way through to the bar Martin ran his hand over the thistle-engraved newel where the stairs descended in a grand sweep on to black and white marble tiles. It had been a familiar gesture. He had used the Club a good deal in times of old and the touching of the thistle on the way down to breakfast had been a kind of talisman for the day.

There were six men in the bar, five in a group of mixed ages talking in loud, well-bred voices. Three of them were greeting the other two and from their conversation they were evidently getting tuned up prior to some kind of reunion jamboree. They wore dinner-jackets and were killing time before the advent of their 'good ladies.' Their clothes and their jargon carried Martin back light-years. Set apart from them, the sixth man was Ian.

He had thickened, and above his ears his hair flicked back in two white ducks' tails, but Martin would have recognized him in the street. He wore a grey mohair suit in a Glen Urquhart pattern, across the waistcoat of which a heavy gold watch-chain hung importantly. A plum silk triangle of handkerchief protruded from a breast pocket, matching exactly the plum stripe in his regimental tie and there were regimental links in the crisp white cuffs of his shirt. Martin, conscious of his own well-worn and faintly shiny suit jacket, buttoned it nervously over his clerical grey pullover and went forward.

"Martin!" The voice was plummy too. More so than over the phone.

"Hallo, Ian." His good hand was grasped, his back slapped heartily. Close to, the genial eyes were traced with red tributaries and under the skin of Ian's nose a matching web of tiny veins was discernible.

"Well, this is good." They took stock of each other. "You haven't changed a bit. You always were a handsome devil, eh? The good life suits you, Martin. I can see that. We weren't so saintly in the old days, what?" He gave Martin a good-natured nudge in the ribs. Martin moved his arm out of the way.

Ian was instantly solicitous. "Sorry, old chap. Forgot about that. How is it these days?" He looked closely at the hand which Martin obligingly manipulated for his wonderment. "Bloody miracle. Damned lifelike, eh? Amazing what they can do. What are you drinking?"

Martin asked for a beer and the barman recharged Ian's glass with a double gin.

"Got to flog the bloody stuff so I may as well enjoy it, what? It pays to advertise. Down the hatch, old boy. Here's how."

Martin took a pull at his beer and to his relief Ian led him away from the bar and over to a table at the far side of the room where they could talk privately. The first half-hour was taken up with reminiscence and 'Whatever-became-of-old-so-and-so', and then Martin asked about Ian's job and Ian returned the compliment. Ian went to all the regimental dinners and reunions, so he was able to regale Martin tirelessly with news of people Martin was ashamed to admit he had either not known or had totally forgotten, and all the time he was wondering how best to introduce the topic uppermost in his mind.

"Why don't you and Sylvia ever come to the annual luncheons? You ought to put your name in for the next one. Jumbo Dawson and Bugs Beddington are coming. You remember Bugs — so-called because of the bed-bugs in the seams of his mosquito net in Tripoli? Dashed amusing. He was bitten to Hades and couldn't find out where the little buggers were coming from. Served him damned well right for being wet enough to insist on a net. They don't touch you if you've got enough alcohol in your veins. Speaking of which — " He made a signal to the steward who came over and took a repeat order.

He hasn't changed, Martin thought, but my God how intensely boring it all is. There was a time when I too was completely wrapped up in all that sort of thing. Were we all like that then? Small boys inside, playing at soldiers? Playing at life? He admonished himself for feeling superior and was even more chastened when Ian, suddenly switching from conviviality and fixing him with a sober eye said, "What's the trouble then, Martin? You've been sitting there looking like a wet weekend and letting me piffle on. It *is* trouble, isn't it?" His voice was kindly and concerned.

"I'm afraid it is." In a gesture of bravado Martin downed his newly arrived drink. He had ordered a whisky this time and his empty glass was replaced by a full one without him heeding Ian's discreet directive to the steward.

"Money or women?"

In spite of himself Martin smiled. There were still only two kinds of trouble to a Forsythe.

"Money," he said. "Ian, I feel terrible about having to ask you, and it would only be a loan for a short time. Maybe a couple of months. I have means of raising it, but I need the cash in a hurry."

"How much?"

"Three thousand pounds." To be on the safe side he calculated to allow for Marian's return fare and any expenses Stuart might incur.

"No problem, old boy." Ian reached into an inside pocket and produced a cheque-book and pen. Martin's white face flushed scarlet. His friend's open-hearted generosity touched him unbearably. The church didn't have the monopoly on charity. He forced himself to say,

"Would you mind very much if it were cash?"

Ian, who had been about to write, halted the gesture. Capping his pen, he returned it to his pocket. If he was curious he didn't show it, but his look of solicitude deepened. Martin was aware of it. A cheque would have to be paid into his account, he had figured. So large a sum, coming in and going straight out again, would doubtless have roused Alan Spencer's curiosity when Martin had so recently persuaded him to extend his overdraft. The fewer people who knew about Marian's difficulty the better, especially if she might have to be extricated from anything outside the law.

"You may have cash, certainly, old boy. But it will have to be tomorrow morning. As soon as the bank opens."

"Thank you." Martin tried not to show his enormous relief. He felt sick and shaky and when he went to take a fortifying swig from the glass in his hand it was empty again. He was drinking too much, but he didn't demur when Ian lined up another, having waved aside Martin's offer of standing his round.

"Not allowed, old boy. My guest."

"I don't know how to thank you. For everything."

"Say no more." Ian made an expansive gesture. "That's what chums are for. You'd have done the same if our positions were reversed."

Martin said, "You haven't asked me what my position is. You have a right to know."

"Only if you want to tell me. I suspect there are reasons you prefer not to. Am I right?"

Martin's silence gave Ian his answer.

"That's OK by me. What I don't know can't harm me, eh? Only thing is, old boy — " he leaned forward confidentially — "it's not a cock-up with the police, is it? Nothing criminal, what?" He made a nervous joke of the last to emphasize its ridiculous unlikelihood.

"Not yet. It could turn into something bad. That's why I'm a bit desperate." Martin stumbled slightly over the three syllables as the combined whiskies and beers hit his consciousness and his gut. "Excuse me. I need to pee." Getting up a fraction unsteadily, he crossed the bar and exited in the direction of the Gents.

Standing at the urinals, the reflection from the strip-lighting dazzled uncomfortably back at him from a shiny white-tiled wall, and the doughnut lurched ominously awash in his stomach. He zipped up his fly and was promptly sick. A few moments later his ignominy was complete when Ian found him sagging against the wall retching into the china bowl. Luckily they were the sole occupants of the place and Ian positioned himself thoughtfully with his back against the door to have warning of anyone's impending approach.

"You're not well. I think you'd better come back with me for the night."

"I'm only pissed. I'm not used to drinking so much in so short a time. I'm out of practice." He tottered across to the basins and cupped water up from the taps to sluice it over his face. He dried himself and combed his hair, avoiding Ian's eyes. "I'm sorry to have behaved so disgustingly. I don't know what you must think."

"For Christ's sake, Martin! You and I have been pissed together many times before and I hope we shall be again. No need to be po-faced with me. How many nights in the past have you undressed me and removed the evidence? Not too many words to Dorothy on that score when you meet her, eh? Esprit de corps and all that stuff, what?"

"But you said you had guests," Martin protested feebly.

"Doesn't matter. You can join us or not, as you please. Dorothy's used to open house. It'll save you coming up to town again first thing." He saw Martin waver. "Come on. For old time's sake. You can ring the little woman from home if that's what's bothering you. I want to hear all about la belle Sylvia. Always was a right little corker as I remember."

"She still is."

"Rather fancied her myself, truth to tell, but I saw her too late. She was already married to you when we met. Wouldn't have been any good. Only took half an eye to see that she was potty about you. God knows why, when you were being such a bloody awkward sod just after you lost your arm. I saw the way she looked sometimes."

He was filling in the awkward pauses, giving Martin time to gather the tatters of his pride and self-possession. They had progressed from the Club out on to the pavement where the fresh air restored some of his colour though his legs still felt decidedly wobbly. Resolving that discretion was the better part of valour, in the end he had accepted Ian's invitation.

When he had rung Sylvia from Chester Square he had wanted to say something to erase the memory of their chilly parting but, cowardly, had not managed to create the opening. She had sounded chirpy enough — a good deal chirpier when she heard his news. Stuart had been making himself useful. He was good company and they had had quite a bit of fun. Was she deliberately laying it on with a trowel? He had had a bloody day. But thank God for Ian. Underneath all that bullshit lurked a steadfast heart and a high degree of shrewdness. "Only took half an eye to see that she was potty about you." Not so shrewd there. "I saw the way she looked sometimes." Beneath that bluff exterior, Martin thought wryly, Ian was an incurable romantic.

★ ★ ★

"That was Martin on the phone. He's going to have to stay up there for the night."

252

Stuart throttled down the Ransom and switched off the petrol and the engine over which Sylvia had been forced to shout. She stood with her hands on her hips taking in his handywork.

"You've certainly made a fabulous job of the grass, and so quickly. It's a day's work for Martin to get this lot cut. He will be pleased."

"I enjoyed the exercise." He was on his haunches cleaning grass off the blades of the mower with a short-handled brush. "So he's not coming back?"

"No."

He was intent upon his task. She looked down at the curve of his neck where the tawny hair was wet with perspiration. A mosquito hovered and settled and he slapped it absent-mindedly, killing it and leaving a trail of blood on his palm. "Big as a horse," he said, inspecting it and showing it to her.

"They swarm at this time of the evening. It's bitten you." She watched the white mark come up against his tan. "Hurry up or you'll be devoured."

"I've finished." He stood up and wheeled the mower into the shed, turning the key in the padlock. "What's the next task?"

Sylvia laughed. "I think I've worked you quite hard enough today. You deserve a drink and supper."

"I told you. I've enjoyed it. I think I could slip into the rural life quite easily. I was going to be a farmer once, you know."

"What changed your mind?" He had a body built for labouring out of doors, Sylvia reflected. There was an easy strength in his shoulders and arms. She had watched him humping the trestles and erecting the scaffolding for the stalls, single-handedly raising the tea marquee and generally doing all the heavy fetching and carrying for the Fayre preparations. After lunch they had had a break and Sylvia had taken him into Hanbury shopping. On their return he had insisted on investigating a noise that had developed in her Mini and had jacked it up and happily spent an hour sorting the problem out. She had enjoyed his company and his jokes and coming back from the village she realized she had probably talked more in the last seven hours than she had for a week. She remembered reading somewhere the statistic that the average married couple conversed with one another for approximately twenty-seven minutes in every seven days. She and Martin were pretty average. She warmed to Stuart even more after Martin's confirmation of his character over the phone. She had felt shabby offering him hospitality with one hand and withholding her complete trust with the other — especially when she wanted so much to believe in him.

"A better opportunity came along."

"Were your parents disappointed? Was your father a farmer?"

"No. He was dead anyway."

"And your mother?"

"She brought me up." They were walking up the garden towards the house.

"Were you an only child?"

"I had a brother. He was killed." He didn't elaborate and she could tell that it was a memory that still smarted.

"I'm sorry," she said. Then, "It takes a lot of adjusting. Losing somebody close. People tell you you'll get over it, but you don't. You just get used to it."

He glanced sideways at her, catching a wistful sadness. "Who was it with you?" he asked.

"A man I used to know."

"A lover?"

She didn't answer. Instead she said, "Oh Lord! I've suddenly remembered. Martin asked me to lock the church." She looked on her wrist for the time. "The confirmation class will be over now. I'll get the key."

"I'll wait," he said, and stood smoothing the gravel drive with the toe of his shoe while she ran up the steps and into the vicarage. The dusk was gathering swiftly and swallows dipped and swooped about the gaunt, grey eaves of the house.

"They're late leaving this year," Sylvia said as she returned and he commented upon the birds. The shrubbery path was narrow and Sylvia walked ahead where the branches of two ancient oaks met above them and where the undergrowth smelled of grass mowings and bonfire ash. She held the wicket gate for him.

"You haven't seen inside our church, have you?" she said.

"They're not usually my scene, but

I look forward to a guided tour of this one."

"It's got an apsidal crypt complete with chancel, nave and two side-aisles. There's only one other in England. Martin occasionally holds celebrations down there on special days."

The old part of the churchyard was overgrown with grass from which the lichened tombstones rose at angles of varying degrees of drunkenness. Away to the right of them a luminosity of flowers on the freshly dug earth of a recent grave marked the ground presently used for burials. There was a light on in the chancel, shining out through stained glass, and as Sylvia and Stuart entered the church they met Peter Cummings on the point of extinguishing it and leaving. Sylvia introduced the two men. They all stood chatting for a moment, then Peter said,

"Well, I'll be on my way, or do you want me to lock up? I can do it."

"No, it's all right. While we are here I'm just going to show Stuart some of our historical treasures, then we are coming."

"Good night, then."

"Good night, Peter. Love to Alison."

He left them and they heard him close the outer door. The church was silent and mellow, mingling smells of musk and chrysanthemums and sanctity. On the altar Saturday's flowers were fresh and there were two pedestals in the nave and arrangements in the window niches.

"Martin had a wedding at the weekend," said Sylvia.

"Are you responsible for cleaning all this? It's beautifully kept." Stuart pointed to the altar silver, the polished eagle lectern, the brass communion rail.

"We have a roster. It works pretty well."

"Can you still get volunteers in this Godless age?"

"So far. Though the congregation does decline. People die off. Here in the country the young ones go to find work in towns. It was more of a challenge for Martin when we were in London, though I hated it. He accepted this parish partly because of me. Not that it made any difference."

"To what?" He was wandering about discovering an early Norman richly decorated font, some thirteenth-century frescoes in a side-aisle, mouldings in a piscina enriched by nail-head carving. "What didn't it make any difference to?"

"To Marian. As far as Marian was concerned, the damage was done. When we were in Hackney Martin had her removed from a school she was doing very nicely at and put her into the State system. That was the beginning of the rot. Going against the Establishment, denigrating all our standards, getting in with a bunch of kids who made fun of everything we stood for. Martin expected her to have enough 'character' to stand up to them. He's such an idealist. You heard what he said last night."

"Yet he has gone to make arrangements to get her the money after all. You said yourself he doesn't always mean what he says."

"He did then and that's when it mattered."

"Is he going to be able to raise it in time?" he asked casually. He was standing in the main aisle, head thrown back, examining the vaulted stone ceiling.

"Yes. Thank God his friend is coming across with it." She came to stand beside him. "Stuart, do you really not mind getting lumbered with this?"

"It was my suggestion, wasn't it?"

"Yes, I know, but it's asking a lot of you to take the responsibility of taking the money out to Marian and trying to convince her. Why should you?"

"I'm fond of her." He ceased his contemplation of the heavens and brought down his eyes to her. "I'm fond of you too, Sylvia. You're taking a chance trusting me."

She flushed.

"But Martin wouldn't do that without having me checked out, would he?"

"There was never any doubt in my mind," Sylvia said a bit too quickly. She grinned. "At least, not for long."

He returned her smile and they resumed their stroll.

"Where's this famous crypt, then?"

"Over here. Watch out. I'm going to take you down the original entrance. The steps over there by the vestry are comparatively modern. This is the way the pilgrims used to have to come in." She motioned him back off a square in the floor of a side-aisle. A chain attached to a winder was secured to the south wall and was looped through an iron ring firmly embedded in the trapdoor. Turning the handle, Sylvia raised the trap. Below, in the hole revealed, there were stone niches cut for their feet and she went down first. Stuart followed. A pool of light from above illuminated the circle in which they stood. Another shaft made a pattern on the floor through a waist-high arch at the west end of the crypt from which the steps rose into the church. Dimly Stuart could perceive that the windows at the east end of the short aisles looked into solid walls, being no more than deep semi-circular recesses. Behind the altar a small vesicular window was the only means of natural light. Through it the gloaming outside now matched the shadow within. The floor was unevenly cobblestoned, and marking off the side-aisles ran a couple of crude stone benches.

"It's creepy, isn't it? It's not much

good this time of day. You can't see the carvings or the plaster on the ceiling at all. We'll come again tomorrow." Her voice reverberated as in a cave, and she lowered it to demonstrate how down here even a whisper echoed. "We'd better go up this way." She moved out of one arc of light towards the other, and he was a step behind. She was a pair of legs outlined against the low arch with the light behind it, the top half of her body in the darkness. He put out his hand and felt her stiffen as he laid it flat between her shoulder-blades. The hair on the nape of her neck rose while she stood quite still and waited for his other hand to cup her breast from behind. Of its own accord her neck arched back, acquiescing to his mouth where it caressed her in the angle of her shoulder.

"Sylvia." He turned her gently round, pulling her against him, murmuring her name between kisses which travelled up the column of her throat until they reached her mouth. "Sylvia."

Sylvia! Sylvia! Sylvia! The sepulchral whispers of a million ghosts threw back the word like tempters, seducing, beckoning, insinuating. She shivered and pulled away.

"No."

"Why not?" His hands were not taking no for an answer.

"You know why not." She stepped sideways to avoid his predatory fingers which had unbuttoned the front of her shirt, and jarred her leg against a rough corner of the stone slab bench. She clutched the air and found herself once more caught in his arms.

"Why not? Because of all that stuff up there?" He jerked his head towards the church above them. "You don't believe in it, do you?"

"It's nothing to do with religion."

"You're right. It's to do with you and me."

"And Martin."

"What he doesn't know won't hurt him. Want to bet he hasn't got secrets of his own? Everyone has."

"I'd take one on his not having been unfaithful to me."

"There are worse betrayals than adultery. Anyway, by his lights you've already committed it in your heart. You and I knew that before I even touched you. Why did you bring me down here, Sylvia?" All the time he had been talking his lips and tongue had been coaxing the lobe of her ear, her mouth which she tried to avert, the hollow between her breasts. "It excited you to be alone with me in this secret place. You wanted to excite me. Well, you have." He drew her hand down and placed it upon the proof. "You're not a common prick-teaser, Sylvia. You want me. Tell me you don't and I'll let you go."

She couldn't, and even if she had, his fingers had now found the places that would have given it the lie.

"Sylvia. Darling." His voice was reverential. No one had called her that since Colin. She was melting in sensuous reminiscence, her lips parted against his.

"You remind me of someone I once knew." It was a rotten excuse but she would rationalize it after. Was it so wrong to want that experience just once again? If there were a cerebral block that inhibited Martin from satisfying her in that way, was she to grow old and wither and waste her munificence? Hadn't he made it quite clear last night? Overwrought had been his description of her. Too damn right! If it was left up to him, overwrought was what she would be for the rest of her life, or until all her juices had dried up.

"You remind me of him. The man I told you about who died."

"Was he your lover?"

"Yes."

"Before or after Martin?"

"Before. There's been nobody since."

Which didn't say a lot for Martin or she wouldn't be pliant and red-hot and moist and ready for him now, Stuart exulted.

"I don't want you to be reminded of anyone but me." He kissed her then, not at all reverentially. At the touch of his lips Sylvia burned her boats. Once, just once, she promised herself, and put both her arms up around his neck.

Something scuttered on the tessellated floor above them like a mouse running in between the pews. It brought Sylvia to an awareness of the discomfort and banality of their cramped and dusty surroundings.

"Not here. Someone may come. Not here, quickly in the dark. I want to see you. I want it to be beautiful. No ghosts."

"All right. But only if you promise that if I let you go you won't change your mind."

"I promise I won't. I can't." It wasn't her mind that needed changing. It was her treacherous, famished body. "What was that?"

Stiffening in his arms, she strained her ears to catch what had sounded like the stealthy closing of a distant door. They both stood listening, but it didn't come again. Conscience and the dankness of the place made her shiver. Taking his hand, she guided him towards the steps and up into the light. The empty church preserved their secret. The vestry door stood ajar, but there was no one inside. Sylvia closed it and turned off the lights. Outside Stuart waited beside her impatiently, listening to the creak of the heavy key in the brass lock.

13

THE six-thirty-eight from Victoria disgorged its daily quota of weary commuters back safely on to Hanbury platform and trailed off through the cutting bordering Brewer's Nurseries and into the distant tunnel. A dozen or so soberly suited city gents mingling with a handful of business girls and some shoppers who had been 'up for the day', straggled up over the iron bridge crossing the track to platform one and the station exit. In the middle of the Meccano-like structure, Billy halted to shake a stone free from its lodging in the heel of his shoe and spit out a pellet of spent chewing-gum over the rail and on to the line below.

With the train gone it was peaceful, the country silence broken only by the sound of footsteps clip-clopping on iron and the desultory conversations of people in ones and twos as they moved purposefully past him heading for home. Nothing had changed much in the two years he and Marian had been away. He caught up with the crowd, passing through the ticket-barrier with them and out on to the road beyond. In the station precinct a short line of cars driven by commuters' wives awaited their wage slaves, and to these some of the grey ants dispersed. Everyone else filtered off in the direction of the bus stop and the village main street.

Billy sauntered along, losing ground behind the others until he was walking alone. He was the only one to part company at the fork where the telephone-box, positioned on a grass triangle, marked the commencement of the bridle path running up through the wooded ridge leading to St Mary's. He and Marian had often come this way. In summertime there had been mossy places just off the track to lie concealed by overhanging beeches, where they had passed many an entertaining interlude, titillated by the unknowing proximity of riders or village matrons taking a short cut to the church. Sometimes she had secreted him in the vicarage on the upper floor, where taking her under her parents' inhospitable roof afforded him a twisted additional satisfaction. He hadn't been good enough for them in spite of all that crap her old man used to spout about all men being equal in the sight of God. To give him his due, it wasn't her Dad that had got up Billy's nose so much as her mother. Stuck-up bitch! And she had never made any secret of her animosity towards himself. But when all was said and done, it was her old man who was the boss. That was good. Billy wouldn't be here else. He had no other place to go, and if he played his cards right Martin might be good for a touch. If he broke the news sympathetically, made a good story out of what he had done for Marian in her last hours, told how he had come specially back to bring them her things, he reckoned they'd be grateful for any crumb of comfort, and their gratitude might take a tangible form.

And it wasn't as if it was all lies. It *had* shattered him rigid, her dying like that. He hadn't realized how much he had come to depend upon her just being there. It wasn't just that she had had the cash to keep them both in the first instance, although that had had its attraction. Even without that, she had class. He admired that — and that brand of confident effrontery that class gave someone like her. Billy had cultivated his own, but it didn't grow on him like a second skin as it had on Marian. And he had been jealous of her devotion to the Shivaan. He had gone along with all that malarky with his tongue in his cheek. Well, it had looked like a free holiday with everything found, and they had both been sick of travelling for the time being when they discovered Durga. He hadn't reckoned on Marian getting properly hooked, though. Nor, once on the island, was it so easy to get off. As recent recruits they had been under surveillance and it hadn't been long before Marian at least had been a willing captive. In fact she had become a proper pain in the arse over it all. It hadn't taken Billy long to become thoroughly disenchanted but he had stayed because of her and because he was lazy and because it was an easy enough meal ticket. Now he realized it had been mostly because of Marian.

Billy climbed and the path narrowed where blackthorn and bracken encroached, with nettles and knee-high grass restricting his passage. Pulling a stick from the hedge, he used it as a switch to clear a way as he went. The right of way had evidently fallen into disuse, which would make it all the easier for him to reconnoitre unobserved the churchyard and the vicarage garden to whose perimeter it lay adjacent. He stopped and looked over the hedge into the harvested field beyond, filling his lungs with the real smell of England at last. Not that his tubes weren't more accustomed to exhaust fumes and the grit and grime of the cities that spelled home to him. He had never seen the real country until Marian had brought him here. He remembered her ankles scratched with the stubble and the way she had taught him to blow through a blade of grass held flat between his two thumbs, making a noise to startle rooks out of the elms. In his mind's eye he could see those same ankles, her long narrow feet, bare and protruding from the white, sheet-like garment in which they had wrapped her in

271

the mortuary. Someone had given him a manilla envelope containing her valuables and a death certificate. The others with him had collected her more mundane bits and pieces and they had loaded her into the Bemo, the private van locally hired. The Bemo had seats down the side with a space in the middle for the coffin. Five of them had been sent to supervise the operation. Three of them were already in the van and one up front in the cab with the clutch let in and the engine running. On the spur of the moment Billy had made his decision. He had closed up the tail-board and slammed home the pins.

"I'll ride in the front," he had called to the others and had disappeared around the front of the vehicle. He put his head into the driver's cab.

"All ready." He gave the man the thumbs up. "I'll give the sign when I'm in." The driver nodded, looking in his wing mirror, preparing to move out into the traffic stream. Billy dodged round the bonnet once more where he crouched and delivered two smart blows with the flat of his hand to the Bemo's coachwork. As it drew away, he had retreated behind the discreetly tinted glass door of the mortuary, and as soon as it had disappeared he had taken to his heels in the other direction and had run like hell. He had been running ever since. He was safe now. They couldn't have followed him this far.

It had taken him four days to raise the money for his fare and to arrange his flight. All the time he had been looking over his shoulder and covering his tracks in case someone from the Shivine had followed him. His uppermost desire was to see the back of bloody Indonesia and to put as many miles between him and it as he could. He had had enough of traipsing the world, and anyway, without Marian he wouldn't have known where to make for next or why. She was the one who had possessed enough of a smattering of language to get them by and the intelligence to deal with or bypass the formalities. His knowledge of English could be termed barely basic, let alone French or German. His grasp of geography was non-existent. What he did know about though was thieving. He had heard that the pickings were likely to be good at Kuta. Visitors descended upon the mile-long beach on the south-west of the island in tour loads, attracted by its unparalleled surfing, spectacular sunsets and the Balinese art shops, trash and treasure drawing American and Australian souvenir-hunters in their droves. It was a pickpocket's paradise. Billy's fingers were selective and productive. It was gratifying to know that they had lost none of their skill. Undoubtedly he would still have been there but for an unexpected coup made late on the fourth day. A party from Memphis — three flabby men in real estate and their well-nourished wives — succumbed to the blandishments of four of the Balinese masseuses who plied their trade with oils and unguents under the sunshine on the beach. Jackets and trousers had been removed and folded in a neat pile upon a rattan mat, watched over by one of the American ladies. There had come a moment when her attention had wavered, drawn to the spectacle of a group of kite-flying children beside a line of beached prahus. Billy had caught her eye and smiled in shared enjoyment and a few moments later he came over at her invitation to explain the intricacies of one of the kite manœuvres. Another member of the group approached, juggling with six ice-cream cornets. Billy's lady took three steps forward to assist. When she had returned to the rattan rug Billy was gone. Gone too, they later discovered, were their wallets and purses. It was criminal the way people, in spite of warnings, carried large sums of cash upon their persons, Billy marvelled!

He still had the manilla envelope inside his leather jacket, but it would never have occurred to him to hock any of its contents for his own purposes. That would be tantamount to robbing the dead and Billy was superstitious. Besides, there wasn't a lot there of any value. A gold watch on a petersham strap, a pair of gold hoop earrings, a string of ivory beads and half a dozen thin silver bangles. He didn't like looking at them much. He estimated they would be worth more to him produced as evidence of his having done the decent thing in returning them to Marian's parents. He might thereby be able to wheedle himself into some kind of favour, even some kind of temporary employment while he saw how the land lay. He had nothing else in sight.

Billy sniffed and wiped his nose on the back of a grimy hand. Resuming his climb, he surmounted a stile and came to the boundary running at right-angles to his path. Here the beech trees ended and a yew hedge marked the beginning of the churchyard. Further up there was a gap, and on an impulse he decided to avail himself of the old remembered short cut. He scrambled through and approached the church, taking care to walk over the grassy mounds and not on the scrunchy shingle of the formal paths. There was no sign of life outside, nor seemingly for that matter within. Billy hovered, listening in the church porch. Tentatively he tried the brass handle but the door was not latched and it swung noiselessly away from him inwards. Almost within arm's length, resting on the back ledge of the end pew, were two wooden boxes with coin slots in their lids. A rack beside them offered picture-postcard views of St Mary's and a potted history of the building in pamphlet form priced at twenty pence and fifty pence respectively. The sight of the boxes proved irresistibly alluring to Billy's magpie mentality. Warily ascertaining he was unobserved, he released the door and stepped right inside. The fifty pence box felt about a quarter full. He turned it upside down and rattled it hopefully. Nothing came out. What sounded like two ten-penny pieces clinked hollowly and slid about in the other receptacle. There was no visible means of extricating the money without prising the boxes apart. Billy had a knife. He had just unsheathed it and inserted its tip between two pieces of wood when he heard footsteps on the gravel outside and several young voices raised in laughter and general conversation. It was worth waiting to have another go if this proved to be only a temporary interruption. Replacing the box on the pew and looking for a means of concealment, his eye lit on the vestry door. Billy slipped through it and closed it before the invaders could discover him.

Peter Cummings's confirmation class clattered in and distributed itself among the front three pews on either side of the main aisle. Billy, lurking behind a row of white surplices hanging from hooks in the vestry, allowed ten minutes to pass before he risked coming out from his hiding-place. Peeping through a chink in the door, he could see and hear the course of instruction was in full swing. The kids were early teenagers with the exception of an older man and woman who sat together slightly apart. Peter was taking them through their duty towards their neighbour. Billy leaned against the lintel considering the impracticability of doing to all men 'what you would they should do unto you'. He was obviously holed up here for at least another half an hour. The vestry was furnished with a desk and a chair. He settled himself in the latter, leaning back with his hands behind his head and his feet up on the desk and waited.

Forty minutes later when the light had diminished and he was sitting almost in the dark came the stampede that heralded the end of the lesson.

"Good night."

"Good night, Mr Cummings."

"Good night, Darren. Richard. Don't

leave anything in the pews."

The last one departed and there was only the man left. Billy held his breath, ready to hide again if he looked likely to come towards the vestry. No, he was on his way out. A panic thought struck. Supposing he locked the door behind him when he went? Billy would have to break a window to escape. There was a mullioned one high up in the vestry wall. He was just wondering what possible excuse he could concoct for his appearance at this juncture were he to make his presence known, when the west door opened and Sylvia and Stuart entered the church.

Billy recognized Sylvia at once. She was thinner but otherwise as he remembered her. He pressed closer to the crack in the door. The man with her was familiar too but he couldn't immediately place him. Then the penny dropped and Billy did a double-take. He was the guy from the hospital in Bali. Marian's friend. He must have beaten him to them with the news. Billy looked more closely at Sylvia. She didn't look particularly devastated or grieved. In fact she looked quite animated and pretty with colour in her face and making small talk to the bloke called Peter. Billy dared to ease the door open another centimetre in order to get a better hearing.

"It was good of you to stand in for Martin," Sylvia was saying. "As things have turned out, he has got to be in London tomorrow as well, so your taking his class has saved him the double train fare, not to mention the wear and tear." She had introduced her companion. "Peter, this is Stuart Balfour. He is an old friend of Marian's who is staying a few days."

It *was* the same man. Billy's eyes had not been deceived. He didn't know so much about the 'old friend' bit, though. Marian had only met him in the hospital. Billy's nose twitched suspiciously. Being well versed in the art of lying himself, he could smell the hint of a rat from a considerable distance. This smell grew stronger. Stuart. That was the guy's name all right, the one Marian had used — but Balfour? That rang a discordant note. It took Billy half a minute to realize why. It had been when he and the others from the Shivine had gone to collect the body from the mortuary. The nurse, making conversation to fill in a gruesome silence had said, "Her friend Mr Coleby was here this morning and it came as a great shock to him." Billy had automatically concluded she was referring to Stuart. Marian hadn't made any other friends in Indonesia away from the Shivine. He could be mistaken. He remembered asking the nurse, "The tall chap? Auburn with a beard? Appendicitis?" The nurse had verified his description. And now the same man was here, but not going by the name of Coleby.

The Peter man was going. Sylvia and Stuart stayed on. They moved away from the vestry and up the church. In his anxiety not to miss what was being said, Billy forswore caution and crept out after them, ducking down behind a curtain that concealed the bell ropes, well within earshot. They were talking about Marian now. *She* was lamenting Marian's snooty school.

"A bunch of kids who made fun of everything we stood for." She meant the likes of Billy. She was right about that. Stuart's next words made Billy prick up his ears. He was saying Martin had gone, presumably to London, to make arrangements to get Marian some money. But Marian didn't need money now, where she had gone. She *had* needed it though. How she had kept on about how on earth was she going to be able to repay for the operation! He strained his ears in an attempt to get the gist of what appeared incomprehensible. Evidently Martin was getting the money for Stuart to take out to Indonesia to Marian.

"It's asking a lot for you to take the responsibility of taking the money out to Marian and trying to convince her."

Billy stood riveted. She obviously had no idea that Marian was dead. Stuart hadn't told her. Was it feasible that he didn't know himself? That he wasn't Mr Coleby? No. What the nurse had told Billy made that impossible. If he did know, why hadn't he said? The stench in Billy's nostrils intensified. For some reason he was bluffing them along. Money was involved. It must be quite a sum. He was smooth. He was inviting them to check his credentials. He was nothing more than a bloody con man. But he was cool. Oh yes. Billy could see from this distance that Mrs High-and-Mighty appreciated both his smoothness and his cool. Cold as the arse of an arctic mule! He remembered the rest of the old rhyme. But not as cold as our poor Willy — for Willy, read Marian — she's dead, poor bugger!

With his mouth hanging open in concentration and amazement, Billy watched Sylvia winch up the trapdoor. They went down. Billy advanced, taking care to stand at an angle where he cast no shadow below to give away his presence. He could see down into the crypt. And then he got his second shock. Sylvia was in the shadow. He watched Stuart reach out to touch her. He too now moved beyond Billy's vision except where the cut-off light glanced down against his legs, from the back of his knees downwards. There was a silence which lengthened, then he said, "Sylvia". The way he said it, it wasn't difficult to imagine what was happening. Billy could hear their hurried breathing, the rustling contact of hands and clothing, the intermittent pauses when they would be kissing and clutching. The sanctimonious cow! Behaving with him and Marian as if butter had never melted in her mouth let alone anywhere else, and here she was having it off with her daughter's boy-friend *and* admitting to having had another lover — maybe lovers — before her husband. And her old man so conveniently away for the night. Her sort struck moral attitudes with the present-day young, but what was she? No better than any of them. Bitterly Billy watched the bracing of Stuart's calves which betokened the thrust of his body further up. Voyeur's curiosity getting the better of him, Billy slid nearer the gap, vicariously horny. The tip of his track shoe kicked a loose hassock which nudged a pencil dropped by one of the confirmation candidates. He froze. He had disturbed them. Guilty consciences would be bound to investigate. Moving silently and swiftly, he made for the door and opened it as quietly as he could. With his heart racing, he gained the churchyard and sprinted through the wicket gate and into the shrubbery. The vicarage was in darkness, the ever-open door unfastened. Billy paused on the threshold, remembering that Martin was away. The house had the feel of being deserted. He had a little torch in his pocket and instinctively he made for the place where he knew he would be safe, taking the stairs two at a time. He knew the attic floor of old. There was a box-room up there, a water-closet and three maids' rooms. The one he and Marian had used was a garret under the eaves. The old iron bedstead and its ticking mattress were still there. The rug with which they had covered themselves lay as they might have left it after the last time they were there, the pillows were still dented. Dust on the floorboards was undisturbed, pigeon droppings thick on the stone sill in the roof, some inside where there was a star-shaped break in the window-pane. The key was still on the inside. Billy turned it and threw himself down on the bed. Unwrapping some gum, he chewed it thoughtfully while his breathing levelled and he turned over in his mind what he had recently learned. He was safe enough here for a bit. He'd have to consider how best to use his new-found knowledge. He'd have to be sure of his facts before he turned the screws on anyone, and that meant looking and listening some more. Fate had presented him with a nice little turn up for the book. Looked like he was sitting on a nice little keg of dynamite which he might send up in any one of three directions. He had yet to figure out which was likely to have the most in it for him. There was no hurry.

His stomach rumbled. It would have to wait to be satisfied. Later he'd go down and inspect the larder. He wouldn't have to wait too long. If his guess was right the others would be dispensing with food. Disgusting hypocrite! She wasn't even young! He'd heard that middle-aged women were the worst. Never fancied one himself. Billy turned over on his empty stomach and lent his imagination rein.

14

SYLVIA ran down in the car to meet Martin off his train. He had stayed up until after lunch and the children were coming out of the village school as she swung into the station yard a full seven minutes too early. It had been another golden day. As she wound down her window and waited, the station-master, Jack Rigby, emerged from his office and glanced her way.

"Let's hope this holds for Saturday, Mrs Dearsley," he called across to her, pointing up at the bright sun three-quarters declining.

"Let's hope so," Sylvia agreed. She hoped he wouldn't come over and start one of his interminable conversations. She didn't feel like speaking to anyone, and that included Martin. Especially Martin whom she would have to face at any minute pretending nothing had happened or was different. Not that anything significant had, or was, but he would be hardly likely to appreciate that if he learned that she had gone to bed with Stuart Balfour! How could he be expected to accept that the act had been satiating in the way that a starving person would find a four-course meal satisfying, but that cerebrally she was still faithful? It was a puzzle to her so why should Martin understand? Sylvia rested her elbow on the open window and ran her hand through her ruffled hair. Stuart had made love to her in the way she remembered, with tenderness and passion and expertise and in a variety of different ways that had given rein to her capacity for sensual expression, but it had been neither his face nor Colin's that she had seen when she had closed her eyes. It had been Martin's features that had got in the way. She had been fired by a desire to recreate the past, but somewhere along the line Colin had faded and in her imagination it was Martin who was making love to her in the way she so deeply craved, a new Martin who was not ashamed to whisper his need of her as he stroked her. The fantasy had stimulated so intense an eroticism in her that she had taken even Stuart by surprise. Afterwards she knew he had been tantalized by her detachment. In his experience women behaved in a variety of ways after coitus — clinging, cloying, remorseful, tearful, possessive, demanding. Sylvia's reaction was none of these. She had accepted him as a pleasurable experience on his own terms. He didn't know that he found that specially flattering and discovered he was the one angling for a more definitive response. If he was justifiably confused, Sylvia was more so. For years she had committed mental adultery in her unsatisfactory sexual encounters with Martin. Now that the fantasy had become a fact it was pretty shattering to discover herself wanting the person who was actually hers by legal right. She loved Martin! She always had. She hadn't stayed all these years through gratitude or any other nobler concept than that he was her life and she wanted to be part of him. Now she had betrayed him. At least, that would be his unequivocal judgement if he ever found out. She could hardly expect him to be grateful to Stuart for opening her eyes.

She had not spoken to Stuart alone today and she was thankful for that. Some time in the early morning she had left his bed while he slept and had crept back to her own room. The sheets were cold in the undisturbed nuptial king-size. She stretched out her hand into Martin's empty half with a sudden yearning for him.

Stuart had kept out of the way until lunch-time. Whether from tact or natural sloth, he was still in his room when Sylvia called him to share the snack she had prepared for the two of them and Alison Cummings. Alison had dropped in with her contribution to the Fayre and for a chat, and her being there made the atmosphere a good deal easier between the two lovers. If you could call us that, Sylvia thought. Technically, yes. In any other way they were poles apart. Strange how this morning it could all seem so unimportant and yet yesterday she had had to have him or die. With Sylvia's encouragement Alison had hung on, and then Stuart had taken himself off to buy cigarettes. She had passed him coming up the hill as she was going down in the car.

The train rattled into the station and doors slammed. A whistle blew, it rattled out again, and Martin came through the barrier looking gaunt and tired. Compassion stabbed her. He was not alone. Dan Rowson, trailing a child on each hand and a plump beagle on a lead attached to his wrist, staggered in Martin's wake and was being shepherded towards the car. Sylvia, putting aside her own problems, recognized a crisis when she saw one. Dan looked dreadful, a changed man since she last saw him less than a week ago. A normally big man, he seemed to have shrunk physically into clothes which looked a size too big and his face was grey with fatigue. She got out hurriedly and went towards them.

"Dan." Sylvia touched his arm sympathetically, not wanting to say anything in front of the children.

"Hallo, Sylvia," he smiled wanly.

Martin said, "Dan's been to collect Jane and Henry from their Granny's. She was taken ill and has had to go to hospital." He spoke brightly, nodding at the children reassuringly. Sylvia looked from one child to the other. Four-year-old Henry clung solemnly to his father's hand, viewing her with big, bewildered saucer eyes. Jane, a couple of years the elder, was jigging up and down, playing with the dog and making him bark.

"Duffer spent a penny in the guard's van," she lisped gleefully through the gap where two front teeth were missing.

"You'll make him spend another if you get him all excited." Dan pulled at the dog irritably. "Stand still." To Sylvia he said privately, "Coronary. Having the children on top of the news about us was too much for the old girl. Always had a dicky heart. Had to come by train. Annette took the car when she scarpered. It never rains but it pours!"

"Why on earth didn't you ring me, Dan? You know I would have driven you up."

"I know you would Sylvia. That's what Martin said, but I thought I'd been enough of a nuisance to you both Sunday night, keeping him up till all hours."

Martin chipped in. "Let's get into the car. It'll be a squeeze but Henry can come on my lap, can't you, Henry?" Somehow they all got in. On the way to Dan's house Sylvia asked, "Are you going to be able to manage?"

"Oh, we'll sort things out, won't we, kids? It's just that tonight I'm meant to be entertaining a client on this new printing deal. He's staying with Sir Herbert Granier over near East Grinstead and I'm on parade there. It's a bit late to ring and cry off now, and to tell you the truth I don't feel much like going into explanations."

Duffer hurled himself against the rear window barking maniacally at a passing labrador. A harassed Dan yanked him back. Avoiding Martin's eyes upon her in the driving mirror, Sylvia volunteered, "You go, Dan. I'll come down and give the children their supper and put them to bed and straighten things out."

"You wouldn't, would you, Sylvia? No, it's too much to ask." Dan's resistance was token, his eyes hopeful.

"Of course I will."

"There's a bed made up with clean sheets in the spare room if you want to stay. I might be late."

293

"Then I will." It was a cop-out, but it would give her a breathing space, time to reassemble her thoughts and features which already she feared were painfully transparent under Martin's perceptive scrutiny. She had the feeling he already knew something was up, but he could hardly dissuade her when she was so patently exercising her Christian duty. She dropped Dan and the children with the promise of her early return and she and Martin drove back to the vicarage in the car steamed up with Duffer's breath and the smell of dog.

"You didn't mind me offering?"

"No, of course not. I was glad you did." It was a lie. She knew he was watching her. "You look tired," he said. There was no suspicion in the statement. Why should there be? It would never occur to Martin not to trust her completely. She felt a pang of guilt, and anger with him for making her feel so. She had given Stuart nothing that Martin wanted for himself. She hadn't hurt him. She was only beginning to think she might have hurt herself.

"So do you," she said. "Was it bad?"

"Not too bad. I got the money." He told her about Ian's kindness, Handyside and Bennett and his interview with Animus. "It doesn't look much, does it?" He took a long envelope from inside his breast pocket and held it open for her to see. Sylvia glanced sideways. Inside she saw three slim packets of notes in fifties.

They had arrived at the house and Stuart was in the drawing-room watching television. He got up and switched it off as they came in.

"Successful trip?" he asked Martin.

"Yes, thank you. I can see you haven't been idle either. The grass looks beautiful. I hope Sylvia hasn't worn you out."

Stuart looked directly at Sylvia and smiled. "Never let it be said."

She interrupted hastily. "I'll go and put a few things together for the night. You two will have to get your own suppers, I'm afraid." She turned to Stuart to explain Dan's matrimonial plight and her offer to look after the children. His look of amusement deepened and his eyes called her chicken and promised that her attempts to escape him would ultimately prove futile. The small chill of fear, foreboding, that she had experienced earlier on his ready acceptance of their hospitality and which she had then squashed, reasserted itself. Starting upstairs to pack a case, she wondered if she was doing the right thing leaving him and Martin alone. She had offered to help Dan on an impulse, wanting to escape, but had that been wise? It was too late to go back on it now. Sylvia zipped up her grip. The children would be expecting her.

★ ★ ★

There were sausages and bacon in the fridge, which Martin fried. They ate it early because of the parish council meeting and stacked the dishes. During the course of the meal Martin produced the envelope with the money and placed it on the table between them.

"There's three thousand there," he said without prevarication. "Sylvia tells me you are prepared to take the money Marian needs out to her. I've allowed for her return ticket and any expenses you may incur. Will you do it?"

Stuart's eyes flickered over the envelope. He passed his tongue across his lips which were suddenly dry. "I'll certainly do it if you are prepared to trust me. What makes you think you can?"

"I spoke to Malcolm Quennell. Besides, I know where to find you." They looked at each other for a moment before both smiled. He thinks he's been so clever, Stuart thought. It will be an added satisfaction eventually letting him know how easily he was fooled. An officer and God's gentleman! No doubt he thinks he's a great judge of character. He was due for a number of enlightenments.

"Fair enough."

"I want you to pay off the Shivaan and make Marian come back. Do you think you can do it?"

"I'll try."

"Tell her we shan't interfere in whatever she wants to do as long as she gets right away from that set-up and keeps out of the drug scene. Tell her what her going off like that has done to her mother."

Stuart nodded.

"Tell her we love her and shan't

make any demands on her. There'll be no recriminations." Martin grimaced. "Personally I'd like to boot her into next week, but you'd better not tell her that." He raised his eyes to Stuart's. "You're fond of her, aren't you? I'm counting on that more than anything she may or may not feel for us. What are your plans?"

"I'll leave tomorrow after breakfast if I may. I have to be at Heathrow early Thursday morning. I want to see and speak to Malcolm myself first."

"In that case you'd better take this now and put it somewhere safe." Martin pushed the envelope towards him. Stuart's fingers closed around the package. The money felt like wadding.

He couldn't wait to get up to his room and see that it was real, and lay it out on the bed and count it, which he did two or three times for the sheer joy of savouring it and what it represented. Not a bad little haul for starters, and easy. He'd be back for more. More of both money and Sylvia, whether she wanted to or not. He had a hold on each of them now and could work one against the other.

Martin had gone off to his meeting. Stuart sat on his bed in the empty house plotting.

* * *

Billy was hungry again. He hadn't saved any of the provisions filched on his foray the previous night, and now it was after two o'clock the following afternoon. He knew the time because he could hear the church clock's chimes clearly up here. Pity he'd flogged his watch to raise his fare before he had encountered the men from Memphis. Marian's gold one, like her, had long since stopped.

As he had expected, Sylvia and Stuart on returning to the house last night shortly after Billy had gained his own sanctuary, had made straight for the sack. They weren't in the bedroom she shared with her old man, but directly beneath him in the spare room, which meant Billy had to be extra cautious about his own creaking springs or floorboards. Straining his ears for half an hour, he had caught the occasional murmur of voices, then he had drifted off to sleep until awakened round about one o'clock in the morning by the flutter of pigeons' wings flapping and settling against his window. All was silence. Judging it safe then to take a chance, he had stolen downstairs and found his way in the dark to the kitchen. A slice of bread here, one Weetabix out of a packet there, a sliver of ham from a cooked joint in the fridge, a couple of biscuits, a small wedge of cheese. He accumulated a picnic of sorts of ingredients unlikely to be missed. A pint of milk was a tempting proposition but he settled for lemon squash made up in one of the empty milk bottles on the shelf by the back door. Too much liquid and he would be peeing non-stop and he only dared flush the WC when he was sure the others were out of the house. He had repaired to his eyrie, feasted and fallen asleep. Jet-lag must have taken its retrospective toll, because it was much later than he thought when he had rubbed the sleep from his eyes and opened his door a crack to hear what was going on down below.

From the ground floor the rise and fall of animated discourse, interspersed with laughter and the rattle of china floated up to him. Stealthily he advanced out on to the top landing and listened. He could hear Sylvia's voice and Coleby's, and there was another woman with them. The vicar was evidently not yet back. It was the vicar Billy wanted to see. He slipped down on to the first floor and hung over the banisters to get a better earful. After a while he heard Coleby leave the two women, announcing he was going for a walk to get some cigarettes. Billy could have done with a fag himself but it was too dangerous. Maybe tonight he could nip out and have a quick drag in the shrubbery while everyone else was in bed. Left alone, the women had dropped their voices to a more confidential tenor and boldly Billy descended the second flight, taking up a concealed stance between the kitchen door and a large coat cupboard which could afford him refuge on the spur of the moment. From this position he could catch every word that was being said and, like last night, it made very interesting hearing. They were talking about Stuart and Sylvia was telling Alison how he

301

had brought them news of Marian in trouble and needing money. Coleby had apparently woven a plausible enough story out of fact and fiction and they had fallen for it. Not only that, but he'd made sure of madam's backing by the oldest method in the world for enlisting a female ally — plenty of soft soap and a bit of the other! Not that she was letting on about that right now to her lady-friend. You had to hand it to this Stuart geezer. It must have taken a lot of brash confidence and subtle nerve to make a toffee-nosed bitch like Mrs Vicar within twenty-four hours of meeting. Twenty-four hours flat! Billy had stumbled on a right hornets' nest and no mistake. As though hardly believing his ears, he absent-mindedly stuck his little finger into one of the afore-mentioned shell-likes to dislodge any wax that might be distorting their reception. In doing so, he caught his fourth digit on the metal hook that pierced his lobe and from which dangled an ivory skull and cross-bones. The ear-ring had been a present from Marian, one of a pair bought off a stall long ago in Leather Lane, and he swore under his breath as the stainless steel scratched him and drew blood.

Dearsley was due back very soon. Mrs D. was going down to fetch him in the car. The friend was leaving. He heard the scrape of their chairs as they pushed them back; he ran noiselessly upstairs. When the house was empty he came down again, but was only able to grab an apple and a banana before he saw Stuart returning from his walk. He was getting braver. This time when he nipped back upstairs he didn't bother to shut himself in. He heard Sylvia come back with Martin and then go off again. Apparently she wasn't coming home that night. He might get a chance to have a go at the vicar alone in that case.

★ ★ ★

The day faded, the evening drew in. Somebody came up on to the first landing and Billy heard them opening and shutting drawers. Water ran. A lavatory was flushed. It was Martin freshening up before supper. As he went downstairs he called out to Stuart, asking him what he would drink. The two men went into the kitchen. Presently the appetizing aroma of sizzling sausages was borne tantalizingly aloft. Billy's gastric juices groaned, his mouth watered. If he couldn't have food then he must have a cigarette. It should be safe enough now with them both out of the way for a while. He smoked it standing by the open window, inhaling the pungent scent of cloves right down into his empty stomach, flipping the butt when he had finished out into the pigeon droppings. Time for another fact-finding mission! Creeping downstairs in the shadows, he stood for the second time that day spying on what was going on in the kitchen. His reaction when he saw Martin pass Stuart the money was much the same as Martin's had been. The envelope didn't look bulky enough to accommodate three thousand pounds. Not that Billy had ever seen that much bread all together in one place before. His eyes grew speculatively greedy. Slowly, mentally, he began reforming his plans. If only he could get his hands on that envelope there'd be no call for ingratiating himself with anyone. He could be his own boss. It would serve Coleby right if he woke up in the morning and found he had been hoist with his own petard. Stuart was tucking the money away into the inner pocket of a safari jacket he was wearing and Billy made a mental note of its exact position. If he had the chance of lifting it he could be on his way before dawn and leave them all to their little intrigues none the wiser that he had ever been around. His pickpocket's fingers could already feel the texture of the lining of that jacket, the smooth envelope, the crinkle edges of the notes. He wasn't going to be able to sleep again for the thought of them. Forget about all the rest. The notes were there for the taking and he knew he wasn't going to be able to resist them.

15

THERE was very little moon. Round about midnight the weather broke and it started raining and the wind got up. Billy, pacing restlessly, watched the raindrops gathering momentum on the roof tiles beyond the window, some of them splashing in through the splintered pane. A bedraggled pigeon huddled up against the glass, its wings sheltering its retracted head, reminding Billy of the meths addicts sleeping rough under newspapers in the Waterloo Road. He amused himself by prodding it through the hole with the tip of his knife and, when it stirred, blowing the smoke from his last cigarette into its blearily opened eyes. The bird took flight and lifted off for another perch where it could get some privacy. Billy had grown blasé about the danger of detection through smoking. He wouldn't be here much longer anyway and he'd had to do something to ease the waiting game and keep his hands and nerve steady. It was too soon yet to make his attempt on the theft of the money. The two men beneath him had retired early but they might have been reading late and only recently fallen asleep. It would be safer to wait until they were likely to be at their most deeply unconscious. While they had been talking downstairs, he had done a recce of both their rooms, paying particular attention to the brass doorknob of Stuart's. It turned smoothly on a stiffish spring that he must remember not to release too quickly. Billy had familiarized himself with the layout of the furniture with special regard to any awkward bits that stuck out. There wasn't going to be much light from the window, so he was glad and proud of himself that he had taken this precaution. The adrenalin tensed his stomach and he resisted and controlled the urge to empty his bowel. Excitement gave him the squitters, though by rights there should be nothing left to go on, he having had only the two pieces of fruit to eat all day. He'd pick up something for the journey on his way out. He had only a half-formed plan as to where he would be heading. He still had a few mates in the Smoke whom he fancied looking up, Doris Clegg to name one in particular. He had been going with Doris before Marian had turned up. She had been a luscious bit of crumpet and all. Not in Marian's class for brains, but suitably adoring and a voluptuous enough handful for any guy. That had been the trouble with Doris. She did spread it about. The money might make a bit of a difference to that. Not that he'd make her wise as to how much. However hard he tried, he couldn't stop thinking about the money. Forcing himself to wait for the witching hour, he sat down on the bed and bit the nails on each of his hands systematically down to the quick.

After an eternity the church clock struck two, chiming muffled through the rain. Billy stood up and zipped on his jacket, satisfying himself that he had on him everything he had arrived with. Quickly and quietly he let himself out of the attic for the last time and crept to the head of the stairs. The fourth tread down creaked under the weight of his foot. He stopped, but the rain blowing and beating against the curtained landing window lower down covered the sound, and he completed his descent safely to where the carpet began. No light was visible under any of the bedroom doors. Billy sidled towards the one he knew to be Stuart's and put his ear to it. With the background racket of the rain it was impossible to distinguish the sound of breathing, but at least there was no sign of movement from within. Experiencing that pleasurable sickness of apprehension epitomized in Billy's language as 'kicks', he slid his palm lovingly around the doorknob, turning it slowly clockwise in one sure, smooth movement. He waited, then inched the door inwards and slid inside the room. Now he could hear the breathing, regular intakes and exhalations accompanied by an intermittent, reassuring grunt of the dreamer. He counted several such sequences before closing the door catch behind him. His eyes, accustomed to the curtainless dark of the attic, were temporarily blind in pitch blackness. Stuart had pulled the heavy drapes across the window and it was a few moments before Billy could adjust and discern three chinks of lighter grey down the sides of each curtain. Now and again they billowed in gusts from the open window behind them. He advanced cautiously into the room, hands stretched in front of him like a sleepwalker. They encountered a spoon-backed Victorian chair over which a pair of trousers was folded. Deftly Billy's fingers sought the pockets. Empty. He ran his palms down to the cushioned seat. A shirt a pair of socks, some underpants. No sign of the safari jacket. Turning left from memory, he shuffled behind his outstretched arms until they touched the wardrobe and his right hand found the knob. Holding the left hand door shut with his other palm, he turned the catch and pulled gently. The wardrobe door opened on a sigh. He listened for any reaction from the bed but Stuart's breathing was still rhythmic. Billy felt carefully into the cupboard, being sure not to rattle any coathangers. The jacket hung alone in solitary splendour. He unhooked it and brought it out. As though they worked independently of him and knew where to go, his fingers delved like ferrets into every nook and cranny but there was no sign of the envelope. No sign of anything. Coleby was evidently a man who emptied his pockets on undressing. Billy felt his way past the chair and headed towards the dressing-table. Ah! That was more like it. His hands ranged over its glass-topped surface, identifying a bunch of keys, a watch, a wallet (he'd come back to that), a lighter and — Christ! The cushion of his index finger came down hard on an upturned drawing pin and involuntarily Billy jerked it back in pain with its spike still impaling him. The edge of his hand caught a tumbler full of some liquid which had been resting on the dressing-table and which now crashed sideways, splashing its contents over everything, and rolled on to the carpet, hitting the skirting with a thud. Seconds before it came to rest Billy had prepared for flight, but he had forgotten the wardrobe door swinging open which now engaged his forehead with intolerable force. The blow brought him up short, gasping, as the lights flashed on in the room and stars burst behind his eyes.

It was a purely reflex action that found his knife. He flicked the blade open, turning defence into attack as Stuart sat bolt upright in the bed.

"Stay where you are!"

Stuart did as he was told, looking from the shining steel to Billy as recognition slowly dawned. Billy enjoyed his astonishment and there was something else in his expression, a wary unease that Billy could well appreciate.

"What the hell are *you* doing here?" He made it sound as if he had found a turd underneath his shoe and Billy's underprivileged hackles rose.

He said ever so quickly, "Same as you, I imagine, Mr Coleby." He accentuated the name. "I come to tell the vicar and his wife about their little girl, didn't I? From what I've heard you got in first, though. Only difference is, again from what I've heard, our stories don't tally, do they?"

"Oh?" Stuart raised his eyebrows. "And just what is it you have heard? And from whom?"

"Just about everything. I know what you're trying to do. You're getting money

312

out of them. You haven't told them Marian's dead, have you? False pretences the rozzers call it. Give a false name, did you? I wonder why. I've been listening, see. Listening and looking." Billy waited for this to sink in before adding, "I was doing both in the church on Monday night. Better than telly it was. That and the other." He winked salaciously and stuck his tongue suggestively out between his teeth. "Prefer older women, do you, Mr Coleby?" He was beginning to enjoy himself. The pain from the blow on his forehead had receded and the knife in his hand and being able to confound Stuart with his knowledge gave him a feeling of power and of having the whip hand. He rocked back on his heels, surveying his adversary with a knowing smile.

"I see." Stuart's face was expressionless. He looked Billy up and down for a moment in silence, weighing up the situation. "Well, since you know so much I won't insult your intelligence by lying. What do you propose to do about it?"

"Me? I wasn't proposing to do nothing about it. Nothing to do with me." Innocence changed smartly to mean avarice. "Let's say a share in the profits, shall we? Fifty-fifty?"

"What profits?"

"Come on, Mr Coleby." Billy tut-tutted more in sorrow than in anger. "I know you've got three thousand quid in cash somewhere in this room." His glance darted over the places he hadn't had time to investigate.

"So that's what you were looking for."

"That's right. I saw the old man give it you last night so there's no use trying to pull the wool over my eyes."

Stuart sighed in a gesture of resignation and looked about him for a cigarette. There was a packet on the bedside table and he shook one out, taking it in his mouth. Swinging his legs out of bed, he reached for the lighter on the dressing-table. As he made the movement Billy re-stiffened into the threatening position which he had relaxed. With his back to him Stuart said, "For God's sake put that knife away and stop behaving like a bad imitation of a B movie gangster. You've obviously got me over a barrel and we're going to have to come to a business arrangement. We're both grown men."

His attitude made Billy feel amateur and unsophisticated, standing over him like a leering villain, and after a moment's hesitation the boy dropped his guard and sheathed the weapon. He stuffed it into his hip pocket and sat down awkwardly in the chair on top of Stuart's clothes. Stuart watched him in the dressing-table mirror.

"That's better," he said pleasantly. "So!" He turned round and rested his back against the piece of furniture. "You've been spying on us. Since when?"

"I come in Monday night. I got the plane back after Marian went. They took her away. I didn't want to go back with them. The hospital give me these." He cast about his person and produced the manilla envelope. Stuart looked inside. "Them's her things. I thought if I bring them back likely the vicar would be thankful." He winked. "You know."

Stuart regarded him thoughtfully. He knew.

"How did you get the money for the fare?"

"Stole it." Billy took the envelope

315

back. "I come up by the church and went in. Hid in the vestry, didn't I? Heard you and her. Heard you call yourself Mr Balfour." He looked up, naïvely expectant of an explanation.

"Yes. Well, I had my reasons."

"What sort?"

Stuart blew a couple of smoke-rings nonchalantly. "I had an old score to settle with Mr Dearsley. I needed a cover."

"Blackmail?"

"I don't care much for that word, Billy. Wouldn't you think someone owed you something if they had been responsible for the death of your brother?"

"Whose brother?"

"Mine."

"Mr Dearsley?" Billy's eyes were round with disbelief. "Mr Dearsley wouldn't kill no one. Him being a parson and all."

Stuart smiled patronizingly but his expression was bleak. "What a simple soul you are, Billy. Taken in just like all the rest. Take it from me, Mr Dearsley is not what he seems. There's no need to feel sorry for him."

"He's always been good to me. Not like her. She wouldn't give me the time of day. But he was kind. Talk about people not being like what they seem, I reckon she's the one. I saw her. And you. 'Ere, what happened to your brother anyway?"

"He was killed in Cyprus in an ambush. Before your time. He and Mr Dearsley were brother officers. Mr Dearsley betrayed their position to the enemy and as a result my brother got killed. Mr Dearsley got a medal for that. Everyone thinks he is a bloody hero except me. It's taken me twenty years to track him down. I'm not letting go now."

The warning was plain enough. Billy digested it together with the fanatical gleam in Stuart's eye. This was a private war with all kinds of ramifications that he didn't understand and didn't particularly want to. It should be worth a share of the money for his promise not to louse things up.

"I'll settle for thirty per cent instead of fifty," he said quickly.

Stuart's eyes narrowed. "Who's black-mailing now?"

"A business arrangement. You said it

317

yourself, Mr — Balfour." Billy smiled ingratiatingly to emphasize that he posed no tangible threat. "Fair's fair."

"Or?"

Billy wished he hadn't asked that. It forced him to take a tougher line than instinct told him might be good for his health, or collapse like a pricked balloon. He said, not altogether convincingly, "There's a number of permutations, isn't there? You and them. You and her. Not that that's any skin off my nose. I just need a few bob and I'll be off. Know what I mean? No one see me come. No one see me go, if you make it right."

"Precisely." Stuart's smile was friendly and relaxed, convincing Billy he had made his point. Live and let live was his motto.

Stuart was calculating his next move. He hadn't come this far to be balked by this snotty-nosed little git, nor did he intend to play host to this grimy little bloodsucker who, whatever he might protest, would inevitably be back for more. There was too much at stake apart from this private operation. Who could say where Billy's nose might lead him as he developed his interest in Stuart's sources of income? Possibly right to Malcolm Quennell himself. Stuart could imagine Malcolm's reaction if any of this led to investigation of their joint activities. Malcolm would shop him and offload him without a qualm. Conjecturing, he examined a number of equally repugnant possibilities as he, still smiling, came to the conclusion that Billy would have to go. He knew too much for his own good. It could be effected neatly. It wouldn't be the first time. Disposal might prove a problem, but there were plenty of places in the gully down in the shrubbery where he had tipped the grass cuttings where a body might lie under leaf loam and the silt of pine needles. Nobody had seen Billy come. Stuart was the only person so far aware of his visit. He would be a light weight to carry. Not much more than skin and bone. He became conscious that his silence had run on and that Billy was waiting for his answer. He made his decision.

"All right," he said. "Done." Moving towards the bed, he bent down and felt beneath one of the pillows. "Here's your cut. You might have guessed I wouldn't have rested easy without it right under my head."

Curiosity and eagerness getting the better of him, Billy came close up beside him, anxious to get a view of the notes. Stuart lifted the top pillow and ran his hand along under the second one. Billy bent forward, holding his breath, then all of a sudden he was fighting to exhale it as his face was slammed nose downwards into the mattress. The back of his head was being held by the pillow in Stuart's hand and the pressure he was exerting was closing Billy's nostrils, squashing his air passages, suffocating him. The surprise of the attack, catching him totally off balance, meant that his flailing legs could find no foothold on the floor, nor could they inflict damage upon his assailant who had both knees astride Billy's buttocks and whose body was well out of reach of his haphazard kicking. His arms, reaching backwards, proved equally ineffectual, and with his shoulders pinned to the bed it took a mammoth effort to release them enough to get his hands up to Stuart's where they held him down on either side of his head. Even then Billy couldn't grasp his fingers with enough strength to prise them open. Desperately he grabbed a fold of skin on the back of each of his attacker's hands and twisted and pinched it with all his might. It was enough to make Stuart relax his hold momentarily and in that second Billy was able to thrust his body upwards and roll over in the confines of that vice-like grip. He was now on his back and the pillow bore down over his face with redoubled force. There was a knee in his guts as well. He coughed and choked, his mouth gagged with ticking and down, his lungs bursting, a roaring, rushing noise filled his ears as every blood vessel in his head filled to breaking-point. He knew he hadn't got long before the moment when the scarlet haze behind his eyelids would turn black and unconsciousness would claim him. The more he resisted, the more determinedly the pillow pressed down. Native cunning and a desperate relic of his instinct for survival told him to abandon contention and go limp. He had virtually ceased breathing but he willed his oxygen-starved brain to hang on. He gave up struggling. One second. Two. He felt Stuart's grip on the pillow relax cautiously. The knee pinioning his stomach slackened its weight, then was lifted as the balance of the man above him shifted. Now! While Stuart was positioned like a dog with one leg cocked, Billy brought up his own sharply pointed knee, catching him in the balls with every ounce of strength he could muster. The pillow fell from his face and he drew in great rasping draughts of air as he lashed out again. Stuart fell sideways, clutching his groin with one hand and Billy with the other, but his slippery prey darted free to trip and stagger and finally sprawl headlong on the carpet. Billy pulled himself up with the aid of the chair arm, but Stuart had his ankle and then his calf and was dragging him back. The boy had no breath to cry out, all his concentration being required for the effort of staying alive. The hands gripped his thigh and he remembered the knife in his back pocket. His fingers and Stuart's closed upon it at the same moment. Billy twisted his right hip round away out of reach. Stuart was still attached to his leg, hanging on grimly. The chair slid away from behind Billy and both men fell to the floor locked in a bizarre and deadly embrace. Without letting go his hold, Stuart tried to get up on his knees. His head and shoulders pinned Billy from the waist, leaving the latter with only his left hand free to defend himself. That hand came down swiftly and decisively in a karate chop on the back of Stuart's neck. It was all over in the space of a second. There was a sound like the severing of a chicken joint in one's fingers, and a small gurgling rattle in Stuart's throat as the air soughed out of him and he became literally a dead weight upon his antagonist.

* * *

Billy looked down at him and then wonderingly at the hand that had delivered the blow. He had copied instinctively an action he had seen a million times in TV movies, and as in those movies, it had had the required effect. The only difference was this was no actor to be resuscitated between takes. This was a real dead man. He, Billy, had killed a man. He was awash now with a different brand of fear. Fear and a deadly sickness and loathing for the thing collapsed across his limbs, contact with which made his flesh crawl. Stiff with horror, he eased himself out from under Stuart's body and somehow stood up. His legs felt like jelly and there was saliva dribbling from the corner of his mouth which he wiped with the back of his hand. It had been self-defence, but nobody was going to believe that. Billy hadn't a deal of faith in the impartiality of the law, having had the rough end of its stick on more than one occasion. Give a dog a bad name! He'd be mad to stick around and try to prove his innocence. Nobody knew he was here or had come within a million miles of Hanbury. Nothing to stop him leaving as he had come with no one any the wiser. It was what he had planned. Only difference was he was leaving behind a body — and the money. He hadn't time to search for that now and even if he had, it would be too risky to take it in case things went wrong. Funny how you lost the taste even for riches when it was a question of saving your bloody neck. He put his fingers experimentally against his Adam's apple and blind panic galvanized him into flight.

The rest of the house was still and quiet. Miraculously they hadn't disturbed the vicar on the other side of the landing. Resisting the temptation of pelting down the stairs two at a time, he went as lightly and carefully as his racing heart would allow. Shit-scared as he was, he retained enough nous to realize that unbolting either the back or front door would point circumstantially to evidence of an intruder, so he opted for the kitchen window as his means of exist. Hopping up on to the draining-board and unlatching the catch, Billy tested it. It was well oiled and heavy enough to drop down when he raised it and gave it a tap with one finger. Climbing out over the sill, he took care not to leave any footprints. Half way out and squeezing through the frame, his jacket caught on the metal, forcing the zip open. It flapped in the wind and

Marian's envelope lodged in the inside pocket was in danger of flying away. He went to stuff it further in, but hesitated. Apart from bringing him bad luck, he wouldn't want her things to be found on him. Safer if no recent connection could be proved if he were ever unlucky enough to be picked up and questioned. There was a drawer under the sink. Billy leaned over and slipped the envelope into it. Cautiously he hoisted himself once again outside into the storm, released the catch and pushed the window shut in one movement. The rain beat against his back and the trees in the shrubbery groaned in travail against the storm. The drop beneath him was inky black. He fumbled for his torch and his rubber soles slipped on the narrow, wet sill. Propelled into the void, Billy felt himself falling. He managed to tense his knees preparing to land safely crouched. Seconds later he went straight through Sylvia's new greenhouse panes.

16

THE light scorched and shimmered like a million altar candles, yet without their mellow incandescence. More like a million neon filaments, bright light, white light, no sight light. It began to form itself into patterns with harsh, jagged outlines, and soon these would weld themselves into the familiar ogre of the nightmare. It was bad. Worse than he could remember. Then he stopped remembering and the light was the only reality. There were electronic noises in his head guiding his movements which jerked to match the changing patterns of the light. All at once it was fluid and melting and infinitely more menacing as the brilliance swam into the shape of his enemy. He groped towards it, silently screaming. He was nearly there. Another step and he would touch it. He strained with a frantic determination to beat the blanket darkness which would envelope him at any second and plunge him into terror. The light snapped off. The noises ceased. Silence and velvet blackness made his flesh crawl with an unspeakable horror. The frustration of not being able to give tongue overwhelmed him. Something gave in his brain and he lost control, lunging, swerving, ducking, feinting, punching, hitting, hitting, hitting. The sense of power was exhilarating and overcame fear. He was aware of being buffeted but nothing could harm him so long as he kept up the attack and took the fight to the aggressor. He hadn't gone this many rounds before without being stopped, and with every punch the adrenalin flowed and his cringing panic of moments before abated. The stench of fear and death embraced him, but it wasn't his fear. Smelling it, he tasted victory and survival. Nobody could stop him now. Nobody. Nothing. Madly, savagely, exultantly he punched. His adversary was down, grovelling at his feet. There was no mercy in Martin as he bent above him to deliver the *coup de grâce*. Trying to raise his foot which suddenly felt heavy as lead, he realized surprisingly that it was booted in steel. It weighed a ton and he could barely lift it to smash in his opponent's head. He visualized with pleasure the damage it would inflict, the crunching skull, the pulp of brains and blood, if he could just aim right and keep his balance. He stood poised, ready to grind his full weight downwards, full of avenging hatred and bitter retribution — when the nightmare took an unprecedented twist and, shockingly, the light reappeared. In the act of stamping Martin recognized his nameless foe. Under his boot it was his own face being crushed, his jaw that cracked, his forehead split, his own eye gouged, bloodied and hanging. Uncomprehending terror and abomination made it impossible to breathe as he struggled vainly with the dog-collar he was wearing in his dream. The badge of his office tightened like a loose-knot at every tug, He choked and everything swirled round. He was falling, fainting, dying. Something hit him and abruptly he was awake.

Martin opened his eyes, shut them, then opened them again. He was on the landing slumped against the banisters at the top of the stairs. Another step and he would have been over the edge and pitching down a flight. He could have broken his bloody neck instead of just feeling bruised all over. Gingerly he tested for more serious injury and, none being apparent, he hauled himself unsteadily up on to his feet. They were bare and, looking at them, he remembered how in the dream he had been shod. A degree of its malignance flooded back over him, leaving him weak and sweating. Thank heavens Sylvia hadn't been around to witness the spectacle of him making a bigger fool of himself than usual. If she had been there she could have awoken him before the nightmare's appalling climax from which Martin now resolutely turned his mind. The faintness was passing and he found he was cradling his good arm protectively against his ribcage. It hurt. Upon examination he discovered a purple discoloration already commencing around the inside of his wrist and up into his hand where he must have hit it against something during the imaginary fight. He had no notion of how he had got out on to the landing, nor to what kind of a shambles he might have reduced the bedroom. He hoped to God nothing was broken.

He turned to go back to his room and for the first time saw Stuart's door ajar. For the time being he had forgotten the existence of their guest and seeing that a light showed beyond, within the room, it was obvious to Martin that his nocturnal antics must have awoken Stuart. Martin wondered how much he had seen. Preparing himself with an apology and excuses, he stepped across to the open door and put his head round it. The bed was empty and rumpled. Martin's first thought was that Stuart had woken and gone to the lavatory, but then his gaze fell past the high back of the chair and upon the crumpled heap on the floor. He stepped into the room and saw Stuart's body lying face down. Martin didn't need to go any nearer to know that he was dead. He had seen enough bodies. Besides, there was that peculiar emptiness in the room that he had experienced a thousand times in the presence of the metamorphosed chrysalis.

He shook himself to reassure himself that this truly wasn't a continuation of the nightmare and, as he did so, initial stunned shock was invaded by an unwelcome shiver of suspicion. Going hot and cold, Martin approached the body and bent over it. Stuart's torso was bare, the lower half of him clad in pyjama trousers. Martin lifted one shoulder and the head lolled slackly forwards. There was a vivid weal on the back of the neck and Martin didn't require medical qualifications to appreciate that it was broken. There was no evidence of much of a struggle, except a tumbler on the floor, the chair marginally out of position, the ruffled bedclothes and a misplaced pillow, but as he looked at the signs self-doubt escalated into a re-kindling of horror. Automatically he rubbed his own bruised arm against his hip and stared down at it.

"Oh God!" He shut his eyes. "Oh Christ! Please — no!" He saw again Colin's bullet-riddled body in the back of the truck. His bowels had seeped as did Stuart's now. He recalled the stench in his dream. He tried another prayer but no words formed. "Father, forgive me for I knew not what I did." He had never been able to say that because it hadn't been true. It was true enough now but he still had no right to use it as an excuse. There would have been no nightmares but for the original sin. "*Mea culpa.*" That came readily enough. He took a grip on himself. It was useless standing here wallowing in self-analysis. Dragging himself across the landing, he gained his own bedroom and, without any regard for what he was doing, started putting on his clothes. One of his socks was inside out and the shirt that he buttoned was the one he had put out for the laundry but his mind was elsewhere. He was thinking of what he was going to say, but his ideas like his socks, refused to match or turn the right way out. After he had dressed Martin called the police.

★ ★ ★

Sylvia, wakened by Dan around twenty past three, struggled up out of unconsciousness and tried to make sense of what he was saying.

333

"There's been an accident at the vicarage. The police have telephoned and they want you there."

"Martin?" She was fully *compos mentis* now, her eyes dark with alarm.

"Martin's all right. They told me that much."

"What accident then?"

"I don't know. They didn't elaborate."

Sylvia hurried into her clothes and slung her night things into her case haphazardly, not bothering to do more to her appearance than run a comb through her hair. Dan hovered, offering tea which she refused as she ran out to the car and jumped in.

"Will you be all right?" he asked.

She nodded and waved, sick with apprehension as she let in the clutch and roared away.

There were two police cars and an ambulance in the drive when she arrived. Two men were closing the back of the latter and there was a uniformed policeman on the vicarage steps standing in the rain waiting for her. Sylvia would have questioned the ambulance men but the constable gently prevented her, taking her arm and shepherding her inside her own home.

"What has happened? Where is my husband?" she demanded.

"Mr Dearsley is inside with Inspector Galton, madam. They are in the study."

She broke away from him and ran down the hall and on to the threshold of the room where a strange man was sitting behind Martin's desk. Martin himself was standing before him like a candidate at an interview. Her first sight of his face made her draw in her breath. There was such a world of pain and suffering in his eyes married to a kind of beseeching appeal which he fastened upon her. Unworthily selfish, her immediate thought was that he knew! Forgetting the ambulance and the law, she hesitated instead of going to him as she felt compelled, anticipating his castigation, his utter condemnation of herself.

It was not Martin but the man behind the desk who spoke first.

"Mrs Dearsley?" He got up and coming round to her, held out a hand and marshalled her into a chair. "Detective-Inspector Galton."

Dazedly Sylvia looked at him. He was of medium height, overweight but powerful, like an athlete whose muscles have run to fat, and he was dressed in a tired-looking suit that looked as if it hadn't seen a hanger for a day and a night. A squat nose and a rather ragged ginger moustache separated two plump cheeks. A broad, high brow terminated in eyebrows that were also whiskery and sandy in hue. From beneath them, button brown eyes regarded her astutely. Detective-Inspector! They would surely not have sent someone of rank for anything minor.

"What has happened?" she asked again through dry, cold lips.

The man cleared his throat like a stage policeman and Sylvia repressed a giggling bubble of hysteria. Why didn't he get it over?

"I'm afraid it looks as though there has been an accident, Mrs Dearsley. You had a young man staying here as your guest, I believe. A Mr Stuart Balfour. I'm sorry to say he is dead." He paused to give her time to take it in which, stupidly, Sylvia didn't seem able to do. Stuart had been in excellent health. But of course the Inspector had mentioned an accident. '*It looks as though* there has been an accident' had been his actual words. Implying what? Surely he wasn't hinting at suicide? Stuart was hardly the type.

"What sort of an accident?"

"Mr Balfour was found in his room almost an hour ago. His neck had been broken." He cleared his throat again, looking from Martin to her before continuing. "I have to warn you that Mr Dearsley has confessed to being responsible."

"Martin!" The name was wrung out of her in total incredulity. "How could a person like Martin kill anyone?"

Galton appreciated that she was referring to her husband's cloth as well as his disability, but all the same he noted that she had asked 'how' not 'why'. She was shocked, that was evident, but had he imagined the expression on her face when she had run into the room, as though what she expected to learn might well justify fears she already entertained?

"I had a nightmare, Sylvia." Martin had his head in his hands in an attitude of abject despair. He wasn't looking at her now. She could barely catch the words and when she did she wouldn't believe them.

"Oh my God! No!"

Galton coughed delicately. "Your husband tells me he is susceptible to bad dreams." The statement was carefully devoid of scepticism.

Sylvia nodded dumbly, her throat suddenly like sandpaper.

The Inspector consulted some notes lying in front of him. "And he has, in the past, been known to assault you during the course of them?" He looked up and the expression in the button brown eyes was widely at variance with the blandness of his enquiry.

Assault! The word implied deliberate violence and threw Sylvia into replying idiotically, "Only in a very minor way."

"Mr Balfour was not so fortunate." Galton's own voice was as dry as her throat. "He died from a left-handed blow delivered to the cervical area by someone who knew what they were doing. Mr Dearsley admits that when he was in the Army he was trained in commando tactics including unarmed combat. He has also sustained a recent injury to his left arm for which he cannot account and which, on his own admission, was not apparent when he retired last night." Galton gestured to Martin, who like a zombie drew up his sleeve and proffered his bruises for her inspection.

"Martin?" It came out as a whispered entreaty for his version, which he supplied falteringly and flatly, like a child intent upon remembering a poem learned by heart. "It was the same dream," he said, "Only worse. And it went on longer. Long enough for me to see him. Oh God, Sylvia, this time I saw him."

"Stuart."

"No. The man who is always there in the nightmare. Always just out of reach. We were fighting. I was winning." Martin shuddered, nearly gagging on the memory of the face beneath his boot. That part could wait — if indeed he could ever bring himself to tell her about it. "I woke up and I was out on the landing. Stuart's door was open. I went back in — and found his body."

"Back?"

He looked at her wearily. "I must have come from there. I don't remember. But the dream was so real. And my arm." He studied it in an academic way as though it belonged to somebody else. "It must have been me, Sylvia. There were only the two of us in the house."

"Someone could have broken in." She was clutching at straws as she appealed wildly to Galton, who sat silently withdrawn like a police chaperone at a prison visiting hour.

"My men have found no signs of an intruder as yet although they are still searching."

Now that he mentioned it, Sylvia could hear them. It sounded as though they were systematically going through the house. The noise of a drawer being pulled out and dropped somewhere above them brought home a disquieting sense of violation, and the realization that evidence of a burglar was not all that they were looking for. Evidence. The word beat in her brain as it was borne in on her just how thin Martin's story would sound to anyone who didn't know him and hadn't experienced his trauma.

"We were alone in the house," he repeated.

"I knew I should never have left you alone together." She was chiding herself, sharing his extremity, but as soon as she looked towards the Inspector she realized that her choice of words had been unfortunate. They had sprung from guilt in the knowledge that earlier in the evening she had accepted Dan's situation gratefully as a personal copout, and they had been uttered absent-mindedly. They sounded as though she were aware of an enmity existing between Martin and Stuart. She hadn't meant them that way. Stuart would never have told. He had been hoping for more of her. Hadn't he promised — threatened her with his eyes?

Sylvia sat dead still, experiencing a numbing chill. An idea spawned by her brain travelled from it down the back of her neck, into her spine and all the way down to her toes. She knew Galton was watching her and that she ought to be explaining her previous remark. She knew too that the enormity of so derisive a suspicion such as the one she was now entertaining must show clearly on her face. The question that spiralled was *had* Stuart told and *was* the story of the nightmare Martin's own cop-out? She could only guess at what might have passed between the two men. Had Martin been so provoked that the restrained force that she knew dwelt within him had overflowed into a fit of rage? Hadn't her first instinct been that Martin knew? Hadn't there been something different in the way that he had given her that first long look? Nightmares? They could furnish the difference between a murder charge and manslaughter.

* * *

Mercifully Galton's attention had been claimed by the appearance of a plain-clothes officer at the door, and he rose to give the man his ear. While he listened, his eyes roved over the room and them, his face not moving a muscle. What was being said was inaudible to husband and wife and the small interlude gave Sylvia a chance to pull her thoughts together. She had been accusing Martin of murder in her heart. Motive? Jealousy of her? She rebuked herself ruefully for her arrogance. Blind passion was hardly Martin's suit. Shouldn't she know that better than anybody else, and what made her think he would consider her worth swinging for? But you didn't swing now. She looked across at him in contrite irony hoping he had not sensed her defection. Some of the chill receded but by no means all. She wished she could speak to him alone for a few minutes but that obviously was not going to be allowed.

The Inspector, terminating his brief conversation, nodded at the policeman who withdrew. Galton resumed his seat at the desk. He flexed splayed fingers that looked like a bunch of sausages on the stubby hands that rested before him.

"Mrs Dearsley, how long had you known Mr Balfour and what was the purpose of his visit here?"

It was a relief to have a plain question — one to which she had a concrete answer. "Not very long. Only a few days, in fact," Sylvia replied. "I expect my husband — "

"Mr Dearsley has told me his story. I

should like to hear yours in your own words if I may."

He no doubt wanted to see if they would catch each other out. He would be disappointed on that score. Whatever Martin might or might not know about her and Stuart, he would never have mentioned that. He would have had the wit to realize that that would be far too incriminating. Though seeing him in his present state of bemused perplexity, she doubted he had the wit for any kind of calculation. Or was it put on? Sylvia trod carefully on what suddenly felt like treacherously thin ice.

"Mr Balfour turned up here on Sunday evening," she began. "He brought us news of our daughter who had been missing for over two years. We naturally made him welcome?" She coloured slightly remembering just how welcome she had made him. Galton watched the blush come and go.

"You had met him before?"

"No. He was a stranger to us. A friend of Marian's."

"What did he want?"

"Nothing, except to help. He told us

where Marian was — is. He had run across her in Indonesia."

"He made no demands of any kind?"

The question appeared to puzzle Sylvia so Galton elucidated. "Did he ask for money?"

"No."

There was a pregnant little silence which she had the feeling he was tempting her to break, and when she didn't he finally said, "According to your husband, he gave Mr Balfour the sum of three thousand pounds."

"Oh, that?"

Galton's raised eyebrows implied it was highly implausible that she could possibly have overlooked such a sum. Somehow he was putting her in the wrong.

"What I mean is he didn't demand it for himself. Our daughter was in need of the money and Mr Balfour was going to take it to her. She had got herself into some financial difficulty and she was far from home." Sylvia hesitated. She didn't want to say too much about Marian's circumstances in case the girl had already gone and done something silly. Now it came home to her with force that they would have to find another way to send her the money and in all probability they would be too late. She wondered whether Martin had also made that deduction and she threw him a questioning glance. Intercepting it, Galton read it as collusive.

"So!" He made an arch of the sausages and contemplated Sylvia over its bridge. "Mr Balfour, a perfect stranger, arrived out of the blue with a story about your daughter requiring three thousand pounds and you handed it over to him without a qualm?" This time disbelief was evident. "Wouldn't you agree that such gullibility on your part sits somewhat incongruously upon two relatively sophisticated and intelligent people such as yourselves!"

"My husband took what steps he could to check Mr Balfour's credentials. He rang the firm for which Stuart — Mr Balfour said he worked."

"So he said."

She resented his tone. "Who was it you spoke to, Martin?"

"A chap called Malcolm Quennell."

"You can check on that," Sylvia said crisply.

"Mr Quennell." Galton wrote it laboriously. "No doubt he will remember your call, sir."

Martin flushed. "Well, no. At least he won't actually know me. I didn't give my real name. I called myself Stanton. My wife's maiden name, you know." He floundered, aware how fatuous it sounded. "I asked him if Mr Balfour worked for him. I made some excuse about finding a lighter." He ought to shut up but he'd got to make the man understand.

"That was a lot of trouble to go to, sir. Very inventive."

"I suppose I was embarrassed Mr Balfour would find I hadn't trusted him," Martin said lamely.

"Which you clearly did not?"

"No. Yes. I mean — "

There was a small speck of dirt beneath one of the Inspector's fingernails which he meticulously set about prising out with a broken toothpick that had been lying in Martin's pen tray. "Three thousand pounds is a lot of money to most people, Mr Dearsley. I imagine it is to you?"

The question made Sylvia acutely

aware of the shabby chair covers and faded curtains and she experienced an immediate desire to rush to the defence of the discoloured wallpaper that twenty years ago had been elegant. These people had a subtle knack of sapping one's confidence. The question had been addressed to Martin, who was considering the pattern of the Axminster beneath his feet.

"A great deal of money," he agreed.

"More than you could afford?"

"Much more than I could afford."

"Ah!" It could have been merely an expression of satisfaction that the nail was now clean as Galton threw the toothpick into the waste-paper basket, but coldly, Sylvia knew it wasn't. Martin's reply and the manner in which it had been stated were evidently obscurely significant. It was like playing chess blindfold with one's opponent employing pieces of unfamiliar value and design. Her apprehension increased as she sensed a surprise up Galton's sleeve and intuition warned her it was unlikely to be a pleasant one. She sat transfixed, hearing the Inspector eliciting from Martin honest answers that fatalistically Sylvia knew were incriminating.

"May I ask, sir, how you came by it?"

"I borrowed it from a friend."

"Not from the bank?"

"No."

"Why not?"

"My account at the bank is substantially overdrawn."

"I see. So you were already in a certain amount of financial embarrassment and you took immediate steps to embarrass yourself to the tune of a further £3,000."

"My daughter's need was acute. She had been ill and needed the money for medical expenses and her fare home."

"Urgently?"

Martin nodded.

"May I have the name of your friend? The one who lent you the money?"

Ian's name and address was written down at Martin's dictation.

"He is obviously a very good friend," Galton observed. "A very close one no doubt?"

"He used to be."

Again the prawn whiskers adorning the

sandy brows twitched in mild surprise.

"We haven't seen one another for some years. We were friends during our Army days."

"Yet you were desperate enough to turn to him over this?"

"It was important," Martin said tersely.

"It must have been. Did you tell him why you required the money?"

"No."

"A very good friend indeed," Galton repeated. He paused fractionally. "No questions asked. And in cash." Abandoning his conversational tone, he looked at them both sharply to have the satisfaction of knowing he had surprised them. "Yes, we have found the money in Mr Balfour's room."

"I don't really see why all these questions about the money are pertinent, Inspector," Martin said acidly. "It is not as if I am trying to cover anything up. I've told you freely how the accident must have come about. God knows, it is bad enough having to live with this." Once again he put his head in his hands. Sylvia didn't know whether he was acting or whether he really was dumb enough not to see that Galton didn't for one moment believe his story and was delving for a motive. She was hardly certain of anything herself any more. She heard Galton carefully explaining.

"In cases where a death occurs and a large sum of money has changed hands we have to consider the possibility of blackmail, Mr Dearsley. Before we can rule it out, that is."

"Blackmail!" Martin appeared dumb-founded. What an innocent he was, Sylvia thought. Or was he? She was still lulled by a sense of false security knowing that, if necessary, it could be proved that the money had been procured long before she had given Stuart any hypothetical hold over them. Only pray God it wasn't going to be necessary. Preoccupied, her mind running along a single track, it was a heart-stopping shock to have Galton unexpectedly switch the points with his carefully timed bombshell.

"Let's stop prevaricating, shall we, sir? Perhaps you would like to tell me for whom the money was really intended. We both know it wasn't to help your daughter, don't we? Because your daughter is dead, isn't she? Was that the news Mr Balfour brought? Alternatively, perhaps you knew already and his appearance was coincidental and unconnected?" His voice was steely.

There was an electric silence and his prey sat turned to stone like a couple of rabbits riveted by a stoat.

"Dead!" Martin gasped the word ludicrously. From a long way off Sylvia half expected to hear him finish the old melodramatic line — 'and never called me Mother!' It was a family joke — as what Galton was saying *must* be. Otherwise . . . She shook her own head which felt quite woolly and said stupidly,

"No. Marian was ill. She got better."

Sighing wearily as though they were insisting on making things unnecessarily tiresome for all concerned, the policeman raised his bulk again out of Martin's chair and went and opened the door. One of his henchmen responded to his call and handed him something. Martin and Sylvia watched him open the contents of a manilla envelope over the desk and a number of objects were scattered on to its tooled leather surface. Marian's watch, a string of beads, a pair of gold hoop ear-rings, some bangles. Two of the latter rolled like wheels across the desk top, their progress halted by the mug of pencils. Sylvia gaped from them to a paper Galton was smoothing out. It was some kind of a document. He turned it round so that they could read the writing on it. It was a death certificate with Marian's full name hand-printed along a dotted line. The date on it was some days before Stuart's arrival.

"But the hospital said — " Martin stopped. He could see himself ringing the Denpasar number at Stuart's dictation. A tingling starburst of white hot shock exploded in Sylvia's breast like pins and needles. Her head wagged independently of her volition.

"No. No."

"Please don't pretend you haven't seen this document before. It was found in a drawer in your own kitchen, Mrs Dearsley. Don't let's make things more difficult."

"No." There weren't any other words in her vocabulary.

"I wonder how it got there then. Now, sir, shall we have the truth? To start with, shall we call Mr Balfour by his proper name? We found his passport along with your daughter's in his effects. We'll find out later what he was doing with that. Maybe it was part of the lever he was using on you, eh?"

Martin listened to him as though he was speaking a foreign language.

"What sort of a hold did Mr Coleby — alias your Mr Balfour — have on you, sir? I would advise you to be frank."

"Coleby!" He could see that was a word Martin had understood. Galton watched the name go home.

"That was his name, as I believe you know, sir."

"I didn't." Martin stood up and stumbled three paces forward.

"Coleby?" Sylvia too was on her feet. Everyone had gone mad. She sought Martin's hand but he was too far away.

Marian was dead. Now this man was saying that Coleby had been alive. No that was wrong. It was Marian that had to be alive. Had to be. Something

354

inside her head disintegrated. Her world lurched and turned upside down like a glass encapsulated snow scene. Sylvia fell, the white flakes mercifully obliterating consciousness.

17

ALISON was there. Everyone else had long since departed, including Martin who had gone with Inspector Galton to Lewes overnight for further questioning. Sylvia had woken in the evening, feeling clear-headed enough for the first time that long day to attempt to express some of her shame for her total capitulation to shock and grief. Alison had hushed her up and the doctor had slid another needle into her buttock and she had gone out like a light again until the next morning. That awakening brought her face to face with reality with no blurred edges. Marian was dead. Martin had killed a man. The police suspected him of murder. Most incredible of all, Stuart had been Colin Coleby's brother and for some obscure reason of his own had set them all up. It was easier to concentrate upon this latter aspect than to dwell upon Marian. Learning about her this way had been crueller than if

Stuart had told them three days ago when he had arrived out of the blue. Up until then Sylvia had had two years to prepare herself mentally for the possibility that she was dead. Having hope and expectation of recovering Marian resurrected, only to be dashed so brutally by Galton, had been a hundred times harder to bear. All that was too excruciating to bite upon for now. There was a lifetime empty of hope stretching into the future where the pain would have to be absorbed, accepted and lived with each aching day.

Meanwhile there was Martin and what could be done for him. And the enigma of Stuart. Why had he sought them out? There had to be more to it than conning two strangers out of £3,000. More than taking advantage of an easy screw along the way. Without making excuses for herself, there had been a calculated predatory sexuality in his manner towards her right from the start. That — and when she thought hard about them — other pointers. With hindsight there had been a number of things about him that had disturbed her. Sylvia's mind went back to the moment in the study when she had shown Stuart the photograph of Martin. There had been that odd intensity in the way he had stood stock still close beside her. She remembered the suggestion of triumph she had surprised upon his face when he had more or less invited himself to stay. Before that, the moment when he had given his name and she had sensed the lie. Discounting the coincidence of meeting Marian, there had to be another special reason why he had come to *them*, his brother's friend, his brother's mistress. He had concealed his identity, made no comment upon Martin's association with Colin's regiment. He had asked all those questions about the way in which Martin had lost his arm and he must already have known. When she had mentioned Cyprus why hadn't he said that his brother had died there? The day before yesterday — was it really only forty-eight hours ago? — he had told her, rawly bitter, "I had a brother. He was killed." She thought about how he had gone on to question her about her own loss and she had told him, little dreaming their mutual phantom was Colin. Why had he not said? But of course he wouldn't necessarily have known about her connection. How much exactly *had* he known — and about what? If extortion had been his sole aim, how much easier to gain their trust by announcing who he was. As Stuart Coleby, Martin would never have doubted him for a moment. Never even thought of checking up on his story. It didn't make sense. Or at least, Sylvia corrected herself, it only began to make any kind of sense if he had an ulterior motive apart from the money.

She began remembering all kinds of small details. How when she had half promised to tell him the story of Martin's experience in Cyprus he had said, "I should certainly be interested to hear it." Had she imagined it or had he spoken ever so slightly sardonically? Stuart's strange smile and his 'That's what I hoped' when she had said they were indebted to him. As though he had ensnared them unconsciously like butterflies on pins. The moment when he had first met Martin. The stiffly proffered right hand issued challengingly. The photograph. Was that what Stuart had been looking for among the pictures in the study. Had he come looking for a one-armed man? Hadn't he been quite sure Martin was the person he wanted until he had seen the evidence? Sylvia was back to that word again. Evidence.

She sat up in bed slowly, blaming the drugs for her fancies, still muddled and confused. Why couldn't she rid herself of the feeling that she was holding one end of a ball of string that, unravelled, would lead her in the right direction? Turning the covers back, she put her feet upon the floor unsteadily and started to dress. In the moment when she stood naked before the mirror, she gazed dispassionately at the body that had made love to a ghost. It would be too facile to excuse herself by saying she had done it because of any fraternal similarity, but all the same it had been strange how as soon as she had met Stuart, Colin had been so much in her mind. There was too much that needed explaining and Galton obviously didn't believe that Martin didn't possess the answers. He hadn't been arrested, Alison had assured her, just held for questioning. If Galton couldn't make anything else stick there would be a charge of manslaughter.

Alison materialized now with a tray of tea and toast.

"Oh, you're up. Feeling better?" She set the tray down and studied Sylvia's pale face. "Silly question," she said. She came and put an arm round Sylvia's shoulders and gave them a tender squeeze, her comely freckled face full of understanding and concern. Anyone else Sylvia might have shrugged away, but sympathy from Alison who had suffered her own share of tragedy in the death of one of her children in a traffic accident was sincere and humbling.

Sylvia said, "I feel so bad that you've had to cope with me when you've got your own family to think about. Peter must think I'm dreadfully wet. I've never gone to pieces like that before."

"More's the pity. It's a mistake to give the impression you're totally indestructible." Alison drew back the curtains, revealing leaden skies and a saturated garden. The storm had passed but it was drizzling.

"Is that how I seem?" Sylvia asked wearily. "Oh God, if people only knew!"

"Not to me, but sometimes I think even Martin is fooled."

"Martin! That's a laugh when I have to school myself to come half way up to his standards."

Alison gave her a funny sort of look. "Perhaps you both try too hard. He is human."

"Yes." Sylvia shivered and pulled a thick jumper over her head. She felt cold through to the marrow in her bones. "It's going to be wet for the Fayre," she said inconsequentially. Some of the awnings Stuart had erected were tattered from the storm and a string of lights had come adrift, straggling across the lawn, some of the coloured electric bulbs smashed. The roses too had taken a bashing, their heads broken and petals strewn everywhere. Two days ago it had seemed that summer would never end.

"Has there been any message from the police?" Sylvia asked. "How long are they going to keep Martin? Am I allowed to see him?"

"Not yet." Alison answered her last question first. "I rang first thing because I knew you'd want to go dashing in.

They're still questioning him."

"What on earth about? He's told them what he thinks happened. Alison, they're trying to say he murdered Stuart. There's something going on that I know nothing about. I saw Martin's face when the Inspector told us Stuart's name was Coleby. He wasn't just amazed. He was afraid. I've never seen Martin frightened before. I wasn't mistaken. That's what I keep remembering. I wouldn't say it to anyone else."

If Alison was surprised she didn't show it. She could see there was more to come so she waited.

"Years ago Martin knew Stuart's brother. So did I. He was killed in the same incident in which Martin lost his hand. All these years later Stuart finds us. Why? I've got a feeling he had been looking all the time. Lots of little things he said and implied while he was here in retrospect fit in. He came here with the intention of hurting us. He had a reason. I feel it in my bones." Sylvia pressed her forehead to the window-pane, staring sightlessly at the drizzle. She was thinking aloud now. "Say it did all happen as

Stuart said. He met Marian out there in the hospital. Marian dies and he sees a way to con us out of three thousand pounds. Wouldn't his story have carried a hundred times more weight if he had told us who he was? The brother of Martin's friend? It would have been a trump card for him, yet he never played it. And why should he plant Marian's things in the kitchen drawer? Something happened that night. Martin couldn't have known who Stuart was all along. He wouldn't have known Marian was dead and not told me." She turned, confused, towards Alison who was making hospital corners on Sylvia's bed, smoothing the bedspread over neatly plumped up pillows. The busy hands became still.

"Sylvia, you're not doubting Martin? You're not getting ideas?"

"No. No, of course not."

But it wasn't true. The ideas were already there. They festered and multiplied during the day that dragged interminably while Sylvia waited for news. The phone rang incessantly with enquiries from the Press and from friends, and there had even been a call from the bishop offering cautious comfort to Sylvia and telling her that arrangements were being made temporarily for a local priest to combine the duties of Martin's parish with his own until 'things sorted themselves out'. Suspension was the word he was too tactful to use. Sylvia unjustly accused him, having to blame somebody for the muddled, mounting suspicions in her own heart. After lunch she managed to persuade Alison she was capable and of sound enough mind to be left and sent her back to her own responsibilities. Gathering her concentration, not for the first time in her life Sylvia embarked upon manual labour as a cure for mental ills.

★ ★ ★

The police had left one hell of a mess everywhere. Drawers that had been emptied had been replaced, but all their contents disarranged and higgledy-piggledy. Grey fingerprint powder clung tenaciously to the polished surfaces of most of the furniture, and unwiped shoes coming in and out of the storm had left muddy-imprints on many of the carpets. Alison had done her best with the downstairs rooms but the bedrooms still had to be tackled. Steeling herself to face the most unpleasant task first, Sylvia opened the spare room door and made herself go inside. All Stuart's possessions had been whipped away. The mattress was turned back and all the bedclothes heaped upon the spring. The room was impersonal, no aura lingering of tragedy, or for that matter of any of the scenes that had occurred in that very same bed two nights ago. Sylvia felt disembodied from that woman in the same way that she was unable to visualize Stuart dead in her imagination. Yet his corpse had reposed upon this very rose-patterned carpet. Methodically she set about tidying the room. After that came her own and Martin's, then the bathrooms and the landing. There was a trail of mud on the attic stairs from a clod that had stuck under somebody's instep. Sylvia followed it up with her dustpan, making it the excuse for a more thorough clean while she was about it. As long as she was physically occupied she didn't have to think too much. Martin had always said she was more of a Martha than a Mary! Her exertions had made her warm and her sleeves were rolled back. Up at this level it was cold and dank and a perishing draught made gooseflesh on her bare forearms. They had left all the doors up here flung open. She went along shutting them to preserve the heat in the lower part of the house.

On the threshold of one of the maids' rooms she was brought up short. It was from here that the current of air was emanating, but the draught hadn't eradicated a distinctive pungency that her nostrils recognized. Someone had been up here smoking Indonesian cigarettes and that someone could only have been Stuart. The scent was unmistakable to Sylvia, who had only smelled it once before. She went into the room and looked around. She couldn't remember when she had last been into it. She and Martin had earlier intended to renovate this floor but there had always been another call on the money. The bed was in disarray where the police had no doubt turned it over. There was a hole in the window that needed stopping up. She would go down and get a piece of hardboard as a temporary measure. Sylvia estimated the size of the gap with her eye. Outside the window there was a crevice where the roof tiles met and ran along to the rain gutter. In the niche there were a couple of cigarette ends and a fresh banana skin. She looked at them, wondering what on earth had brought Stuart up here long enough to smoke two cigarettes and eat a banana. Why had he come up here at all? But then he had probably inspected every inch of the house. For what purpose they might never know. She and Martin had been spied on. Of that she was becoming increasingly convinced. It wasn't a comfortable thought. It was getting prematurely dark and a ghost walked over Sylvia's grave. She was suddenly conscious of the big empty house rambling beneath her and she fought down a desire to ring Alison and ask her to come back.

A distant door shut and her heart jumped cravenly into her mouth. She went out on to the landing and looked over the banisters, calling out bravely,

"Who's there?"

"It's all right. It's me."

"Martin!" Consumed with relief she ran on down to meet him.

He was standing alone in the hall and Sylvia involuntarily looked for his escort. "Where are the others?"

"They brought me back. They let me go."

"You're free?"

"For the moment anyway. There may be more questions later."

"But how — ?"

"They haven't got enough to go on to charge me with murder. If they decide on manslaughter Ian is standing surety. They've already got his three thousand."

"So it isn't over?"

He looked at her flushed, hopeful face. "No, it isn't over," he said shortly. "It's never been over. It's never going to be over."

She thought he was rambling. "What do you mean?"

"It was bad enough before, but now — " He seemed to have forgotten her presence. He looked deathly tired

369

and he hadn't shaved. Blue-black bristles shadowed the lower half of his pale, grey face, running darkly into the clefts from nose to jaw. He frightened her.

"Martin. What has never been over? What was bad enough before?"

Her fear and suspicions showed nakedly in her eyes. Recognizing them for what they were didn't appear to upset him. He merely said in a dead kind of voice, "You're not sure either, are you, Sylvia? Don't deny it. I saw it in your expression when Galton had us both in there." He nodded his head towards the study. "I don't blame you."

"I shall believe whatever you tell me now," Sylvia said steadily. "I don't care what it is so long as it is the truth. I've had all day to think about this. Did something happen between you and Stuart last night after I left? Did Stuart say anything?"

"No." Her question seemed to have aroused a faint glimmer of interest. "Should he have? Anything about what?"

"I don't know. Did he for instance say anything to precipitate a quarrel?"

"You mean, did I kill him, but not in my sleep?"

"I mean, did you know who he was?"

"He never told me."

"But did you guess?"

"No. I never guessed." He let out his breath on a long sigh. "But I suppose I should have known that one day — "

It seemed to Sylvia that he looked at her conjecturally and her guilty conscience convinced her that what he had been going to say was that one day someone would come along and remind her of Colin. Under his scrutiny, she flushed.

"Did he remind *you* of Colin?"

She stared at him wondering if he knew what he was asking. "A little. But not until I thought about it afterwards. I too never guessed. Martin, why didn't he tell us? It would have been an easier way to ingratiate himself with us. I've been talking it over with Alison and we both think there was something else. Something brought him here apart from the money. Do you know what it was?"

"You're beginning to sound like Inspector Galton."

"Why? Did he ask you that?"

"Let's say he's not convinced Stuart Coleby had nothing on me. That one is going to dig, Sylvia. He's going to dig and dig and dig — until he shovels out mud. And when he does . . . I need a drink." He moved heavily in the direction of the kitchen.

"And when he does?" She followed him.

He didn't answer but found the whisky bottle and poured himself a measure, clanking the neck of the bottle noisily against the tumbler, unable to steady his hand.

"And when he does?" Sylvia insisted.

Martin gulped the liquid down neat and refilled the glass. He realized Sylvia hadn't got one. "I'm sorry, do you want — "

"No. And I don't think you should have any more either. Not before you've had something to eat. Martin, what are you afraid of Inspector Galton finding?" There was something. She had known it all day. Fear twisted her own guts, but this time not for herself. The second draught of whisky seemed to have steadied him. She saw him drop his shoulders and straighten his frame in an attitude of weary acceptance. He turned round, his back to the sink, and looked down into her dread-filled eyes, his face curiously naked. He said simply, "The truth."

During the pause that followed Sylvia had the impression of standing, one foot poised over a precipice. She wanted to withdraw but she had been the one to ask for the truth.

"The time has come for it, Sylvia," he was saying. "I wish it hadn't, but you've got to know now because Galton eventually will, and I want you to be prepared. I may not be free then and you deserve some kind of an explanation."

She couldn't ask the question that hovered between them but he answered it for her. "No. I didn't murder Stuart. At least, not intentionally."

Sylvia wilted with relief. It wasn't that, at least. Nothing else could be as bad as that.

"Nor was he blackmailing me, although I'm sure that was his intention. You were right when you said something brought him here apart from the money. It was revenge. Revenge for his brother's death." It was as though he couldn't bring himself to say the name, so she said it for him,

"Colin?"

"Yes. I killed Colin too. Funny, isn't it, how it's all come full circle, and all through Marian? There must be a moral in that somewhere."

"You — killed Colin? But you weren't responsible for that."

"Oh yes I was, Sylvia. My treachery led to that." He saw her eyebrows angle sharply at his turn of phrase. "I'm not being melodramatic, my dear. I was a traitor. There's no way of wrapping it up. I betrayed my comrades in arms and my country. For money. Because of what I did Colin got killed. I think you had better sit down."

She numbly allowed herself to be steered into a chair. She had begged to be told the truth but now that she was about to learn it she didn't want to know. What you didn't know couldn't hurt you, and from Martin's expression she had the feeling she was about to be crucified. After he had sat her down she tried to retain the reassurance of his hand in hers, but he put her aside and took his own seat across from her. The width of the kitchen table between them made her feel bereft of comfort and terribly alone. When they were both settled Martin started speaking.

18

"**I** KNOW you always thought I was hard on Marian," he said. "Strict and stern. Even harsh sometimes."

Sylvia blinked. It was not the opening she had expected.

"It had nothing to do with the fact that she wasn't mine. You may not always have believed that. I was so anxious she shouldn't make the mistakes I had made. I learned self-discipline from my father. By present-day standards he was pretty tough on me, and it should have been an invaluable lesson. I wouldn't have gone far wrong if I had stuck to his precepts. You can't go against the rules, Sylvia, and not come a cropper. I wanted Marian to appreciate the importance of them and if I was strict it was only to save her from pain." He made a little wry moue. "I know now that's impossible. Nobody's going to learn from another's experience. Least of all the younger generation. I didn't.

"I was a dull little boy, Sylvia. Not at school. I did rather well there, but I suppose I must have seemed a bit of a colourless goody-goody to my contemporaries. There wasn't much money and I wanted badly to get to Cambridge to please my father. It took a lot of hard work and there wasn't much time or cash for fooling around with girls or motor-bikes or any of that sort of thing. I didn't mind. It had been so dinned into me that nothing in this world comes easily or is achieved without blood and sweat and that they in themselves were character-forming. I used to get good reports. From my housemaster's point of view I was eminently satisfactory. A conformist. I expect I was a little smug although I can't remember ever feeling quite good enough. I had few friends. Nobody close. I suppose I was old before my time and the other boys my age all seemed a bit juvenile. I sound as if I was an insufferable prig." He gave her a wan, apologetic smile. Sylvia imagined the earnest child deprived of fun. She said nothing.

"And then I went up to Cambridge,

and I came across Ian. I'd never met anyone like the Forsythes in my life. They were a rollicking, boisterous, uninhibited crowd. There was I, nurtured on the principle that diligence and virtue were rewarded and that profligacy and intemperance brought damnation, and here was a set of people whose profligacy with money and goods and generosity confounded me and who hadn't experienced a temperate emotion in their lives. Far from being damned, the fates appeared continually to smile upon them and I knew they were good people — warm and kind and not giving a damn what anyone else thought. *They* made their own rules and changed them when they didn't fit a new circumstance. At first I was shocked and then found myself envious of so insouciant a flexibility. My father would have said I was seduced. I suppose I was."

"You were growing up," Sylvia said.

"Yes. I thought so too." His voice was tinged with irony. "I was broadening my ideas all right. It was impossible to be a friend of Ian's and take life too seriously. He was the sort of chap who could pass exams without swotting, not like me. We spent more time than was good for me debating and carousing and playing games and getting up to all those stupid pranks for which undergraduates are renowned. Or at least were then. He didn't have to worry too much about his future. His place in the regiment was more or less assured with his ability and at least three of his ancestors having served in it. My situation was different. I scraped through the first year exams but began to fall hopelessly behind in the second, and still hadn't the fortitude to chuck in the foolery and get down to serious work. I kept telling myself it would be all right. I worked a lot harder than Ian and if he could pass I kidded myself that I should deserve to also. And then towards the end of our second year Ian got bored with Cambridge and announced his intention of joining the Army a year earlier than intended. By then I knew I hadn't a hope in hell of catching up academically without the kind of effort I was beginning to question my ability to make. I'd gone soft. I seemed to have lost my goal and I

379

didn't any longer know for certain what I wanted to do with my life. Ian said had I thought of the Army for myself? He painted an attractive picture of Service life and said he thought I'd make a good officer. He said his family could pull some strings. I began thinking about it seriously.

"There was no one else to advise me and the mistake I made was not signing on — but of going into a regiment that was far too expensive for me. All the other subalterns had money or came from families capable of backing them substantially financially. They were chaps who thought nothing of placing a hundred pounds a go on a horse and betting high stakes on a game of poker. They could also put away the drink, and what with that and guest nights and paying for the other regimental customs and uniform, my mess bill began to get out of hand. I was in straits before I went to Cyprus."

Martin broke off to get himself another drink and this time Sylvia didn't refuse one herself. They were coming to the crunch and she suddenly needed something to warm the icy void in her stomach. He came back to the table and sat pensively running his finger round and round the rim of his tumbler making it sing.

"I got involved with a girl there," he continued. "She was a Greek Cypriot, the daughter of one of the civilian clerks on the base. Her name was Ariana Nicolaides." Seeing the name rang a bell he said, "She was the sister of Jannis Nicolaides, the prisoner I told you about." He had only ever mentioned the man once but Sylvia had not forgotten — nor the telling. It was coming now. She hung on tightly to herself now as she had then.

"It was madness because the political situation being as it was we weren't suppose to fraternize, but we were a long way from home and several of the lads had someone on the quiet. Ariana came to a Christmas party on the base and it started from there. I had never had a woman. Ian would never have believed that. I boasted like all the others, but I hadn't ever made love to a woman before. There hadn't been much opportunity and I suppose I was still hung up with my puritanical upbringing. I don't know what I imagined, but when it happened it was a revelation. At the time it seemed like the abandonment of the last of my father's rules and like the others, once broken, it only went to prove that he hadn't known what he was talking about. He had always gone strong on purity and self-respect and the sin of lust, the degradation of animal passion — that sort of thing. It simply wasn't true. It was the most marvellous thing that had ever happened to me. We both went a little mad. At least I did. Ariana proved in the end that she had kept her head but I lost mine, totally. Terrible things were happening all around us but they didn't seem to have anything to do with us. I bought her presents I couldn't afford and my pay packet was by now mortgaged several months in advance. The President of the Mess Committee took me aside and gave me an ultimatum about settling my mess bill which was now nearly three months in arrears, or proceedings would be taken. I knew what that meant. Resigning my commission. Ignominious dismissal. I couldn't borrow from Ian or anyone else in the mess. I didn't want my affair with Ariana to come to the CO's ears. I was off-limits on that as well.

"Then Jannis Nicolaides got picked up and I was in charge of the escort for his transfer. Ariana knew I was in financial trouble. God help me, I told her that as well as everything else. It's hard to believe how the flesh — " He wiped his mouth with the back of his hand and couldn't meet her eyes. "She made me a proposition. Naturally I wouldn't listen. She asked me to betray the route of the escort vehicle so that Jannis's friends could waylay it and free him. If he were tried he would inevitably be executed, she said. Didn't I love her enough to save her brother's life? 'No harm will come,' she said. 'No one will know what you have done. No one will be hurt. I give the information. Nobody will know how I came by it. We know that it is best that we do not ask questions,' she said. She would be paid much money. She named a sum that would see me well clear of all my debts. I was horrified. I went on refusing. She threatened to go to the Colonel and tell him about us. With her brother a captured terrorist, that really would have spelled ruin for me. Her father had already been relieved of his post at the base. The despicable thing was that even as she was blackmailing me I still wanted *her*. I'd have moved heaven and earth still to keep her." His voice shook. Sylvia's face was a mask.

He raised haunted eyes to hers. "I did it, Sylvia. In the end I told her which way the truck would pass."

The kitchen clock ticked the seconds away like a dripping tap and Sylvia found herself counting each and waiting for the next.

"I justified myself. I had her promise that no one would be hurt. All they were interested in was freeing Jannis. I was criminally naïve considering the daily reports of killings and atrocities, but I clung to Ariana's word and I didn't credit her with her brother's fanaticism. I didn't want to. The rest of it happened as I told you." He got up and started walking up and down. "There's not been a day, a night since, when I've not remembered that it was I who prevented Colin from firing. Who denied him the right of self-defence. Not a day when I haven't seen him and the others as they were." Seeing her ashen face he said hastily, "What I told you was true, though. It was quick. He didn't suffer. But Oh God, if only it had been me instead." He stopped in his tracks and shuddered and felt his amputated wrist. "I'd have given both of these. This wasn't punishment enough." He turned an agonized look towards her but it was impossible from her frozen features to see how she was taking it.

Martin went on painfully. "They flew me home and they gave me a medal. You can imagine how I felt. I wanted to tell someone but I was ill and in shock when they told me my name would go forward, and soon after I had found your letters and I had met you. It seemed to me then that here was some positive retribution I could make. Nothing could bring Colin back or undo the ghastly thing I had done, but you were in deep trouble and I could right a small part of the wrong for you and for his child."

Sylvia had been fixated by the sight

of Martin's feet traversing the kitchen tiles. Sometimes his foot fitted exactly into one of the squares. In fact more times than not. Every now and then he stepped on one of the joins. 'Walk on the crack — break your mother's back' the old hopscotch adage rang in her ears. Now she raised her head stiffly, like one coming out of a hypnotic trance.

"You could have told me," she said. "You owed me that. Why didn't you?"

"Because I owed you much more than that. You wouldn't have married me if you had known, would you?"

She stared at him. "I would have hated you too much."

There was a blue vein standing out prominently in his temple. "I know. Knowing that has been another part of my punishment."

Her mind, like an Advent calendar, started opening windows to reveal a series of pictures behind. She said dully, "So you put me on like a hair shirt. Like your arm. I said I didn't want to be married out of pity but this was even more insulting." It was all becoming so clear. No wonder he had withheld the core of himself from her all these years. Once upon a time he had allowed his emotions to run away with him and he had been punishing himself ever since. She had been part of that punishment, a constant sore reminder of the past and a means of expiating his crime. It wasn't flattering and it was so appallingly hurtful that if she didn't get angry she would cry until her heart would break. It was worse than losing Marian. Much worse even than Colin. Nothing he had told her about his act of treachery, his responsibility for Colin's death, his idiocy, his cowardice — not even the suspicion that he might yet have murdered Stuart — had so shocked and cut her to the quick. As if that wasn't bad enough, she was shot through with the deadliest of all the seven sins. A furious jealous envy of Ariana Nicolaides, of whom Martin had spoken in terms of the flesh. Ariana who had possessed the key to release the pent-up passion locked inside him. 'The most marvellous thing that had ever happened to me' he had called her. Shutting all that away had been another act of penance. Sylvia tasted again the tears upon his cheek after he had first taken her.

She said steadily and bitterly, "And to think all these years I've been so grateful and thought I wasn't nearly good enough. How many times have you let me say it?"

"I've always refuted it. I've never done anything to make you feel that way." He thought she was still talking about what he had done to Colin.

"But you did, all the same. With your goodness and your seeming inability to condone weakness. I was so ashamed to think you might have read my letters to Colin. You were at such pains to tell me that you didn't want me 'in that way'. And now I find — " Tears were on the threshold so she got up and took their glasses to the sink. Hardening her voice, she said, "Well, you wouldn't, would you? I'd be the last person for you for that. I realize now why. It must have been embarrassing for you when I made all the advances. What a fool I made of myself."

"Don't say that, Sylvia. You've got it all wrong." He came to her and would have touched her in an attempt to explain but her shattered pride shook him off.

"I suppose you're afraid that when Galton finds all this out he'll have his motive. I must admit that it's a weightier one than the motive I had worked out for you, laughable though that one seems now in the light of your recent revelations."

"What do you mean?"

"It doesn't matter now." Nothing seemed to. "What are you going to do?"

"I don't know. I might as well tell him too. It will be a relief, and now that you know there's no point in keeping quiet any longer." He could see that she thought he must be stark staring mad. "It's only a matter of time before they'll find out anyway. They never let these things sleep. They'll go to Cyprus. I told you, they'll dig. It'll look much worse than if I haven't been honest."

"Honest!"

She had the pleasure of seeing him flinch.

"I deserve that."

His acceptance, his docility antagonized her.

"You're not even going to fight?"

Martin shrugged. "What difference does it make? I have killed two men. Whichever way the law interprets it, I shall have got away with one. That's a burden I shall still have to carry."

He was unbelievable! "What are you, Martin, some kind of crazy masochist? For Christ's sake! You're always preaching about forgiveness and a God of Mercy. Can't you forgive yourself?" His attitude was totally incomprehensible to her. Unless . . . She was so angry she couldn't prevent herself saying it. "Unless your determination to be martyred is a cover for what you really did. You knew who Stuart was. You meant to kill him. You knew about Marian." Her voice, rising to an unsteady crescendo cracked upon the name.

"No!" She had provoked him too to shout. In his eyes there was an expression that made her bitterly regret her accusation but hadn't he forfeited the right to her trust? It served him right.

He said more quietly, "I loved Marian too. I would never have done that to you. You know me better than that."

"I don't know you at all. You're a stranger to me, Martin. How should I guess how a stranger would behave?"

The vein was really black now and his face went even whiter, the shade that it had been in the hospital when they had actually been strangers. Touching him on the raw salvaged a crumb of her self-respect after what he had done to it, but it was cold comfort to her heart which was crying out to retract the words.

He said, "I'm too tired to go on with this. I'm going upstairs. I'll sleep in Marian's room."

★ ★ ★

It was only early evening and still light and neither of them had had any supper. The futile normal punctuations of life, the minutiæ that framed and segmented each day supplying the purpose and pattern of habit had crumbled with the foundations of her existence. It was imperative to hang on to some relic of routine. There was a collection of crockery upon the draining-board — the plates from hers and Alison's toasted lunch sandwich and their coffee cups that needed washing as well as the glasses. Instead of smashing the lot as she would like to have done, Sylvia rinsed two milk bottles and carried them out to the back doorstep. The priory cat who was hunting in the shrubbery leaped, startled, into the open and disappeared around the corner of the house. She watched it go and saw the broken panes of glass lying shattered in the grass under the kitchen window. Damn! The storm must have been responsible. Sylvia ventured forth to inspect the damage. There was no fallen branch anywhere near nor evidence of a tile having fallen off the roof. It would cost a pretty penny to replace, not that it mattered to them any more. The cat had been lucky not to have cut its paws. She bent down and picked some of the jagged pieces out of the grass for safety. It was heavy and thick and whatever had hit it had done so with a considerable force. A severed white shoelace lay among the wreckage.

After Sylvia had made it as tidy as she could she went back in. The detergent bubbles floated a million tiny rainbows in the washing-up bowl as she cleaned the china. They glug-glugged down the wide jaws of the waste disposal unit and so too did one of the Stanton crested silver teaspoons before Sylvia could stop it. Pulling back her sleeve, she plunged her hand down into the maw to rescue it from the mangled fate of its predecessors she had been too negligent to save when the machine had been in action on other occasions. Martin was always warning her about dropping things down. Martin! Don't think about him, not yet, not until tomorrow. The tips of her fingers fished gingerly among the blades and came up with the spoon — and another object that fell back in again. Sylvia delved again and retrieved it. It lay in the palm of her hand, recognizable and familiar, but not making immediate sense. The object was an earring. An ivory skull and crossbones. The looped steel hook to which it was attached was what had caught in the spoon handle and tinkled metallically in the drain. It was Billy's. There was no doubt of that. The last time Sylvia had seen him wearing it had been the night of the row the four of them had had, she and Martin, Marian and Billy — when Marian had flounced out of the house with him two years ago.

19

FOR all of five minutes she must have stood there stupidly holding the ear-ring and marvelling how it could possibly have remained in the waste disposal unit all that time before common sense asserted that it couldn't. She turned it over. It wasn't damaged in any way, which must mean that it had come only recently to its resting place, certainly within the last day or two. Sylvia had last used the waste disposal before going off to Dan's. Martin and Stuart had left their dishes for the morning. In the event it had been Alison who had cleared those. If Alison had used the bowl in the other side of the double sink she might not have had cause to send anything down the unit. Therefore Billy had been here. In the vicarage. Billy! Sylvia was beyond telling herself that it wasn't possible when everything else impossible had already happened! Billy had been here lately. How lately?

A flicker of excitement stirred. If her reasoning was right, could he have been here on Tuesday night? It was crazy, but no crazier than what had been going on since Tuesday. Sylvia stood very still, thinking. If Billy *had* been here he must have hidden. He knew the house and it was a big enough one with several rooms unused. She held her breath, startled by her own line of deduction. Of course! The attic room. The cigarette smell of occupation. Billy too had been in Indonesia. What if Stuart had never set foot up there? She remembered the banana skin and flimsy suspicion strengthened into cautious certainty. She went on thinking about Billy up in that room. Spying? Biding his time for something? Just using the vicarage as a free doss-down? What had he come for? Had he left with or without it? He must have covered his tracks if he had been there on Tuesday night. The police had found no sign of a third party. Perhaps they hadn't tried very hard. They had been so anxious to pin it on to Martin. If Billy had been about the sight of them would surely have scared him off pretty damned quick. The police were no friends to Billy. He had left no other clues. Sylvia hadn't noticed anything else strange in her clearing up. Nothing missing. Nothing out of place. She checked herself. Wait a minute. Nothing *missing* — but she was forgetting: something had been added. Something had been found in the house that hadn't been there before. Right where she was standing. The drawer right by the sink. Spellbound, she opened that drawer. There were only knives and forks in it now but on Tuesday night someone had slipped an envelope in there. She hadn't been able to understand that at all. How Marian's things had turned up in that drawer. But if Billy had stood in this place — beside this drawer! He had been near enough the sink to lose his ear-ring. Probably leaned across as Sylvia did when she wanted to open the window. The drawer. The sink. The window. They were all in a line. If he had opened the window it wouldn't have been because he wanted fresh air! More likely a means of escape!

She reconstructed his actions to fit her hypothesis. In her mind's eye she saw him jumping up on to the draining-board in those dirty old scuffed-out rubber-soled shoes he always wore. Half the time the laces were all frayed and undone. The hairs on the base of her spine tingled as she thought about laces. She stopped her hand mid-way in the action of closing the drawer. Where had she seen a single white shoelace not half an hour since? Outside. In the grass. Her pulse began to race with her imagination. Supposing he had opened the window and jumped? It must have been dark or he would have seen the sheets of glass. They would have made a noticeable noise breaking too, unless the sound had been masked by the turbulence outside. On Tuesday night there had been a storm.

Sylvia ran outside again and inspected the damaged panes more closely. The police, if they had noticed them, most likely wouldn't have attached any significance to their breakage. There was a lot of junk littering the shrubbery side of the house and it was conceivable that broken glass among it would not have been specially noteworthy. The dustbins were here and all the rubbish from the preparations for the Fayre. It must have been a hefty fall. Six five-foot panes broken into sizeable, wickedly jagged rectangles and wedges and eight or ten smaller sheets splintered into thousands of smaller fragments. If someone *had* gone through that lot it would be a miracle were he not badly cut. After the torrential rain there wasn't much point in looking for signs of blood, but feeling like Sherlock Holmes, Sylvia did retrieve the shoelace from where she had thrown it. It was like a hundred others and could have been lying there for days, but her intuition told her that it had not. She had built up a picture in her mind of what might have happened. All of it was conjecture, but the ear-ring was real and so was the evidence that somebody had occupied the attic room. Billy had definitely been here. Once again she looked at the glass. He might even still be around if he were hurt. It was a long shot and she was certain that the police must have searched the outbuildings as well as the house, but she was compelled by some inner conviction to look for herself before handing over her new-found evidence to Galton. She wasn't at all confident that he would take her seriously anyway. She could hear that bland voice suggesting that she had planted the ear-ring herself, and that he had only her word for it that Billy had been the owner. Her other clues were too fragile to constitute concrete evidence, and as the wife of the police's main suspect for the crime she could be expected to lie in her teeth to get him off the hook.

The light was fading fast as Sylvia collected a torch from the kitchen and went out into the yard. The outbuildings on three sides of the cobbled quadrangle had once been stables. Two of them had been converted into garages. The old haylofts above were approached by staircases built on the outside walls, and the lofts themselves ran through into a rabbit warren of raftered garrets under the roofs of the old dairy, a potting shed, Sylvia's box store and the Victorian laundry. Up there a small child could stand up straight under the highest part of the roof but an adult would have had to go on all fours or wriggle along prone to make any progress. Some of the timbers were dangerous and the garrets were colonized by bats who were preparing for their nocturnal sorties as the light from Sylvia's torch bounced off the potting-shed wall. The door of the shed, sagging on its hinges and ajar, rested heavily on the uneven ground. She had to lift it to move it back and gain entry. Nothing in there. A few rusty tools, a stack of empty seed-boxes, a pot of dead chrysanthemums. It smelled musty and on the floor there were mouse droppings where a bag of peat had split its sides. Sylvia moved on. She explored the garages and the lofts above, the box store and the laundry, stopping every now and then to listen and feeling increasingly ridiculous in her amateur sleuthing. Yet something drove her on. The silence was eerie and she was afraid of bats. Billy or anyone else could be a hundred miles away from here by now and indeed, if he had any sense at all, would be. Darkness had swooped down like one of the dreaded bats and Sylvia swore as she caught her trousers on the rusty metal edge of the old copper just inside the laundry door. It was high time all this stuff was cleared out and dumped.

Perhaps the next incumbent would attend to it. Hobbling outside, because she had knocked her shin as well, she shone the torch on to the three-cornered tear in her pants. The light fell down on the ground. Beside her feet a channel, cut into the cobbles, which had originally served to carry water away from the laundry, joined another from the dairy at a junction where both sluices ran through a grating into a drain. On the circumference of the pool of light and teetering on the grating lay a fag-end. No filter tip. Sylvia knew what they looked like by now. It lay as though having been cast down and instinctively she pointed the beam upwards. High up there was an air vent close to the ninety-degree angle of the buildings.

Her heart was drumming and she thought of going back for Martin, but she could still be wrong. Sylvia knew, she just knew she wasn't. Somebody was up there. Somebody had thrown that butt out, just as he had on to the attic roof. If it was Billy she could handle him. She wasn't afraid of Billy. If it was a stranger, he might be dangerous. She hesitated for a second. Whoever it was might already have seen the light from her torch and if she went for help might get away. She made up her mind. Turning off the beam, she waited a second more, listening and allowing her eyes to grow accustomed to the shadows. The bricks of the staircase up to the hayloft were worn and covered here and there with a slippery moss. Carefully Sylvia ascended them well away from the edge, her back against the wall and testing each step for any loose pointing. From a three-foot-square platform at the top there was a waist-high wooden lintel to be negotiated, and then she was over and in the loft.

There were signs that the dust up here had been disturbed, scuffings and footmarks most likely made by Galton's legions. Keeping well away from the unguarded overhang into the garage beneath, she turned left into the roof and found the narrow entrance to the garret warren. The aperture only came up to her knees so she had to drop on all fours to crawl through. Resolutely averting her eyes from the shadowy clusters of bats among the rafters around her, she followed the boarded passage straight ahead, stopping now and then to cast a burst of light in the direction she was taking. A third of the way along there was a dark stain like congealed oil mixed with the dirt. Further ahead there were more stains, bigger than the first, the last one of all having spread to the size of a tea plate. Sylvia touched it with her finger. It was tacky and dark brown, like a scab. Forgetting caution, she increased her pace, scrambling along now heedless of the racket she was making, as the torch in her hand banged against the deck with each forward movement.

She wasn't sure whether she called his name, but as she came upon him Billy turned his head feebly and recognized her with glazed eyes. He was lying with his head propped against one angled timber, his left arm nursed painfully against his chest that shallowly rose and fell on short, severely hampered breaths. The sleeve of his jacket was torn and a good deal of blood had seeped into the leather and run down to cover the whole of the front of his T-shirt. The other source of bleeding was his foot. One of the soles of the rubber gym shoes which were pointing upwards in Sylvia's direction was cleanly cut under the instep, Billy's foot inside had evidently been similarly lacerated, how deeply she could only guess, but it was terrifying to see the blood oozing from it was red instead of brown, and that its flow appeared continuous. Any exultation that Sylvia felt at having her suspicions verified was swamped in horror and concern.

"Billy!" She groped her way up beside him. "Billy, do you hear me? It's Mrs Dearsley." She took his head gently in her hands and cushioned it from the hardness of the wood. It was a dead weight, his neck muscles slack, and she realized the futility of attempting to move him an inch without help. "Billy!" She patted his cheek firmly enough to bring round his eyes, which had wandered away, and fix his attention upon her. "I'm going to get Martin. Martin." She purposely repeated the name to give him reassurance. As far as Billy had been known to respect anyone, Sylvia knew he respected and trusted Martin. Laying his head down again in a more comfortable position she said, "I'll leave you the torch."

She was relieved when he nodded weakly, and even more thankful that he was able to raise the effort to whisper, "Matches." She understood that she was meant to feel somewhere in his pockets and on the first attempt she found a half-used book.

"Thanks. I won't be long." She turned back along the way she had come and crawled away from him as fast as she could into the darkness. On gaining the hayloft it was a relief to be able to stand up straight again, and striking a match to guide her to the lintel, she clambered over, this time taking the steps down at a reckless gallop.

★ ★ ★

Martin, thank heavens, had not undressed. He wasn't even in bed. He was standing at the window of Marian's room looking into the garden. He couldn't be seeing much because it was dark outside. Dark too in the room. He had not switched on the light and in a moment Sylvia, racing to find him and flinging open doors, would have passed on in her search. He didn't even turn when the room was illuminated and could have been in a world away from her, deaf and blind to his present surroundings. His withdrawn stillness bespoke his separation from her universe more significantly than any of the words that had passed between them, and for one fanciful moment it occurred to her that he might have been contemplating suicide.

"Martin. Come quickly. I need your help. Billy is hurt. He's in the rafters above the dairy. I think he's bleeding to death."

"Billy?" That brought him back to consciousness. He turned round, looking dazed.

"Yes. He's been hiding here. In the house. Martin, he may have had something to do with all this. We've got to get him down. Come on."

He was alert now, crossing the room in a couple of strides and following swiftly on her heels as she ran down the stairs. In the hall he said,

"Better ring for an ambulance."

While Sylvia obeyed he went and got a Tilly lamp from a cupboard and by the time she found him waiting for her by the door he was also armed with a deckchair. "We'll need something to get him down on," he explained. He was completely switched on now, competent and cool, and she was thankful to be in his hands.

"Will the men know where to come?" he asked.

"I told them the back entrance by the yard."

"Good girl."

Between them they carried the chair up the steps, Martin leading with the light grasped in his artificial hand and held aloft. When they got to the opening into the rafters he said, "I'll go first. You come after and push the chair along in front of you."

There were holes in the knees of her trousers from her previous trip, but Sylvia was impervious to pain from splinters or grazing. She concentrated all her efforts on negotiating the deckchair up the narrow track behind Martin, and prayed that they were going to get Billy down alive. And then Martin had stopped and he was speaking and encouragingly Sylvia could hear Billy's voice, a little stronger now.

"It's all right, old chap. We're going to try to move you out of here. I'm coming round to get your head." Martin side-stepped into the unboarded rafters and came round behind the boy. Taking the weight of Billy's head on his own chest, he gripped the waistband of Billy's jeans on either side with his good hand and his hook. "Come ahead of the chair and lift up his legs," he commanded. When Sylvia had completed this manoeuvre he said, "On the count of three I'll lift and you slide the chair under him like a stretcher."

She was sweating and trying not to hurt the damaged foot which looked horribly as though it might be cut right through with only the top part of the shoe holding it together. She banished a wave of nausea and waited for the count.

"One. Two. *Three*."

Sylvia heaved and shoved and miraculously the chair moved at the right moment and seconds later Billy was lying on top of it. They both stood panting, looking down at him. Sylvia had read about people who in extremis and the direst necessity managed to lift objects like cars singlehanded and thought she must be one of those. Talk about faith moving mountains! The boy had winced and closed his eyes, but then he opened them, focusing and to Sylvia's relief, looking more lucid. She knew it wasn't the appropriate moment but the ambulance men would soon be here and Billy would be whisked away and she had to get through to him before anyone else did. She bent over him and said, "Billy, what were you doing here?"

"He's too ill," Martin remonstrated but she took no notice.

"Billy. Tell me."

It was Martin he looked towards. "Marian." He licked his dry lips. "Marian's things," he whispered.

"You brought Marian's things?" Sylvia prompted. "You left them in the house?"

"In kitchen drawer."

"Why didn't you give them to us?" She nodded coaxingly.

"Sylvia!" Martin was getting impatient.

"Saw Coleby first."

"Stuart Coleby?"

"Liar." Billy said.

In spite of himself Martin couldn't help being interested. "What do you know about Stuart Coleby, Billy?"

"Blackmail. Said you killed his brother. But I knew."

"And you told him you knew?" Sylvia held her breath. "What did he do?"

"Tried to kill me. Fight."

Sylvia looked across him triumphantly at Martin. From below Billy only saw that she was pleased with herself. Always pleased with herself. Didn't care about him. He could wipe that smile off her face. He made a supreme effort.

"I knew." Again he addressed Martin. "Her and Coleby. Saw them. In church. In bed. You ask her. Whore!" He looked directly into Sylvia's eyes, making her shiver with the realization that she was hated. For the blackest moment of her life that hatred was reciprocated with a vehemence that would have gladly allowed him to bleed to death if only they hadn't needed his testimony so badly. Then any further words were drowned

411

by the ambulance siren down below and the shouting of the attendants. The whole exchange had taken only seconds but there wasn't the slightest chance that Martin had not heard or understood.

He said, "Careful," and gave the makeshift stretcher a shove. Sylvia pulled at her end, crawling backwards this time and shouting to let their rescuers know where they were. By the time they reached the hayloft the men beneath had heard them and seen Martin's lamp.

"I'm afraid we couldn't help jolting him a bit. He was right up in the roof." Martin's face was set as he put down his end of the chair. Billy's eyes were closed and he had slipped mercifully over the edge where the pain was temporarily alleviated.

"You did a grand job, sir, madam. We'll take over now." Arrangements for a proper stretcher to be winched down were being swiftly and expertly made and Sylvia and Martin stood side by side watching the safe execution of the operation, feeling spare now that their part in it was over. Neither spoke. Sylvia's mind was in a turmoil and there was no hint of any emotion except extreme fatigue on Martin's face. She herself was almost too tired to put one foot in front of another and she stumbled getting across the lintel. He let her pick herself up without offering any assistance and came down the steps behind her.

"I'll go with him." The men held the door for him to clamber tiredly inside and before they closed it Martin called to Sylvia, "Ring Galton and tell him to come to the hospital immediately."

She was left with the lantern and her cut and bruised knees, shivering and shaking in the dark. It was finished anyway, she told herself defiantly. It had never really begun. Not so far as he was concerned.

Her teeth were chattering so much that she had trouble stringing together the message for Galton but somehow she did it. After she put the receiver down she leaned her head against the wall and for the first time in her life Sylvia gave way to despair.

20

TEN minutes after the ambulance had deposited Billy at Casualty the police arrived. Galton was not with them but his side-kick Raymond Bentley, listened to Martin's version of the evening's events, then went away to find a doctor to see if Billy could be questioned. Martin was left sitting alone with his thoughts in the middle of a shiny white corridor. Out of the confusion of these, uppermost was dawning the realization that it had not been he who had killed Stuart Coleby. That fact would still have to be proved to Galton's satisfaction and Martin wasn't at present allowing himself to think what might yet happen if Billy died before he could testify, but at least he knew that on this score his own conscience was clear. The knowledge, however welcome, did nothing to lift his spirits. It had come too late to save him and Sylvia. Twenty-four hours earlier and she would have been spared his own bitter revelations and things could have gone on as before between them. He cursed himself for having been precipitate in telling her anything, then more honestly accepted that not all of his motive in doing so had been altruistic. He had come to a breaking-point beyond which he could not go without the self-indulgence of the confessional. She would say he had purged himself at her expense. She had been impatient of his acceptance, almost his eagerness to assume guilt which he now saw as a sickness that had tainted their lives. Ironically, he had let himself out of the cage but the price of freedom was the loss of her.

"I would have hated you too much," she had said. From her attitude tonight it was clear that she wouldn't have changed that view. It would be so much easier if he could whip up some hatred of his own, and he tried to by remembering the cold slap of Billy's accusation and the look on Sylvia's face when he had made it. Martin didn't know if it were true. That was something else that would eventually have to be faced between them — if indeed she was still there when he got back after all this was over. Against the likelihood of her leaving, even the possibility of her infidelity paled into insignificance. It was alarming not to be able to vilify her. He only knew he loved her beyond any wrong that either of them had perpetrated.

Bentley, a lean streak of a man like a rasher of wind, was approaching, the steel-tipped heels of his shoes breaking into the silence and Martin's thoughts.

"He's having an emergency operation to try to save the foot. It may take some hours. They've given him transfusions. They think he'll make it. He talked again before he went under. It seemed to be on his mind. One of our men was there and we'll be near by the moment he comes round. There's nothing more you can do here, sir. I've got your statement. I suggest you go home and get some sleep."

"If it's all the same to you I'll stay until it's over. He has nobody else."

"As you wish, sir. I'll see Inspector Galton is advised as soon as he gets back."

Martin sat down again and waited. He didn't know how many hours passed. A nurse came by at some juncture and brought him a cup of tea and occasionally the night staff came to ask him how he was, but they had no news. Early in the morning when he was dozing upright in the chair, someone shook him by the shoulder and he opened his eyes to see a staff nurse standing over him. Billy's surgeon was with her.

"How is he?" Martin got stiffly to his feet.

"He'll do. We'll have to see how the foot comes along. With luck he'll keep it although he may not ever regain full mobility, but he'll survive."

"Thank goodness."

"You look as if you could do with some care and attention yourself. Are you all right for getting home? Shall we ring your wife for you?"

"No, it's all right. I'll get a taxi."

"Don't worry about him. I'll take care of him." They turned and Martin saw the familiar figure of Galton in the corridor.

"Come along, Mr Dearsley."

Martin went with him meekly. In the vestibule and out of earshot of the others he said, "Are you arresting me?"

"Not today. I'm taking you home."

Outside there was a plain dark saloon and a driver waiting. Martin clambered into the back while the Inspector went round the other side and got in beside him. The leather seat sagged and bounced under his weight.

"I gather you've had quite a night of it. Bentley's told me. Which is lucky for you, Mr Dearsley, because it looks as if this lad's story is going to put you in the clear. Let's hope he remembers it tomorrow. It was lucky you finding him like that."

Martin said, "It was on my wife's hunch. She had found Billy's ear-ring in the house. I gave it to Inspector Bentley."

"*Constable* Bentley I shouldn't wonder after this little lot," Galton said grimly. "My men should have found him. A head or two will roll."

"Well, you were only after mine at the time." Martin had begun to feel he could make cautious allowance for the hapless policeman.

"That's as maybe, though you could hardly blame us. Your story wouldn't have held a teaspoon of water in court, sir. I was right about Coleby being a blackmailer. He evidently held a lifelong grudge against you, sir. The lad told us that. You say you never knew?"

"I never even knew of his existence. I didn't know Colin Coleby even had a brother. As for a grudge, I can only assume Stuart had become fixated by the circumstances of his brother's death. You see — " Martin told him the story of the ambush, the original version that he had first told Sylvia. "What I reproach myself with now and have done all these years is that when they opened up the truck I gave the order not to fire. It was an error of judgement and one which I have lived bitterly to regret. I blamed myself and evidently Stuart blamed me too. These things can get out of proportion if you have too long to dwell upon them. That's why the name came as such a shock to me and my wife." Martin wiped the palm of his hand with a handkerchief. "We were completely taken in."

"From what I've lately discovered, you

weren't the only ones by a long chalk. Slippery customer, our Mr Coleby. I haven't been idle since I last saw you. That's why I wasn't here when you brought the boy in. I have been making enquiries into Messrs. Coleby, Balfour and Quennell. Balfour was only one of his aliases. There's a profitable little racket being run under cover of Handyside and Bennett's Holborn branch. Mr Stuart Coleby's demise has left Mr Quennell holding a red-hot potato."

"What sort of racket?"

"Drugs. Mr Coleby did a lot of business in the Far East."

Martin felt sick and for one blinding moment he wished with all his heart that it *had* been he who had murdered Stuart. It was all becoming very clear now. His plans for the devastation of every one of them had been carefully laid and they had all fallen like ripe plums. All except Marian. He didn't know how he would bring himself to tell Sylvia all this.

Seeing his face Galton said, "He was a nasty piece of work."

"He'd have got away with it if Billy hadn't turned up."

Martin was thinking of Marian, enlisted, enslaved — if she hadn't died.

"Not that he's much better," said Galton. "He tried blackmail too. But he's young and he's had a bad fright. He may not be irredeemable."

"What will happen to him?" Martin asked.

"He can plead self-defence. He may get away with a short, sharp shock." Galton leaned forward and tapped the driver on the shoulder.

The car started and they drove out into the early morning traffic of people on their way to work. Martin looked at his watch to remind himself what day of the week it was. It was Friday and he hadn't slept a night through since Monday.

It was eight o'clock when they got to the vicarage and Galton pushed across him to open the door.

"Go in and put Mrs Dearsley's mind at rest," he said. "I'll be along later in the day to tie up some loose ends and we'll both go and see the boy." He wound up the window and the car swung about on the gravel as Martin went into the house. His first impression was that Sylvia had gone. The hall echoed hollowly and nothing stirred in the kitchen or the study which he cursorily inspected before going upstairs. The bedroom doors were all open as Sylvia had left them in her search for him last night and none of the beds had been disturbed. Martin pulled open a cupboard in which some of her clothes hung, but he never noticed what she wore enough to know whether anything was missing. His brain didn't seem capable of organized thought and he went downstairs again aimlessly, forgetting once there that his intention had been a cup of coffee.

★ ★ ★

A sound from the drawing-room reminded him that he hadn't yet looked there, so he went in and found her just waking from where she had been huddled on the sofa. She was in the same bedraggled state she had been in when he had left her, having crawled there in her abject misery and curled into a foetal position without concern for the mess her filthy clothes and bleeding knees would make of the covers. His relief at finding her still there superseded every other emotion. When she sat up her cheeks were caked with dirt where she had last night brushed away the tears.

"What happened?" Her voice was barely a croak and the tears were still thick in her sinuses.

"He'll live. They operated last night. They hope the foot will heal. He talked to the police. He admitted it. He may revoke, but Galton doesn't think he will. He believes him."

She let out the breath she had been holding tightly on a long shuddering sigh.

He said, "I know. It's a tremendous relief to know I didn't — I can't quite get used to it."

"Did you tell him?"

"Who? Galton? No, there was no need."

"That was lucky." It was said sarcastically. She meant she wished she had been as fortunate. He knew what she meant.

"We both learned a few home truths last night, if it comes to that." She hadn't the monopoly of bitter pills. It was too late for pretending. "Is it true?" he asked. "Is that what you were afraid Stuart might have told me — what might have caused a disagreement between us? Is that what you meant when you talked about a motive?"

"Yes."

"You and — him?"

"Yes." Her voice came out stronger. Defiant. Feeling at a disadvantage sitting down and having to look up at him, Sylvia got up and went to stand by the mantelpiece. She turned round and looked him straight in the eye.

"That night you were in London we went to bed together. He made love to me. I wanted him to. I made love to him."

"Bed? Billy said something about the church," he said fatuously, as if it mattered where it had happened.

"We went over to lock the church. I showed him the crypt. He kissed me. It started there. Billy must have been spying. He must have heard us when we came back to the house. Now neither of us has any secrets."

His face had sharpened into rigid planes and there were deep pinch marks on either side of his nose. She could tell that she had wounded him deeply and she was both pleased and afraid.

"I don't understand. You hardly knew him."

"I'm sure you don't and in the biblical sense I did."

"A man like that. A confidence trickster, a cheat, a man who makes his money out of drug-running and corrupting children like Marian." He hadn't meant to tell her this way but now he was committed to repeating all that Galton had discovered. It was her turn to look shocked and she had the grace to cover her face with her hands. After a moment she threw her head back and said,

"I didn't know that then. Neither did you. It didn't matter to me what he was like. He was a man who wanted me. I needed that. I was starving and he gave me bread. Why should you care? I didn't give him anything you wanted."

It became so quiet that suddenly she found she couldn't look at him any more.

He had come to stand quite near her and the pain in his face sent a dagger into her own heart. Her legs were shaking and she had to get away.

"Excuse me."

He moved to let her pass and she walked as steadily as she could away from him.

"Where are you going?"

"Does it matter? I don't think we've got anything else to talk about." She would rather die than turn round and let him see she was crying.

"Sylvia, I love you." It was said so quietly she didn't believe she had heard it. She hadn't thought he would stoop to that and though she despised him for it, it made the ache worse all the same.

"Please don't."

"I've always loved you."

Oh, he was cruel and much lesser than she had thought.

"That's not true, and even if it were it can't be now."

"What you've just told me doesn't make any difference."

She swung round. "For Christ's sake spare me your tolerance. I'm sick of being used to cleanse your soul." The wet tears stained her cheeks anew and her eyes were blazing.

"There's no point in hiding it from you any more. This may be my last opportunity of telling you. I think we should speak the truth."

"Look who's talking!"

"You've every right to be resentful, to hate me." But that was the trouble. She didn't. She had said she would have. That Sylvia. Then. "I accept that," he said meekly.

She lashed herself into fury as a balm against despair. "Must you always be so bloody perfect? Must you always put people in your debt and in the wrong? If you love me, as you say, why don't you give me a thick ear for boasting that I was unfaithful? You're a sham, Martin. You don't give a tinker's cuss. All you're afraid of is I might leave you and how it will look. Of having no one around to make you feel a better person than you are."

That had got him on the raw. She thought he was going to hit her, and she dodged his hand as it came up towards

427

her face. Instead of the slap she had expected, she felt herself grasped by the chin and impelled backwards until her shoulders were up against the wall and she was held there in a vice-like grip. The hook on his right hand was embedded in the wooden door strut behind her ear and his eyes glittered dangerously inches from her own.

"I've always shared you with another man, in bed and out, so if the fact that you slept with Stuart doesn't inflame me as much as you hoped it's because I'm used to the idea. Colin was always there, wasn't he? In your heart. In my mind. But you're wrong if you think I didn't care. I wanted you all right but he always held me back. Knowing you wished I were he. Knowing that but for me you could have had him. Should have had him. You're right too about by being afraid you would leave me. We might have made it come right somewhere along the line if I could have brought myself to talk about what happened, but you see, my dear — you said it earlier — you would have hated me once you knew and I couldn't risk that. Selfishly

I couldn't risk that. You accuse me of being high-minded and sanctimonious and rigid and setting myself up to be better than others, but it's because I know I'm so much worse than they that I have to hedge myself about with standards. I know what is inside me."

He drew a deep breath and the anger left him. She felt the grip on her chin relax and his fingertips lightly trace her jawline in a renunciating featherweight caress before he dropped the hand to his side. He stood away from her and she was free to go but she was unable to move.

"I should never have married you," he said wearily. "You were quite right. It was self-indulgent. But you did something to my heart standing there in the hospital wearing your efficient grey suit and your courage. I thought I was beyond feeling anything at that time. It wasn't till later that I realized." He laughed humourlessly. "You say you can't live up to me. In fact I have always been painfully aware that the boot was on the other foot. You were so capable and long-suffering and you made such a success of everything you undertook. I know what a wrench it was for you when I went into the Church. I couldn't even be honest about that. How could I tell you that I couldn't face my men any more? It was easier to let you think I'd lost my nerve. But you buckled down as you always do and made a good job of being a clergy wife, although you don't hold with any of it."

"I never said so."

"No." He sighed. "We've both never said the important things. That has been our problem. I know it's my fault. I'm trying to say them now as time is running out. There's a price to be paid for what we do, Sylvia. I'm only sorry you had to pick up my tab."

She remembered Alison's remark about Martin thinking she was indestructible and wondered where she had gone wrong. It seemed that they had been at cross-purposes forever. He had said he loved her, but the idea was too fragile and novel for her to grasp. Some words she had once read came into her head: 'If a man in some part does not love himself, then he cannot love others.' She realized he was asking a question.

"Where will you go? Whatever you want, I'll accept your decision. I shan't make things difficult. If you want a divorce eventually I shan't stand in your way."

"What about the Church?"

"That's something else I shall need to examine. So many things will need to be gone into. I don't know whether after this — "

"I shan't want a divorce."

"I don't want you to make any more sacrifices on my account. You may want to marry again."

"No."

His mouth tightened. "Yes. I dare say you feel once is enough."

"Yes."

The way she said it made him look at her sharply and she saw the dawning of an incredulous hope at what he read in her eyes. He took a step towards her and she saw the tears spring into his. This time they tasted good mixed with all the muck and grime.

Other titles in the
Ulverscroft Large Print Series:

TO FIGHT THE WILD
Rod Ansell and Rachel Percy

Lost in uncharted Australian bush, Rod Ansell survived by hunting and trapping wild animals, improvising shelter and using all the bushman's skills he knew.

COROMANDEL
Pat Barr

India in the 1830s is a hot, uncomfortable place, where the East India Company still rules. Amelia and her new husband find themselves caught up in the animosities which seethe between the old order and the new.

THE SMALL PARTY
Lillian Beckwith

A frightening journey to safety begins for Ruth and her small party as their island is caught up in the dangers of armed insurrection.

THE WILDERNESS WALK
Sheila Bishop

Stifling unpleasant memories of a misbegotten romance in Cleave with Lord Francis Aubrey, Lavinia goes on holiday there with her sister. The two women are thrust into a romantic intrigue involving none other than Lord Francis.

THE RELUCTANT GUEST
Rosalind Brett

Ann Calvert went to spend a month on a South African farm with Theo Borland and his sister. They both proved to be different from her first idea of them, and there was Storr Peterson — the most disturbing man she had ever met.

ONE ENCHANTED SUMMER
Anne Tedlock Brooks

A tale of mystery and romance and a girl who found both during one enchanted summer.

CLOUD OVER MALVERTON
Nancy Buckingham

Dulcie soon realises that something is seriously wrong at Malverton, and when violence strikes she is horrified to find herself under suspicion of murder.

AFTER THOUGHTS
Max Bygraves

The Cockney entertainer tells stories of his East End childhood, of his RAF days, and his post-war showbusiness successes and friendships with fellow comedians.

MOONLIGHT
AND MARCH ROSES
D. Y. Cameron

Lynn's search to trace a missing girl takes her to Spain, where she meets Clive Hendon. While untangling the situation, she untangles her emotions and decides on her own future.

NURSE ALICE IN LOVE
Theresa Charles

Accepting the post of nurse to little Fernie Sherrod, Alice Everton could not guess at the romance, suspense and danger which lay ahead at the Sherrod's isolated estate.

POIROT INVESTIGATES
Agatha Christie

Two things bind these eleven stories together — the brilliance and uncanny skill of the diminutive Belgian detective, and the stupidity of his Watson-like partner, Captain Hastings.

LET LOOSE THE TIGERS
Josephine Cox

Queenie promised to find the long-lost son of the frail, elderly murderess, Hannah Jason. But her enquiries threatened to unlock the cage where crucial secrets had long been held captive.

THE TWILIGHT MAN
Frank Gruber

Jim Rand lives alone in the California desert awaiting death. Into his hermit existence comes a teenage girl who blows both his past and his brief future wide open.

DOG IN THE DARK
Gerald Hammond

Jim Cunningham breeds and trains gun dogs, and his antagonism towards the devotees of show spaniels earns him many enemies. So when one of them is found murdered, the police are on his doorstep within hours.

THE RED KNIGHT
Geoffrey Moxon

When he finds himself a pawn on the chessboard of international espionage with his family in constant danger, Guy Trent becomes embroiled in moves and countermoves which may mean life or death for Western scientists.